Love's Labours

By

Simon Truckle

Chapter 1

The first labour of Hercules landed right on their doorstep in the unlikely form of a hen party from Newcastle. Scott and Oliver had just finished the morning chore of dragging two pedalos and a collection of windsurf boards, sails and life jackets onto the beach, and were recovering with their first iced coffees of the day, when Vanessa appeared.

'Nessie, you're up early,' said Scott, raising his coffee. 'Want one?'

'Just had one, thank you,' she said, dropping into the spare deckchair and kicking off her flip-flops. 'Airport pick-up and the plane's delayed, so I thought I'd come and see what you chaps are up to.'

'Not much,' said Scott, waving at the assorted paraphernalia dotted around their shed. 'Business is still a bit slack.'

'Could that possibly be linked to you offering windsurf lessons when neither of you can actually stand up on the things?'

Scott shuffled his feet and looked down. 'There is that.'

'Plus, there's bugger-all wind,' added Oliver, who had a natural talent for finding the crux of the situation and firmly planting his thumb on it. 'We can't even hire the bloody things out.'

Oliver was reclining in the second of their tatty deckchairs in his customary position, outside the shed that housed the equipment. This they liked to call the Operation Nerve Centre. The shed was leaning at an alarming angle, and if it were an operation, it would be a triple heart bypass performed with a rusty Stanley knife. The pronounced lean was caused by the nightly presence of five windsurf boards, which, had there been any justice in the world, would have seen them raking in cash. Sadly, justice had disappeared into the distance with its arse on fire, and the boards had recently been christened Chardonnay, Stephen Fry, Gobi, and Rot, because they were all very,

3

very dry. They'd run out of things to call the fifth so Oliver just called it Wanker.

There they sat, in mute but defiant testimony to the triumph of mindless optimism over sound business sense.

'Well, goodness knows why you both look so glum,' said Vanessa. 'If you're going to be a bit broke, then a lovely warm Greek beach seems as good a place as any.'

'I'm alright, Nessie, this is just my morning face. Having the time of my life, me.' Oliver paused before adding, 'Although, granted, the rest of it hasn't been up to all that. It's your man Scotty there who's less than chipper. What with all the old Hercules stuff and that.'

'I thought you'd be loving it, a break from teaching kids irregular verbs – hold on, what did you say? What Hercules stuff?'

'Oh. I thought you knew.'

'Knew what?'

They both looked at Scott, Oliver a little sheepishly.

Grinding his deckchair more firmly into the sand, Scott assumed a confessional look. 'Well, it's not exactly a secret and I've been meaning to tell you, Nessie. There's a bit more riding on this Greek adventure than just a few extra drachmas. I've got to make enough dosh to buy a sailboat and sail it home.'

'A sailboat!' Vanessa's face left no doubt as to how much confidence she placed in Scott's ability to travel the 2,800 nautical miles back to England under his own steam. 'You'd be better off in a pedalo. Why on earth have you got to sail home?'

'My uncle Ted died last year and in his will left me his house and record collection. It's a nice house, too – worth a bit. Only it came with a few strings. You see, he had quite the sense of humour. That's where Hercules comes in.'

'This I have to hear,' said Vanessa.

Oliver leant forward, nodding happily. 'This is the really good bit,' he told her.

'Before he died, he wrote out a list of the labours of Hercules,' Scott went on. 'I've got to complete seven of them before I can meet the conditions of the will. And God only knows how I'll manage that,' he added. 'Anyway, I got a one-way ticket here and I've got two years to complete the labours, buy a sailing boat and sail it home. Only then will my dad stump up the cash.'

4

'Blimey,' said Vanessa. 'How exciting is that! Sounds like great fun – all that to look forward to and you get to do your Baywatch impression here all summer.'

'True … but.'

'Ah, I recognise that look. It's her, isn't it? Your ex back home?'

Oliver nodded. 'Can't do a thing with him, Nessie. He can't sleep, can't eat, can only down endless cans of cold lager.'

'That's a lot of cans, mate,' said Scott, who was keen to move on from the subject that haunted far too much of his waking moments.

'And all that drinking is eating into our profits,' continued Oliver.

This drew an appreciative nod from Scott despite himself. 'Which means no sailboat,' he said glumly, 'and no going back home just yet.'

'Don't suppose you could add us to your entertainment schedule?' Oliver asked Vanessa. 'We could give you a group rate for windsurfing and pedalos.'

Vanessa worked as a tour rep, a job that entailed keeping groups of tourists just the right side of having their stomachs pumped. At twenty-eight she was four years older than Scott and Oliver, and kept thinking of herself as thirty, which annoyed the hell out of her.

She was five foot seven, with lots of naturally curly hair of an indeterminate colour. It looked like it could be blonde if it could be arsed but was quite happy being what it was, sort of not-very-blonde. She had a very small nose and very big eyes and was unimpressed by most things, particularly boys. As a great deal of her professional life was spent fending off the unwanted attentions of either local Greek men or drunken tourists, she was highly adept at looking after herself. Having elevated sarcasm to an art form, she found most people only bothered her once.

'Send my lovely punters over to you boys? Not a chance. I shudder to think of the risk assessment that would involve. Nothing personal, you understand.'

Oliver nodded. 'Fair enough.'

'Well, I'd love to hang about to hear all about it but I should probably get moving. Just popped by to see if you two fancied going to Moe's tonight? If you're not too busy slaying bulls and the like.'

'Sounds great,' said Scott, mustering a smile.

'See you chaps later, then.' She jumped up from her chair and headed off down the beach.

The beach she was walking down was a beautiful strip of white sand about five miles outside the city of Volos. The road ran parallel to the beach until it hit an olive grove and turned up towards the mountain villages. The stretch of road nearest the beach sported an assortment of bars, restaurants and clubs and fed a number of smaller lanes that ran away from the sea, lined with tourist apartments. It was the busy part, easiest to reach from the apartments and with handy places to grab lunch or snacks.

The windsurfing shack's end was a lot quieter, due to the lack of amenities and the strong possibility of seeing naked Germans. Just past Scott and Oliver's spot, the beach turned a corner and had become the accepted place for those naturists that liked to let it all hang out. To Scott's enduring enjoyment, Oliver had convinced himself the correct term was 'naturalists', and Scott had no intention of disabusing him of this notion. He enjoyed the look of mild confusion each time it came up in conversation and he asked if David Attenborough had been past that morning.

The olive grove behind them had been converted into a campsite and was their temporary home for the summer. Once autumn rolled around, they would have to strike camp and go back to civilisation in the form of centrally heated flats and their day jobs teaching English to resentful Greek children. But for now, they could take advantage of the cut-price rental on the shed, which the campsite owner had offered them in exchange for deals on windsurfing for his campsite clientele. Even at reduced rates, though, the lack of any sort of wind meant that business remained stubbornly slow.

As Vanessa dwindled into the distance, Oliver, the one person possibly more indolent than Scott, peered down the beach from his deck chair, his hand shielding his eyes against the sun.

It was the tops that had grabbed his attention as the girls manoeuvred their sun loungers into position. Rather unusually for the beach, they were dressed in matching black and white striped football shirts. According to one of the National Geographic magazines Oliver had devoured in his youth, zebras had developed stripes not so that the animals could be well camouflaged on the dusty brown plains where they lived, but rather so they would look like other zebras. It was all about blending in. Thanks to one of evolution's more subtle ploys, it was virtually impossible for a predator either to work out how many zebras there were or to pick out an individual to attack – a trait that in human terms, thought Oliver, was embodied by politicians and newsreaders, who all seemed to be designed from the same mould.

While pondering this evolutionary oddity, Oliver also noted that he was not the only anthropological enthusiast to have had his interest piqued. A group of young gentlemen a little further down the beach had all simultaneously discovered a need to tweak their hair and apply suntan lotion, a task that required them to stand up and stretch whichever muscle group was best defined or most intriguingly tattooed. Someone, clearly, was working out which individual to 'attack'. Oliver leant forward in his deck chair, craning his neck to see which of the male herd would strike first, in the process upending his delicately poised plastic cup of iced coffee.

'Fuck,' he said, mildly and to no one in particular.

'What have you done now?'

He looked up to see Scott, who had reappeared carrying a large and battered canoe. Scott propped it up against the shed next to the sign advertising their hourly hire rates. If you looked carefully, you could tell the rates had already been revised downward. Twice.

'Nothing yet,' said Oliver.

'Comfy?'

'Got a slight crick in my neck.'

'Must be tiring, sitting down all morning. You probably need a nice rest. Don't, under any circumstances, help me with this heavy lifting.'

Oliver ignored this and nodded in the direction of the girls in black and white.

'Can you count them?'

'Count what exactly?'

'Those girls. How many are there? Quick glance only. No lingering.'

'What, the five that walked past a minute or two ago?'

'Imagine you hadn't seen them before and this was the first glance. How many would you reckon there are? In total.'

Scott toyed with the idea of asking for some kind of explanation, but assumed from painful experience that Oliver would eventually make his point. Squinting against the glare, he said: 'There are two girls lying on towels and three on sun loungers.' He crouched down suddenly in the shade of the deck chair. 'And thanks to you they've just caught me staring at them.'

'Hmm. Probably need to see them mingling a bit. Your zebra's not renowned for lying on sun loungers.'

Scott nodded to himself.

'Ah. It's a zebra thing is it?'

Oliver explained the stance taken on zebra evolution at National Geographic.

'Interesting theory,' said Scott from behind the deck chair. He had his head on one side and was squinting more tightly to see if it had any effect. It didn't.

At that moment, three of the girls stood up and began hopping in the direction of the sea. Scott noticed that they had names stencilled onto the backs of their shirts: Learner, Captain and Pole Dancer. Not likely, he thought, to be their real names. He was just toying with the idea of offering to sand down one of the supporting beams of the equipment shed for Pole Dancer when another member of the party got up and started walking towards them.

Oliver hadn't noticed. He was drawing in the sand, freshly damp from spilled coffee, with the tip of his big toe.

'Makes you wonder,' he said, 'whether the same effect applies to badgers.'

Scott, ignoring this remark, slowly rose up from his hiding place behind the deck chair to greet the visitor. As the full vista came into view, he wondered if his eyes were playing tricks on him. But no, the girl in black and white kept coming, looming larger and larger until he and Oliver were engulfed by her shadow. Scott looked up at a face towering above his. She was at least six foot two inches tall in bare feet, and there didn't appear to be any bit of her that wasn't gorgeous. Oliver, sensing that something had blocked out the sun, also looked up.

The girl pointed to her camera, smiled and gestured back towards her group of friends.

Scott grinned and said, 'You fancy a nice group shot, I take it?'

8

'Oh, are you English, pet?'

'As English as a pork pie.'

'I love a pork pie, me.'

'Can't help you with that,' said Oliver.

'But we can take a photo, can't we, Oliver,' said Scott smoothly, taking the camera and striding purposefully towards the rest of the group. Oliver looked over, looked back at the sand, sighed, thought about levering himself out of the deck chair to follow, then didn't.

'Group photo, girls!' shouted the tall girl, breaking into a trot. The others began bunching up on one of the sun loungers to fit in the shot.

'What's with the shirts?' Scott asked.

'We're on a hen party, pet. Sharon, that's her there, she's getting married in four weeks.' Sharon, unsurprisingly, was the one with 'Learner' on her back.

'Well, if you want to hire a canoe or pedalo, or learn to windsurf, we're here every day,' said Scott. 'Say cheese!' He handed back the camera and headed back to where Oliver was sitting.

'Some sort of hen party,' Scott said.

'Hens dressed as zebras – unusual, that,' said Oliver.

Scott, sat himself down in the second deck chair.

'That one you were talking to,' Oliver continued. 'Nice-looking girl.'

'Hmm.' Scott was thinking of a sunny afternoon in Bournemouth and a beautiful curly haired girl in a swimming costume.

'I said, nice-looking girl.'

'What? Oh yes, she's certainly very tall.'

'That'll be the Amazon thing.'

'Amazon?' asked Scott.

'She's got Amazon written on the back of her shirt.'

Oliver looked up and was pleased to see Scott doing his 'cat's arse mouth' thing. When struck with a sudden thought, he had a tendency to purse his lips together and go all squinty, a look Oliver found unflaggingly amusing.

'Amazon. Amazon. That sounds familiar. Where's that book?'

Scott reached for a beaten-up canvas satchel which was leaning against the side of the shed and began rummaging around in it. He came out with a battered paperback and began flicking through the pages.

'Here we are. For the ninth labour, Hercules was sent to the land of the Amazons to get the belt of Hippolyta, the Amazon queen.'

At this point he was interrupted by another of the girls asking to rent a pedalo. This time it was Pole Dancer who approached.

'How much is it to rent one of those wee boats, like?' she asked.

Scott was about to reply when Oliver stepped in. 'Well, seeing as it's a special occasion, you can have it for just 1,500 drachmas for an hour,' he said.

'Thanks, pet, champion.'

As she went back to tell the others, Scott turned to Oliver.

'Are we a charity now? What's with the 1,500?'

'Give it five minutes,' replied Oliver

In fact, only three minutes twenty-two seconds passed before the group of glistening, over-groomed young gentlemen appeared to hire the second pedalo at a price that had just trebled.

Scott had no chance to strike up any kind of conversation with the Amazon girl as they pushed off into the water. An hour later, as he helped the girls back out, he only managed to discover the fleeting information that her real name was Debbie and they were in his friend Vanessa's tour party, staying for a week.

That evening, as he and Oliver dragged the pedalos up the beach and locked the equipment in the shed, Scott asked himself, not for the first time, how they had managed to find themselves accidentally running a beach sports business and trying to complete the labours of Hercules while so clearly lacking in all the essential ingredients to make a success of either.

Chapter 2

Poseidon's was a restaurant on the seafront which they had christened Moe's, since the owner, a guy called Dimitris, looked exactly like the character of Moe the bar owner in the Simpsons. The comedy value in his face would have been reason enough to visit, but as well as serving fantastic authentic local dishes he also had a pizza oven and a location at the end of the beach with water lapping just a few feet away from the tables.

'It's in the bag, mate,' said Oliver confidently through a mouthful of pizza. He rotated the piece of paper towards Scott and Vanessa, and pointed to the ninth line:

The labours of Hercules

1 Killed the Nemean lion
2 Killed a Hydra, a nine-headed snake
3 Captured a golden-horned reindeer
4 Brought back a bull from Crete
5 Captured the Erymanthian Boar
6 Cleaned the Augean stables in a single day
7 Chased away flesh-eating Stymphalian birds
8 Captured the horses of King Diomedes
9 Got the belt of Hippolyta, Queen of the Amazons
10 Captured the cattle of Geryon, the three-headed, six-armed giant
11 Brought back the three golden apples from the Garden of Hesperides
12 Went into Hades and brought back the three-headed hound of hell

'There you go: number nine, pull the tall girl, get her belt and that's the first labour done. What do you say?'

Vanessa raised her eyebrows. 'What could possibly go wrong?'

Scott, noting the heavy sarcasm in her voice, nodded in agreement.

'Exactly, Nessie. I wish I could share your confidence, mate, but I'd like to refer you to a minor obstacle. She is called Amazon for a very good reason: she's six foot lots. I, on the other hand, am five foot eight.'

'Six inches goes a long way, you know, boys!'

'Thank you for that, Vanessa. As I was saying, I don't think "pulling the tall girl" is going to be quite the cakewalk you are assuming, Mr Pond.'

'Podium dancing,' offered Oliver enthusiastically.

Scott raised his eyebrows in weary enquiry.

'Get yourself on a podium, she won't notice you're vertically challenged.'

'I am not vertically challenged – I'm just not...' He searched for a suitable simile, failed and tailed off lamely, 'very tall.'

'Or you could try rollerblades,' added Vanessa, joining in. 'They'll make you look taller.'

Scott stabbed an olive with a cocktail stick and glared at the giggling pair across the table.

'You're enjoying this, aren't you? Sod it. I'll just ask her for it. I'll tell her about the whole Hercules thing and offer to pay for it.'

'You can't just ask for it. Old Hercules wouldn't have just *asked* for it, for fuck's sake!' said Oliver, appalled at the prospect of his week's entertainment being whisked away from him. 'What if she says no? What're you going to do then?'

Scott shrugged and looked at Vanessa for help, but she was staring thoughtfully into the distance.

Vanessa, who liked to embark on an adventure with a good sense of what she was getting into, had spent the months before her arrival in Volos reading up on Greek culture and history. Unlike either Scott or Oliver, she had a good grounding on the myths surrounding Hercules.

'Nessie.'

'Sorry, what?' She put down the slice of pizza that was halfway to her mouth.

'You know about this stuff, so – remind me of the details of the Amazon queen thing, would you?' asked Scott.

'Interesting use of the word "remind". It would suggest that you had learned it previously and forgotten it, which would not strictly speaking be true, would it?'

'Not as such, no.'

Vanessa rolled her eyes.

'Well, you've heard of Zeus, right?'

'Yep, got him, he was a god,' replied Scott

'Not just a god, *the* god. The head of the gods,' said Vanessa. 'He was smitten with a mortal woman so he disguised himself as her husband in order to make love to her. The son she consequently gave birth to was Hercules.'

'Right, so Hercules is the son of the big cheese! Nice,' said Oliver.

'That's right. But Zeus had a queen, Hera, who was the jealous type.'

'And presumably welcomed him home with the mythological rolling-pin,' added Scott.

'Succinctly and correctly put. Now are you going to leave me any of that or should I order some more?'

Oliver looked down guiltily at the shared plates he had just munched his way through and gestured to the waiter to come over.

After ordering another bowl of chips, vine leaves, souvlaki, more salad and a round of drinks, Vanessa continued.

'When Hercules was just ten months old, Hera sent two serpents to kill him in his cot. Hercules just grabbed a snake in each of his tiny little fists and strangled them.'

'Not someone you'd want to mess with then,' said Oliver.

'Quite. When he grew up he married the daughter of a local king, had three children and looked set to become King of Thebes when his father-in-law died. Hera, however, was having none of it. She nipped down to earth and sent Hercules mad.'

'Mad? Like angry?' asked Scott.

'Mad as in clinically insane. In this delusional state he mistook his sons for enemy soldiers and shot them all with poisoned arrows before coming round and realising what he'd done. His wife promptly died of a broken heart and he was banished from the kingdom. In this sorry state, he went to work for the king of Argolis, in the southeastern part of the Peloponnese. This king was a thoroughly nasty piece of work who, with the help of Hera, came up with a number of jobs that he thought certain to result in the death of Hercules.'

'And those are the twelve labours,' said Oliver. 'Impressive knowledge there, Nessie.'

Scott was looking thoughtful.

'What do you think, Nessie? Any chance of putting in a good word with the Amazon for me?'

'None whatsoever. I am a tour guide, not some dodgy pimp catering to your sordid ambitions.'

Oliver shared a grin with Vanessa as Scott looked indignant.

'Just thought you might introduce us or something. What do you think of my chances?'

'I think it's in the lap of the gods,' she said enigmatically before tucking into the newly arrived plates.

Scott looked around at the other tables. A week ago, they had practically had the place to themselves. Now every other table was taken, and Moe and his brother were hurrying around, balancing trays laden with plates and glasses. Apart from the odd family, it was all couples. He wondered where the Amazon girl was and how he might go about finding her. This led him, inexorably, as all thoughts about girls did, back to Abi.

It had been a dark day the previous November when his girlfriend Abigail, or Abi as she liked to be called, had finished with him, stating that although she loved him, he was never going to do anything with his life and she wasn't prepared to wait any longer for him to shake himself out of it. But to Scott, she wasn't just a girlfriend; she was The One.

He had fallen hopelessly in love with her the first time he had seen her, which was when he was seventeen and she walked into the Kings Arm pub in Salisbury. He had watched her go out with a string of his friends and acquaintances for nearly seven years before they finally got together about a year ago. The 3rd May at 11:33 pm, not that he was counting.

They'd lasted six months – six months that had been a mix of the best and worst days of his life. Best because he was spending time with the woman he loved; worst because he was never fully at ease with her. He had spent so long loving her from a distance that he had put her on a pedestal, and whatever metaphorical stepladder he used never quite reached high enough.

She had once asked him about it. She had avoided the love word and tactfully said.

'Why do you have such a high regard for me.' He had looked at her with something bordering on amazement. Wasn't it obvious? He had held her shoulders tightly, looked into her eyes and said.

'Saying I have a high regard for you is like saying that Shakespeare could knock out a limerick, that Elvis could hold a tune, that.. that, Marylyn Monroe scrubbed up well. I don't have a high regard for you, I love you, I loved you the moment I first saw you, I love you now and I'll never stop loving you.'

At least that is what he said in his head a few hours later, what actually came out of his mouth was;

"Well, you know, you're, well you're great."

Which just about summed it up. Generally, when dealing with other people, Scott was confident and self-assured, but with Abi, he inexplicably found it hard to find the right words and often came across as a bit hopeless. She rather liked this quality at first but as the months passed it wore thinner and thinner.

The other thing that affected their relationship was a condition he suffered from but was totally unaware of. He had something called hodophobia. It was an anxiety disorder which had its origins in a family day trip to the beach when he was four years old.

It was a hot Saturday at the end of two hot weeks, and consequently the Poole family were far from alone in their decision to spend a day at the beach. It was packed, and the young Scott, having wandered a short way from their beach rug, found himself hopelessly lost. His four-year-old brain had unwisely decided to navigate by seagull, and he kept walking towards the one that he thought he'd chased away from his bucket and spade. This took him further away with each step, and with everywhere looking the same, he walked around in circles trying and failing to find his mum and dad. It felt like hours for young Scott but was in reality no more than ten minutes before his dad found him sobbing uncontrollably.

After that, he developed a nervousness around travelling. It wasn't so crippling that it made it impossible to go anywhere, but the thought of going any great distance induced a sense of dread and panic that he just couldn't shake off. Abi, though, absolutely loved travelling and spent her time between dull jobs planning her next trip. She would suggest places and ideas, and he would find himself offering excuses and counterarguments, not really knowing why but aware that he would never be able to join her. That, plus his curious inability to be himself and act naturally, had been the final nail in the coffin of their relationship.

Her actual words were:

'You're lovely in so many ways and part of me loves you to bits but I really don't think you will ever go anywhere or do anything interesting.'

She hadn't been unkind about it – she'd said it rather sadly – and he had known she was right and he would have to do something about it.

If he hadn't been living in a small town in Wiltshire, England in 1985, there would probably have been any number of routes he could have taken to find help. Unfortunately, any form of mental illness or anxiety was not yet a 'thing'; you were just a loony or lazy. If there had been some sort of way of accessing, I don't know, let's say the entire accumulated knowledge of the world via a device in his pocket, he would have been able to self-diagnose his problem and find a number of appropriate treatments. But that was a few years away. This was 1985 and he was on his own.

Now, six months later, he'd managed to get himself as far as Volos, thanks to a massive mental effort and the aid of four pints of Guinness in the Gatwick departure lounge. Pulling his thoughts away from Abi with a wrench, Scott looked across the table at Vanessa and Oliver chatting away. They look good together, he thought to himself – a thought that surprised him.

When the vine leaves, chips and souvlaki were finished and they'd paid the bill, the boys were keen to go for more drinks in one of the beachside bars. But Vanessa declined, claiming she needed to head back to the office, ostensibly to do an hour or two of paperwork but in reality to delve into her Greek mythology book to learn more about Hippolyta, Queen of the Amazons.

The next week found Oliver scouring the village for the hen party in the hope of getting to know them. Three times each day he would walk the length of the beach, but to no avail. He had roped in an assortment of mates to help him in the search, one of whom liked to announce his arrival with a loud and discordant version of 'I've Got a Lovely Bunch of Coconuts'.

PG Wodehouse once described a gentleman as someone who could play the accordion but didn't. Billy was no gentleman.

He was a colleague of Oliver's, a peculiarly intense English teacher who supplemented his earnings in the summer when his school was closed by playing said instrument. Although it was only slightly more portable than a grand piano, he insisted on carting it around with him even down to the beach. His desire to inflict his 'talent' on casual passers-by would have marked him down as a thrusting young executive in the Spanish Inquisition, but as the contact pages of certain specialist magazines bear out, there is always someone, somewhere, who likes that sort of thing. He made a reasonable living – often, it has to be said, due to people realising the best method of getting him to sod off was to pay him.

His most disconcerting habit was to play his accordion in a low-slung position while dressed only in a pair of skimpy Speedos, which gave him the appearance, when viewed from the front, of being totally naked apart from a, ahem, large instrument. Given Billy's physique, this was not calculated to give him a competitive advantage. In truth, he was not that bad, musically speaking – he could play it and was indeed a talented pianist – but an accordion is an accordion, after all.

This morning he had been in full flow, as was evident from the large space at the far end of the beach.

'Whisky in the jar?' offered a quizzical Oliver.

'My money's on "The Wild Rover" – difficult to tell at this range,' added Scott.

Billy, who was standing at most three feet from him by this time, grinned nervously and hoisted the accordion off his neck. He did most things nervously. He had a trusting soul, thought the best of everyone and was always open to constructive criticism. The jester's hat had been Oliver's idea and seeing the thick rivulets of sweat running down Billy's face gave him a warm sense of satisfaction.

'Alright, Billy, how's it going. Still wearing the hat then,' said Oliver.

Billy looked pained.

'You know I'm not sure about it really.'

'You must be joking. Everyone loves it – that hat is the talk of the village.'

'Well, perhaps I'll stick with it a bit longer,' said Billy dubiously.

'Never mind the hat,' said Scott. 'Any luck on finding the hen party?'

'Nope, sorry. There is a group of girls down the beach but none of them were very tall and they didn't match your description.'

'Oh well. Keep your eye out, won't you – they must be around here somewhere.'

'Righto,' said Billy, heaving his accordion back into place before wandering off up the beach in search of new victims.

'You'd think Vanessa would be a bit more bloody helpful,' moaned Scott for possibly the tenth time that morning.

'Wouldn't disagree, mate. Very unreasonable not to tell blokes where vulnerable female guests are staying.'

'Vulnerable? Did you see the size of her – she's almost as big as you. She would kick the crap out of me if I tried anything.'

'Not the point. Nessie's got a duty of care, or something like that. That's ethics.'

'Doesn't sound remotely like the Essex I know. Round Romford way you could stalk a girl to your heart's content and they'd generally thank you for it.'

In fact Vanessa was discharging her duty of care that very moment, by sourcing aloe vera gel for the worst of the sunburnt tourists in her party of Geordies. She hadn't dropped by the boys' shack much in recent days, choosing instead to spend her time brushing up on the details of the ninth labour. She had learned that the Amazons were a nation of very warlike and scary women and there were quite a lot of them. It was their custom to bring up only the female children; the boys were either sent away to the neighbouring nations or put to death.

Nessie had been intrigued when Scott had suggested asking Debbie for her belt because that is exactly what Hercules had done in the original story. He'd travelled in peace to the island of the Amazons and explained his mission to Hippolyta, the queen, who generously agreed to give it to him. However, Hera, watching from amongst the gods, decided to stick in her usual troublesome oar. She sneaked onto the island disguised as one of the Amazon warriors and told them that Hercules planned to kidnap their queen. The resulting contretemps saw the whole horde descending on Hercules and his mates to give them a good kicking before they'd been able to limp back to the ship and escape with the belt.

In her role as the tour rep for the group, Vanessa had got to know the hen party pretty well over the week and had been increasingly amused by Scott's attempts to get news from her about their whereabouts or any snippet of information that might help in his belt hunt. It was the girls' last night before heading home and a leaving party had been planned in the local club, the Blue Parrot. Vanessa had made the arrangements and made sure that Scott and Oliver were both invited. Now, with everything set, all the evening needed was a Hera – a role Vanessa was looking forward to playing.

Chapter 3

The club was heaving. Ninety seconds after they got their drinks at the bar, Scott and Oliver found themselves separated in the crowd, with Oliver swept up in the wake of a neon-clad girl from Spain. Being tall (six foot three) and generally amiable, he did well with girls; they liked that he looked at them as they talked and noted that his eyes, unlike those of the other males, were not constantly flicking around the room checking out other people. It helped that they were a piercing blue that looked like they should belong to a film star. The irony was that his concentrated focus on the person in front of him was due to his appalling eyesight. He was so short-sighted that he could see bugger-all beyond a five-metre radius and found contact lenses a pain in the arse to use. He did wear glasses from time to time, but on balance preferred his world to be more blurry than not.

The Newcastle girls were standing in a group at the bar with Vanessa, sinking after-shots and surrounded by hopeful-looking types that a previous generation might generously have described as suitors. One group of which was represented by the pedalo renters from the beach, who were obviously very keen to make further acquaintance with the hen party. They were on a stag week and were not helping themselves by being impressively drunk for so comparatively early in the evening or by all sporting bright yellow T-shirts with an assortment of sexist slogans written on each. 'Tit fancier' had already made a grab for Nessie's bum, which had seen a glass of beer thrown at him. Seemingly oblivious to being drenched, he turned his attention to Debbie.

'Hello sweetheart, d'you know you've got a really nice arse.'

Debbie leant forward and replied, 'And you've got a face that makes my arse go all ten pence five pence.' He was still trying to work it out when his mate chipped in.

'Hello darling, like the shirt. Pole Dancer – is that what you do for a living, then?'

'No, pet, I'm a salsa teacher from Warsaw, now are you going to fuck off or what?' At this he had finally dragged himself and his equally annoying companions off, muttering about dykes, to search out more willing victims of their particular charm.

Nessie was just congratulating Alice on the Warsaw line when Scott appeared. The girls all shouted hello and messily clinked glasses, spilling shots all over the floor.

'Thank God for that, a normal man!' said Vanessa, giving his arm an affectionate squeeze. 'Where's Mr Pond tonight, then?'

'Talking of normal men, he's over there standing on a chair.'

Nessie followed his arm and saw Oliver peering intently at her from the other side of the room.

'Why is he standing on a chair looking like a psycho?'

'He's counting zebras.'

'Course he is, silly me,' said Vanessa.

Scott shrugged, took a swig of his beer and looked around at the girls. They were all wearing the football shirts, apart from the Hen who was wearing an extra large t-shirt that clearly belonged to someone else and a baseball cap, which, again, was far too big.

Turning to his right, he found himself at eye level with a pair of breasts. Reluctantly forcing his eyes upwards, he eventually came to the face of the tall girl. It was worth it. She was looking lovely; long dark hair and sparkling green eyes with just the start of a few laughter lines heading out from her eyes and mouth.

He had a tendency to compare everyone he met, invariably unfavourably, with Abi. It was something he had been doing for so long that he didn't really notice himself doing it any more. Distance and time had not stopped this process entirely, but right now, for once in his life, he was living in the moment and focused solely on the vision in front of him.

The idea that he'd ever have been able to seduce her into giving him her belt now seemed quite ludicrous, and with this thought in his mind he felt far less nervous about talking to her.

'How's it going? Had a good week?' he asked.

She looked down at him, put her hand to her ear and shook her head.

He tried again, shouting this time, but the fact that her head was barely two feet from a speaker was proving an insurmountable barrier. She smiled and, to his surprise, slipped her hand into his. Pointing to the garden, she strode through the crowd with him trotting along in her wake. Once outside he was propelled towards a table at the end of the garden with a view of the beach.

'That's better, couldn't hear a thing in there,' she said, eyeing him coolly before adding, 'I think you want something from me, don't you?' Her tone of voice would have been enough to send all the red corpuscles speeding towards his groin; by licking her lips as she said it, she ensured that all the white ones went along for the ride. Scott didn't trust himself to formulate a complete sentence.

'Vanessa?'

'She said you wanted my belt.'

'I don't make an item of taking women's habits.'

She raised her eyebrows.

He closed his eyes and tried again.

'I think you should know I don't make a habit of taking items of women's clothing.'

'Well, that's a shame,' she purred, gently stoking his arm. He gulped and, to his annoyance, found himself giggling like a schoolboy. In his list of fantasies, the idea of being seduced and dominated by a powerful, stronger woman had not featured. He couldn't for the life of him work out why he'd missed it. He hadn't felt this turned on for ... well, ever. Pulling himself together with a conscious effort, he said, 'I think I'd better explain.'

She leant forward as she listened to his story. He talked about his father and his uncle and the inheritance and the labours of Hercules. He was deliberately vague about the details and addressed most of what he said to the table. On the few occasions he risked looking at her face, he ended up stammering and losing the thread.

When he'd finished, she leant back in her chair with a wicked glint in her eye and whispered, 'Well, lover boy, if you want my belt you might have to give me something in return.'

'Sure – I mean of course – I don't expect you to give it to me, I'll pay you for it.'

'I have something in mind,' she said, taking his hand. 'Let's go somewhere a little more private.'

Five minutes later, Scott was flat on his back on a sun lounger, convinced that Father Christmas was about to pop up out of the darkness with a winning lottery ticket and the keys to a small island in the Caribbean. Her magnificent legs were astride him either side of the lounger as she looked down at his supine form, her eyes lingering on the prominent bulge in his jeans.

'I think we'd better take that shirt off, don't you?' she whispered as she lowered herself onto him and wriggled against his straining erection. She deftly undid the buttons of his shirt, pulled it over his head and, holding his arms firmly above his head, rubbed her breasts against his bare chest. He groaned as he felt the pressure of her nipples against his through the cheap nylon fabric of her top. Releasing his hands and pulling his shirt free, she moved her attentions to his jeans. Her long, powerful fingers quickly and efficiently undid the buttons on his fly as he whimpered gently to himself. Removing his shoes, she insistently tugged at his jeans until he felt them slip off. 'Now close your eyes, there's a good boy.'

He heard a gentle click as she removed her belt and then groaned with pleasure as the leather flicked against his nipples. He felt his arms again being forced above his head as she bound his wrists with the belt, leaving him exposed and vulnerable. The anticipation reached a fever pitch as he awaited her next touch.

Twenty seconds later, he still had his eyes tightly closed despite the nagging doubts that were flooding his mind. If he counted another ten seconds without opening them, he promised himself, then he wouldn't find himself alone, on the beach, naked. He got to twenty-nine before accepting the inevitable.

Back in the bar, the girls were waiting in anticipation. Nessie, a veteran of more hen nights than she cared to admit to, had given the girls the idea of collecting a complete set of blokes' clothing for the Hen to put on. So far she had a hat, a t-shirt, and one flip-flop. The reappearance of Debbie clutching Scott's jeans and shirt reduced them all to hysterics.

Oliver, who had given up his zebra experiment and was busy pouring drinks down the neck of Pole Dancer, or Alice as she was normally called, was more delighted than most. For the last ten minutes he had been uncomfortably aware of the girls eyeing his trousers, and if he was off the hook at the expense of the humiliation of his mate, then all the better. Debbie, breaking free from the howling girls, turned to him and said, 'Look, I'm sorry about your mate. He's down on the beach if you want to rescue him. Tell him it's just a joke and I'll buy him a drink.'

Oliver looked at his drink, looked at Debbie, felt Alice squeeze up against him and said, 'I think he'll be alright for a while.'

Chapter 4

Scott was surveying his options, none of which were particularly attractive. Stay where he was and get eaten alive by mosquitoes, or wander through the village bollock naked. He was just coming down in favour of the latter option when the sound of drunken voices threw up a third possibility. As he listened, a snatch of conversation drifted his way that made his spirits soar. It was a nasal female voice intoning the most beautiful words he'd ever heard.

'Well, are we going fucking skinny-dippin' or what?'

He rolled onto the sand and wriggled commando-style, in every sense, towards the voices until five figures appeared out of the gloom. There were three guys, two of whom seemed of a similar build to himself, and two girls. They were all tearing at their clothes, racing to be the first into the sea. Taking care to keep out of sight behind an upturned lounger, he waited until the splashes and shouts had drifted away from the shore before making his move. He darted out, grabbed a pair of baggy shorts and a top and legged it back to his hiding place. He wriggled into the shorts, which were way too big, and slipped on the t-shirt, taking care to listen for any commotion from the skinny-dippers. He needn't have worried; they had far more interesting things on their minds than what might or might not be happening on the beach.

Even the most fashion-conscious are unlikely to be too picky when stranded naked on a beach, but there is a reasonable chance that Scott would have looked around for another top had he realised he'd put on a distinctive bright yellow t-shirt bearing the legend 'Pussy Hound'. Unfortunately, this was a fact to which he was oblivious as he headed back towards the lights.

Officer Panos enjoyed his job as the village policeman. It gave him a status in the local community, paid reasonably well, had a decent pension that he was only two years away from taking and, most importantly, involved doing very little. Most evenings he just drove around a bit, stopped at a bar or two for a coffee and had his photo taken with tipsy northern European girls who had borrowed his

... ᴜᴇ occasion. But earlier this evening, his routine had been broken by a phone call from his sister in-law, Christina, known as the noisy one in the family.

Right now, Christina was leaning out the window of Panos's police car, shouting at Scott and jabbing a heavily ringed finger in his direction. He was standing on the pavement by the beach and had been deciding on his next move when the police car pulled up alongside. He didn't need to be an expert Greek speaker to tell this woman was less than pleased about something, and her ire seemed to be directed entirely at him. Next thing he knew, she was out of the car shouting in his face and poking him in the chest as he tried to get a word in over her tirade. She was followed a little more slowly by Officer Panos, who carefully levered his portly frame out of his seat and said something that, temporarily at least, calmed her down. Scott looked between the two of them and addressed himself to Panos.

'Hello, I am English and speak only a little Greek. Is there a problem?' he asked with a lot more politeness than he was currently feeling.

Officer Panos nodded. 'Problem. She say you run away from taverna and not pay. You come with me.'

'I haven't been to a taverna, I have just been...' Scott thought about the likelihood of his story being either understood or believed, and ended up shaking his head in frustration. He was put into the front seat of the police car and they drove through the village. Scott knew enough Greek to have a few basic conversations but could think of nothing that might be vaguely appropriate for this situation, so searched around for some other way of establishing a rapport. He noticed the car ashtray was full of butts and could feel a packet of cigarettes digging into his hip from the pocket of the unknown bloke's shorts. Thinking of all the kidnap movies he had watched, he felt sure it was important to create a relationship with your captor.

'Cigarette?' he said, digging out the packet from his pocket.

Panos nodded and looked across to take one, at which point the headlights of a car heading in the opposite direction illuminated, to Scott's horror, the packet of condoms he was waving in Panos's face. Panos looked away in disgust and came out with a stream of the swear words the kids in Scott's English class were always trying to teach him. Scott moaned softly to himself and sank a little lower in his seat.

After they had driven for about a mile, Panos pulled in at a large group of apartments that were grouped around a taverna. The apartments were small and cheap, catering for the low-rent end of the market. If you were British, aged between eighteen and twenty-five with a propensity for binge-drinking and urinating wherever you happened to be standing, then this was the sort of place you would book.

The car came to a stop and they climbed out. The woman in the back seat, presumably the owner of the place, had kept up a non-stop stream of high-pitched complaints all the way. Panos had responded to her ranting a couple of times in a fairly non-committal manner. Scott guessed from previous experience of anyone in an official role that he would not be keen on doing any paperwork and hence would be looking for a non-official resolution. He had an uncomfortable feeling that this might involve someone hitting him very hard a number of times.

In the taverna were four family groups sitting at various tables, and all eyes turned to Scott as he entered. Policemen always excite interest and it was pretty obvious that everyone in the room had immediately figured Scott for the bad guy in this situation. Scott's concern for his physical wellbeing was not helped by the emergence of a bearded, heavyset guy wearing an apron, who appeared from the back room sharpening an enormous carving knife while glaring at Scott.

Christina went to the cash register and came back with a bill which she slapped onto the table in front of him. Whoever Pussy Hound had been with, they had clearly done themselves very well and managed to rack up a bill that was the equivalent of nearly a week's takings from his and Oliver's meagre windsurfing hires.

Scott stretched his arms out with his palms pointing up in the classic 'what can I do?' shrug before indicating that he had no money by standing up and patting his pockets. In doing so, he discovered that there was in fact a wallet in the baggy shorts he was wearing. It was in a low pocket on his thigh and looked promisingly plump. He opened it and discovered that his skinny-dipping friend had come out prepared for a no-holds-barred night on the town; it was full of cash. Finally, things were looking up.

He examined the bill, counted out the notes slowly to cover the charge, then paused, looked directly at the aggrieved owners and put his hands together in a praying motion, while looking as shamefaced as he could manage. Then he continued counting out the rest of the cash.

This went down well. The knife-sharpener nodded grimly and disappeared back into the kitchen. The owner picked up the money and spoke to Panos, who turned to Scott and said, 'We go now.'

Scott didn't need telling twice. They walked outside and Panos gestured that Scott should get back in the car.

'Problem?' he asked.

Panos, who on the strength of his evening's work could look forward to a number of free meals in the coming weeks, shrugged and said, 'No problem.'

He dropped him back where he had picked him up, which was directly outside the Blue Parrot.

Scott stood for a moment as the police car drove off, and listened to the music and laughter drifting his way. The way the evening had panned out up to now suggested that he should cut his losses and just go back and lie in his tent in a foetal position until someone's nan arrived to put a tartan blanket over his knees and tell him it was all going to be okay. The other option was to tip some strong alcohol down his neck until either things started to improve or he passed out. To do the latter, he needed cash or someone to supply the drinks, so in the end he elected for the Blue Parrot.

They spotted him walking towards the bar and he felt his face burning as he headed for their hysterical laughter. Immediately Debbie strode towards him and before he could react with a stream of recriminations, her lips clamped onto his, rendering speech impossible. Her hands held each side of his face as her tongue insistently searched for his. The whoops of the others faded as he lost himself in the sensation of her and his rising confusion. She pulled back and looked down at his face and said, 'You've no idea how much I've wanted to do that. Now I'd better get you a drink.'

His face now red with embarrassment, he wheeled around dazedly in the middle of a crowd of girls all laughing and slapping his back. As soon as he saw the Hen wearing his jeans and shirt in addition to the baseball cap, t-shirt and lone flip-flop, the reasons for Debbie's actions fell into place.

'Cheers!' she said, pressing a bottle into his hand before leaning forward and whispering, 'Here's to unfinished business.' And she kissed him on the cheek.

'To unfinished business!' replied Scott, clinking glasses.

'And I thought you only loved me for my belt.'

Scott took a swig of his beer and considered that despite all that had happened to him in the last hour, it looked like the evening was going to end about as well as he could possibly hope.

He was leaning forward towards her lips when suddenly he felt a rough hand on his shoulder, pulling him backwards. Turning round, he was confronted by an ugly mass of tattooed muscles.

'You sure this is the one, Trace?'

'That's him, Pete, he's the one. He grabbed my arse when I was dancing, and he tried to grope Jen when she was waiting for the loo. It's definitely him, I recognise the t-shirt.'

He didn't even see the punch. One minute he was standing, the next he was on his back with a massive pain above his left eye.

Scott awoke unsure of where he was. He closed his eyes and luxuriated in the slow clicking of gears as his brain slowly pieced the clues together. He remembered being dragged to his feet by Debbie and then leaving with her to go back to her apartment. At the thought of what had then happened, his face broke into a smile, causing him to wince at the throbbing pain in his head. He was in her bed, but she was no longer in it.

It was the first time he had been with anyone since Abi and he wasn't entirely sure how he felt about it. On balance, he thought, he felt pretty good. Hearing the bathroom door open, he rolled over, expecting to see a beautiful naked woman. What he actually saw was Oliver Pond's testicles swinging in the breeze. Oliver had them cupped in his hand and was examining his cock with a good deal of fascination.

'Morning' Scotty, you awake then? Will you look at that? Me old fella's more polished than a pensioner's Rover, smashin'.'

'Please tell me I'm still dreaming and when I wake up you'll have disappeared.'

Oliver grinned and scratched his arse. 'The girls have gone for breakfast. That eye's looking a bit tasty.'

'Which is more than could be said about you. Do you know I think I've spent more time looking at your cock than I have my own. Can't you put it away for a change?'

Oliver grinned some more and continued scratching. 'Quite a night, eh?'

'You really don't know the half of it,' said Scott.

'And you got this,' said Oliver, holding up a long leather belt with a silver buckle. 'First labour chalked off. Now, are you going to get dressed? I'm starving and the girls are waiting for us.'

It was a nice enough breakfast – omelettes, fresh coffee and attractive company – but a pall of depression hung over it that couldn't quite be shaken off. Debbie and Alice were leaving on the afternoon flight and were understandably less than enthusiastic about returning to home and work. There was a lot of clumsy embarrassment of the type that can only exist between comparative strangers who have spent the previous night experiencing an advanced degree of intimacy. No one really knew what to say or how to act, and in truth it was a relief when the time came to say their fond farewells. They swapped addresses and Scott promised to keep Debbie posted on his Herculean efforts before they hugged and kissed goodbye.

Chapter 5

When Scott was ten years old, he'd had an epiphany. Not for him the career of a train driver, or an astronaut, or an owner-manager of a haulage firm like his father and his grandfather before him. He knew, with absolute certainty, that he wanted to own a club and he wanted to play the best music that anyone had ever heard and he wanted people to dance and be happy.

The inspiration for this decision was Scott's Uncle Edward (Ted to his friends, Teddy to his extended family, 'that useless little shit' to everyone else who knew him). Some might say Ted was a visionary who had realised the 1960s was the most exciting decade the world had yet seen and one to make the most of. Others would point out that he was a lazy bastard. Either way, within six months of his father's death, Ted had sold his half of the inherited haulage firm to his brother (Scott's father) and carefully invested the proceeds in a record collection to rival that of a medium-sized radio station, plus mind-expanding drugs, vintage cognac and, rather surprisingly (or not, said his friends), ukuleles.

Scott's father had always complained that his brother lacked ambition, but as far as Scott was concerned, if your ambition was to get happily drunk while listening to Sister Sledge first pressings and playing the ukulele, you couldn't argue with Uncle Ted's application.

Uncle Ted had created the equivalent of a Victorian library, but for records. All four walls were filled from floor to ceiling with custom-built shelves. He even had one of those ladders on wheels and the young Scott loved to scoot along on it, watching the titles on the spines pass by as he went: Jackson 5, The Tornadoes, Marvin Gaye, Chuck Berry. In the middle of the room was a record player, and around the edges were four speakers as big as the ten-year-old Scott.

As soon as Scott was old enough to get a job, he took up the family baton and amassed a pretty impressive record collection. Ted encouraged him and once a week Scott would take round whatever he was listening to, and they would sit and play records and chat while Ted drank his trademark Courvoisier and Scott sipped lemonade – and, if he was lucky, beer.

On one memorable occasion Scott took a cassette of a new band and a Walkman, neither of which had gone down well with Ted. He could remember the conversation now.

'What on God's earth is that fucking thing?' Ted had demanded.

'It's a … You know what it is.'

'I most certainly do fucking not.'

'It's a Walkman, Uncle Ted.'

'What is it doing in my house?'

'You should get one, you can listen to music wherever you go and you can copy some of your old stuff onto them.'

'They can copy my arse before I will touch one of those things.'

Ted shifted in his chair, hooked his long grey hair behind his ears with his left hand and swirled his brandy around the glass with his right.

'Fuck off with your Walkman while I listen to some proper music.'

But Scott stayed. Whatever his uncle called him (and he called him many things), Scott always stayed. Ted then put on a very old single by Muddy Waters.

'Listen and you'll hear a hiss and crackle, and you'll hear scratches, and if memory serves it jumps on the second chorus and that is all how it should be. Music means something different to everyone who hears it and it should sound different too, don't you think? Unique?'

Scott sat back, hands behind head, as the needle hit the first groove and the scratchy sound of Muddy telling the world that his mojo was working filled the room. Scott found his feet tapping and his head nodding. He caught Ted's eye and smiled as the needle jumped.

'It's great. Reminds me of someone.'

'Well, it would, dear boy. You see, music is like the Olympic torch. Each new generation picks it up, adds something and runs with it. Mick and the boys were always listening to this.'

'Mick?'

Ted pushed himself up from his chair, stood still for a moment pulling his lip as he considered and then skipped across the room to pull Out of Our Heads (US import version) by the Rolling Stones from the rack. Scott watched him and marvelled at how everything changed when Ted was listening to music. He carried a fair bit of weight and tended to waddle and wheeze his way through most tasks, but when he wanted to find a song to play, he glided across the floor like he was on rollers.

'Even a youthful worm like you will have heard of the Rolling fucking Stones. 1965, they made this.' A dreamy look came across Ted's face. 'A bloody good year that was.'

The first track, 'Mercy, Mercy', started up and Ted took a long pull on his brandy.

'Sound familiar?'

Scott nodded as the obvious similarity between the two songs hit him.

'Bowled the bugger out, once. Loves his cricket, does Mick. Not a bad batsman. Chucked him down a complete bastard of a googly. Bloody good bloke. Mind you, Charley was the man for me. Charley's a gent. Shite at cricket, mind you.'

Scott grinned to himself and just listened as Ted got into his stride. This was how their evenings played out. In the 60s, Ted had been a rich young man, with the proceeds of his part of the business at his disposal, and had always been more than generous with whatever cash or substance he happened to have about his person. From what Scott could gather, he had never exactly been in with the in-crowd, but had bobbed along comfortably on the edges for long enough to meet a few people and have a few anecdotes to tell. The beauty of Ted's stories was that many of them were somewhat lacking in anything approaching reality. But some were true. And it really didn't matter to Scott which was which. He suspected that it didn't matter to Ted either. More likely, he could no longer tell the difference.

'Didn't have cassette fucking players back then. Didn't want 'em. Still don't.'

By the time Keith Richards's classic, fuzzy riff from 'The Last Time' had begun its scratchy fade-out, Scott was converted. From then on he had spent on vinyl any money he could get – which, once he started working for his dad at weekends, turned out to be quite a lot.

As his collection grew, he became more and more in demand to play at friends' parties and school discos. Each occasion reinforced what he had always known: that all he really wanted to do was play records for people.

He even had a venue in mind for his club. One of his many short-term jobs had been in a plumbing wholesaler's situated in an old warehouse next to the railway track in his hometown of Salisbury. The place still had the old cranes and chutes that had been used to load coal into steam trucks, and he could picture it converted into a club, but still with the old machinery as features. He had even worked out the costs, which were considerable. The warehouse was for sale at £150,00 he reckoned he would need at least £20,000 more to kit it out, but he had no concrete idea of how he would ever get close to earning the money to turn his dreams into reality.

Sadly, his opportunity came in the demise of Uncle Ted, whose lifestyle had finally caught up with him and not so much bitten him on the bum as gained a vice-like grip on his aorta.

It was two weeks after Uncle Ted's funeral and Scott was still dealing with the loss when his father called and asked him to come to the family home to talk.

Scott wasn't looking forward to it. What his dad described as a 'talk' would be far more appropriately categorised as a lecture about his failings. That was how it usually went, and it was with some trepidation that he trudged up the path to the front door.

It had been a difficult interview. They sat down in the kitchen, which was not Scott's natural habitat and made him nervous from the outset.

'Scott.'

'Dad.'

They stared at each other for a few moments, each unsure of how to continue.

Mr Poole coughed and said; 'What are you doing with yourself lately, then? I hear you've got a new job.'

'That's right,' said Scott brightly. 'I'm working for a mobile communications firm.'

'Mobile communications!' echoed his father, raising his eyebrows. 'Sounds very grand.' He stood up and walked towards the French windows. 'Mobile communications,' he repeated dreamily, looking out at the pristine lawn. 'You wouldn't care to elaborate on that at all?'

Scott licked his lips and thought to himself it had all been going too well. 'Um, well, I suppose you could say that we deal in communications that are, um, mobile.'

'You're a push-bike dispatch rider, aren't you?'

'No.'

Mr Poole turned around.

'I mean, yes.'

His father went back to staring out the window.

'Yes, but it's …'

'Only temporary,' interrupted Mr Poole. 'Of course it is, Scott. It's always "only temporary" with you. But, then, of course, you're right. Life is only temporary.'

The conversation was taking a melancholic tone in Scott's view, and a silence followed that neither of them seemed inclined to fill. His father moved away from the window, came to sit at the other side of the kitchen table and took a sip of his tea. He put it down with great care and raised his eyes to look piercingly into those of his son. Scott was surprised to see a tenderness there he hadn't seen since he was a child, a tenderness more pronounced because fathers so very rarely look at their grown-up sons with such burning intensity.

'I want to talk to you about your Uncle Ted, and I want you to listen. When I was two years older than you are today, and Ted was exactly your age, our father – your grandfather – died.'

Scott moved his coffee cup nervously but didn't say anything.

'We both had to take on a lot of responsibility, a lot of work, a lot of money. Teddy wasn't as strong as me. He thought he knew best, he thought he knew what he wanted from life.'

Scott heard the crack in his voice and was startled to see tears welling into his father's eyes.

'Now he's dead, and I miss him terribly. Losing a brother is bad enough. I'm damned if I'll bury a son, too.'

Scott felt himself welling up, too, at the emotion in his father's voice. But his principal reaction was confusion. What was the old fella talking about?

'Dad, you've lost me. Push-bike dispatch isn't that dangerous, you know.'

His father gazed at him wearily and shook his head.

'I'm not talking about riding a bloody bicycle.' He paused to collect himself, straightened his tie and walked over to a French dresser that contained the set of china that they only ever used at Christmas. He opened a drawer, pulled out a manila folder and handed it to Scott.

'What's this?'

'Go ahead and open it.'

Scott did so and found what appeared to be an airline ticket, £200 in cash and a handwritten note. He opened the note and recognised Uncle Ted's neat script.

'Well, young Scott, as you are reading this it would appear that I have chipped a long hop to silly mid-on and the umpire's finger has gone up. Looking back, I'd say I'd had a bloody good innings so I want no moping about or sadness from you, my boy. It's time you started living – there's a big old world out there and I wish I'd seen a bit more of it when I had the chance. Nothing wrong with sitting around listening to music, but you can't spend your whole life doing it, so here's the thing. You can have it all – the records, the house, the whole damn shooting match – but first of all you've got to get off your arse and earn it.'

When not listening to music, drinking or playing the ukulele, Ted had indulged his other passion. He had a fascination with ancient history and in particular Greek mythology. The seeds of this interest had been sown by the classics teacher at his boarding school, Mr Bay, who had also run the school cricket team. Mr Bay's favoured teaching technique was to compare the figures of classical mythology to famous cricket players, so Zeus would be WG Grace,

Agamemnon Jack Hobbs, and the feats of the gods would be compared to those of the cricketing greats.

A typical lesson might take the form of an explanation of how Paris had sailed to Troy and unleashed Agamemnon against his enemies just as Jardine had travelled down to Sydney and set Larwood on the Aussies.

Ted and his classmates had lapped it up.

Ted had always regretted that he hadn't travelled to all the places he wanted to. He'd been to Rome but had never made the trip to Turkey, Greece, North Africa or any of the other ancient sites. That regret had clearly been washing over him when he was writing his will.

Scott read on.

'I, Scott Poole, do agree that I will travel to the city of Volos in the country of Greece and will, within two years, complete seven of the labours of Hercules. On completion of said labours I will purchase a sailing boat and sail home to England. On arrival and presentation of proof that said labours were completed in a manner acceptable to Mr Richard Poole, I, Scott Poole, will inherit the estate of the late Mr Edward Poole.'

He put the note down and looked up at his father, who was looking back expectantly at him over his teacup.

'So you see, Teddy had decided to leave you everything, but it worried me that you would repeat his mistakes and drink your life away. We talked before he died and agreed that if you were going to inherit then you needed to prove yourself up to it. This is your chance – what do you say?'

Scott didn't know what to say. He didn't even know what to think. The insistent voice of a character from a sitcom his parents liked came to him, saying, 'Don't panic, don't panic!' Could he do this? Of course, the money would be great – but more than that, this was a chance to prove to Abi that he could be the man she wanted him to be. It was also quite literally Ted's will that he do it. It would be hard and terrifying, especially the bit about getting on the plane. But perhaps for Ted and Abi he could do this.

He looked up at his father, gulped and to his surprise heard himself say yes.

'Good lad. I have every faith in you. If you can do this, I will happily pass over your Uncle Ted's estate. He didn't leave much money, but you will get his house and of course, his possessions. I hope this will be the making of you.'

Scott thought about the record collection and what he could do with it. Then there was the house, a big, sprawling pile in an expensive part of town. It had to be worth enough to buy a venue and kit it out. This was his opportunity to make his dreams into reality. He just had no idea how on earth he was going to manage it. One thing was certain – he was going to need some help.

The phone conversation was brief.

'Mate. Do you want to spend two years in Greece and help me earn enough to start a club?'

'I'll start packing,' said Oliver.

Chapter 6

The town of Volos had been chosen by Ted as it was the location from which Jason set sail with his Argonauts. It had changed much in the intervening years, not all for the better. An earthquake in the 1950s had destroyed most of the older buildings and their replacements ran to functional concrete rather more than was ideal.

Its setting, however, was magnificent. The town was squeezed between the sea and the mountain range of Pelion, so that from most vantage points it was possible to see either the ludicrously blue water of the Pagasetic Gulf or the verdant green of the mountains. Pelion was tall enough to be snow-capped in winter, and melting snow seeped into the thousands of tiny streams that criss-crossed it and gave it its unusual greenness. Whereas most of Greece ran to pale olive groves and dusty fields, Pelion stood out as an oasis of forestry. As the town had grown it had encroached on the lower reaches of Pelion, but higher up it was studded with tiny identikit villages all with a traditional square or *platea*, café, restaurant and springs of the clearest, coolest mountain water.

On arriving in Volos, the boys had swiftly discovered that the only obvious employment for two non-Greek speakers in a provincial Greek town was to work as English teachers. To their surprise, Volos had around forty English schools of varying size and repute. Finding work had therefore proved something of a breeze.

Oliver was somewhat lacking in teaching qualifications, but he wasn't going to let that stand in his way. At the age of fifteen, prompted by the small ads in the back of Private Eye, he had bought two O Levels with a month's wages from his milk round and had been struck with how simple the documents were. With the aid of a printing set, a calligraphy book from the library, and a large amount of painstaking practice facilitated by a correspondingly large amount of cannabis, he discovered he had something of a talent for forgery.

As a result, he left school at sixteen with ten O Levels, five A levels and a degree in Philosophy.

And so, after a trip to the Volos stationer's, Oliver could boast an English degree to rival Scott's genuine one. Within two weeks of their arrival they had both found jobs, each of which came with a flat, the rent for which was taken from their pay each month.

The pay was the downside. On examining what was left in their envelopes after the first month, it was clear they would have to either spend the next twenty years scrimping and saving or come up with some other money-making ideas to complete the labours, buy a boat and fund the trip back to England.

As they settled into their new life, Scott found that his anxiety about moving around diminished the more he got used to his new surroundings. Volos was not so huge and the trick was to not think about being so far from home, but rather to think about where he was right now as home. Abi still popped into his thoughts unbidden countless times a day, and he would often imagine bumping into her around the neighbourhood. In these daydreams he would construct whole dialogues in his head, in which he invariably sounded cool, interesting and in control.

Pretty much all of the English teachers met up once a week in an ugly pizza restaurant alongside a main road. The food was not particularly good and no one knew why they met there, but somehow it had become an ingrained habit passed from one set of transient teachers to the next.

One night, after they'd been working at the school for a few weeks, Scott and Oliver were taken along to it by an English colleague named Carl. As they strolled along, Carl explained that, broadly speaking, the teachers fell into two categories. The majority were like him: recent graduates who didn't fancy a real job just yet and had signed up to a kind of paid gap year. He called these the 'first offenders'. The other group consisted of those who had mistaken the job for a profession and were generally an odd mixture of superiority and embitterment. Carl referred to them as 'lifers'.

Lifers were, for the most part, hugely qualified, some with master's degrees in languages and additional teaching qualifications plus years of experience. In any other profession they would be highly paid, respected and probably in management positions. As it was, they worked for an hourly rate on short-term contracts, often for unscrupulous school owners who offered no pension, holiday pay or any other benefits that would recommend the job to a sane individual. They were, as Carl succinctly put it, a miserable bunch of fuckers – but there were enough people in the other category to provide an entertaining and varied social crowd.

Most of the people at the restaurant were in their early- to mid-twenties and the vast majority were female. Scott and Oliver were therefore something of a novelty, and each found himself being quizzed on where he worked and where he lived and what he thought of Volos so far.

Oliver was chatting about music to an Irish girl when he noticed Scott talking to two pretty girls at the other end of the room.

Women liked Scott, and on the face of it, it was difficult to work out why. He had a natural tendency towards smiling, dark eyes and a mop of naturally curly dark hair, but not even his mother would claim he was drop-dead handsome. Granted, he was funny and interesting and could be very charming, but none of this really accounted for his success.

Oliver had a theory. After years of seeing his mate succeed with attractive women, he'd given it considerable thought. He reckoned it was down to the size of his head. It was really big. This, Oliver reckoned, made Scott look like a baby and brought out the maternal instinct in women.

He had once tested this 'big head' theory. One evening Oliver had been invited to a party where he met and fell into conversation with a very attractive Leisure and Tourism teacher from Chelmsford. He had in fact quite literally fallen into conversation: turning from the bar, he'd got his leg caught in the strap of a handbag and pitched headlong into a firm and shapely pair of breasts. Having already reached second base, so to speak, he'd found it quite easy to return to first and start a conversation.

She was lovely and he was absolutely delighted to get back to his flat with her address. Except he hadn't, exactly. Since neither of them could produce a pen, she had told him it as she was leaving and he'd memorised it, then written it down as soon as he could borrow a pencil from his cab driver.

The next morning, he had written a masterpiece of wooing that would have made Cyrano de Bergerac toss it all in and get a job writing birthday card messages. Which would have been all been great if he hadn't written her address down as number sixteen rather than the number sixty that she lived at.

A day later, Sarah from number sixty had written to tell him that she could safely say she'd never read wooing quite like it and if he cared to write again she'd be delighted to hear from him. Within a week, they'd got to exchanging photos, and this was where Oliver had seen the opportunity to test his theory about Scott. By painstaking cutting-and-pasting he'd managed to graft a 150% image of his head onto a 100% body so that you could barely see the join.

In retrospect, his big mistake had been to choose a torso shot that had no recognisable inanimate objects in it to give a sense of perspective. Sarah from number sixty, on receiving the photo and discovering her dream man had a horribly wizened body and appeared to weigh about six stone, had abruptly stopped writing.

Reflecting on the injustice of this, Oliver sipped his beer and looked around the pizza restaurant at his newfound fellow teachers. His eyes settled back on Scott and the girls he was chatting to. They were looking in his direction and smiling in a conspiratorial way. One of the girls walked over and tapped him on the shoulder.

'Hi, I'm Su,' she said, and then did the most surprising thing that had ever happened to him. She lent down and whispered in his ear. 'Your friend Scott says you might be up for a foursome.'

Now any fantasies that Oliver had in that direction – and there were many – generally consisted of him and a number of other women, and didn't feature other men. Particularly not Scott. However, he was open-minded and prepared to give it a go.

In his head he had practised for this moment for years. This was where he lazily raised an eyebrow and, smiling confidently, said, 'I thought you'd never ask.'

What he actually said was:

'Smashing. Thank you very much.'

'Great. Finish your drink and we're on then,' she said.

They all left together. Su's friend, who was called Samantha, flagged down a passing taxi and within ten minutes they were being shown into her kitchen.

'Give us a couple of minutes, just need to get everything set up,' said Samantha, disappearing into what Oliver assumed was the bedroom.

He turned to Scott and whispered, 'What the fuck?'

Scott grinned. 'We just got talking and it came up in conversation that they liked it, and, well, I haven't done it for ages, so I thought why not.'

'You're being very cool about this, mate,' said Oliver. 'I'm off to have a bit of a scrub up.'

He disappeared into the bathroom. Scott heard splashing and guessed Oliver was rinsing the parts of his body that were about to see some unexpected action.

When he came out, Scott nipped in to use the loo, leaving Oliver in the kitchen with Samantha. She smiled as she edged around him in the narrow space.

'Just need to rinse these glasses.'

'Can I help?'

'No, you're fine.' She squirted some bright yellow liquid into the washing-up bowl. 'I'm really looking forward to this. Scott says you're really good.'

It was fortunate she had her back to him, as it meant she missed the look of shocked incredulity on his face.

'Did he?'

'Yes, he said you were a natural,' said Samantha.

'Right, yes, no, nice,' Oliver stuttered.

Scott bigging him up in the love stakes was possibly the least likely thing he could imagine – but clearly tonight was a night of surprises. Scott reappeared from the bathroom as Samantha, having dried the glasses and grabbed a bottle of wine from the fridge, said, 'We're all set. Come on through.'

The flat had just the small kitchen, two bedrooms and a bathroom, with no shared living space, so the room they entered was Su's bedroom. Su's preparations had involved folding her bed away and setting up a table and four chairs in the middle of the room.

Su indicated the seat farthest from the door.

'You don't mind being North, do you?' she asked Oliver.

In something of a daze, Oliver found himself sitting at the table and staring at the pack of cards in front of him.

'Ah, bridge, great, nice, hmm, bridge,' he said.

Scott grinned at him from his seat opposite.

'You alright, mate? You look a little like your crest may have fallen.'

'What, eh, no, smashing, bit of bridge, lovely.'

'You weren't expecting something else, were you?' asked Su, who had very big, pretty eyes and was doing her best wide-eyed innocent look.

'You gits,' said Oliver as the three of them dissolved into helpless laughter.

Eventually they calmed down enough to start the game. After the first couple of hands, as the smirking and occasional bursts of giggles began to subside, and Oliver's disappointment and embarrassment faded, they fell into the rhythm of playing the game and chatting between hands.

'Noticed you speaking a bit of the old Greek to the taxi driver there,' said Oliver.

Samantha nodded.

'This is my fourth year, so I've picked up quite a lot. It's not too bad when you get used to it.'

'You've been here for four years?' said Scott.

'Not here in Volos, no – this is my first term here. I was in Crete for three years.'

'What was that like?'

'Amazing. Really beautiful place and incredible people.'

Su caught Samantha's eye at this point and raised her left eyebrow. Samantha continued, 'Well, lots of nice people and one complete arsehole.'

It transpired that she had spent two years in a relationship with a guy before he finally got round to proposing. Unfortunately, not to her. Hence she had felt it was time to move on and so had taken a job in Volos. She didn't seem to think a great deal of the place, and was clearly missing Crete as she talked about it a lot and in very glowing terms.

With three years under her belt, Samantha was just on the right side of becoming a lifer. This was a fact of which she was only too aware, and she made them all promise that if she was still there for the next school year they had permission to take her to the nearest beach and drown her.

Su was a fairly standard first offender: she had a degree in psychology and was toying with the idea of completing a master's, and thought a year in the sun might help her decide. The evening rolled on until three a.m., when the last bottle of red wine had been demolished. At which point they said their drunken goodbyes, agreeing that they should play again soon.

Chapter 7

May 1991

It was the morning after another epic bridge marathon that Scott first met Vanessa

He had woken to a hangover so bad that his hair hurt, crawled out of bed and pulled up the shutters to the balcony. They covered double doors, which opened onto a marvellous view of the mountain. Blinking at the light, he stepped through the open doors, breathed in the fresh morning air and found himself standing in a drying pool of vomit. Looking down at his feet, he scratched his head. He couldn't remember being sick the night before, but the evidence seemed pretty irrefutable. He hopped into the bathroom, rinsed his feet, made his way into the kitchen and discovered he had run out of coffee. At which point he sat down heavily on his one chair and moaned softly and pathetically to himself.

Although at that precise point Scott would have claimed to be the most miserable being in the world, he would have been wrong. There was someone feeling even worse, and that person was only twenty feet away from where he was sitting. Her name was Vanessa and she had just moved into the flat above his.

This was her first morning in Greece. The day before, she had been shown to her flat, given a whistle-stop tour of the city and then taken to a restaurant by her boss and poisoned. The poisoning had been accidental (the result of a dodgy swordfish) and hadn't kicked in until about two in the morning, when she was back in her new flat. It was on the top floor in a block that sloped inwards; hence, if she were to drop anything over the edge of the balcony – the contents of her stomach, for example – it would land on the balcony below.

Up all night suffering from the effects of food poisoning, and in the knowledge that she had been sick on her new neighbour's balcony, Vanessa felt she had got off to a bad start. The four words of Greek she felt confident enough to successfully pronounce were not designed for use in the tricky social situation ahead, unless of course she were to copulate with her as-yet-unmet neighbour while suggesting he might have an interest in masturbation. With the help of some prescription drugs for dysentery, which she had kept from a gap year in India, she made it to the office and enlisted the help of her new boss as translator.

Scott's low, moaning wail was interrupted by a knock on the door. He didn't get a lot of visitors and naturally assumed, from the way his day was panning out, that it would be some variety of Greek Jehovah's Witnesses. He hobbled to the door and found himself facing a girl who was so pale she looked translucent. To add to Scott's confusion, she appeared to be wearing a pair of canary-yellow Marigold rubber gloves. She was standing next to a suited middle-aged man with a moustache.

The vision in canary yellow spoke, and to his surprise she spoke in English.

'Hello. My name is Vanessa and I've moved into the flat above.' She pointed upwards and smiled weakly. The suited man repeated what she had said in Greek to Scott, who nodded sagely.

'Last night I ate something that was not good and was sick. I think I may have created a mess on your balcony, and I've come to clean it up.'

Again, the stream of Greek from the suit before an expectant silence fell. Scott grinned at Vanessa, looked at her Marigolds, and said:

'Scott Poole, delighted to meet you, I've a few dishes that need doing now you come to mention it, won't you come in and have a cup of tea?'

Over the following few weeks, he, Oliver and Vanessa became firm friends. They would meet up and, being English, moan about the shortcomings of their adopted home. That they invariably did this in lovely cheap restaurants while drinking lovely cheap booze, surrounded by lovely people, was somewhat ironic and somehow typically British.

The lovely cheap restaurant they were in tonight was called a *tsiperadikos,* which meant it sold *tsipero.* Of all the delights their new home of Volos and its environs had to offer, *tsipero* took some beating. This was the region's own particular brand of ouzo that was served in numerous *tsiperadikos*, or *tsipero* restaurants. It was served in tiny bottles slightly smaller than those used for whisky miniatures and which the locals called 'soldiers', the idea being to collect a small platoon as the evening progressed. Each bottle came with an appetiser, which improved in quality as more bottles were consumed.

Their local was just around the corner from Scott's school and was owned by a man they had, within minutes of meeting him, nicknamed Taffos, a typically friendly and well-connected local who had rather taken them under his wing. In a culture where most things got done through the patronage of a cousin here and an uncle there, Taffos possessed a supreme advantage. He was that rarity known as a Greek Catholic from a family whose devoutness firmly embraced the sin of family planning. The resulting Taffos clan was frankly vast, with a network of cousins that extended throughout Greece and most of the rest of the world. Taffos could pull more strings than an overworked piano tuner.

It became Oliver and Scott's favourite spot and they would drop in most evenings after finishing work, often meeting Vanessa for a quick drink and to chat with the owner. In reality there was very rarely anything like a quick drink when it came to *tsipero*. It had a narcotic quality and made you feel a mixture of euphorically drunk and stoned at the same time. After the first two, they invariably developed fixed grins on their bright red faces and a compulsion to keep them coming.

An additional temptation, as if it were needed, was the improvement of the dishes the more they drank. On one of their earliest visits they had worked their way up from a few random olives and a bit of bread, through little fish and potato skins to the exotic delights of king prawns and stuffed crab. The next dish to arrive had, somewhat surprisingly, appeared to be a whole pickled cauliflower. Taking the slight disappointment manfully in their stride, they both assumed they had been round the clock, so to speak, and were back at the start. It tasted a bit odd and it was not until the waiter had proudly asked them if they had ever had sheep's brain that they realised why.

They were currently on the deep-fried whitebait, having demolished four drinks before Vanessa arrived. She sat down and looked at the notepad in front of Scott.

'What you are you doing there?' she asked.

'Trying to work out how to make some money,' said Oliver. 'We were writing some ideas down before you arrived. We don't get paid in the summer and don't fancy washing up in a bar for eight weeks.'

'Don't most of you lot go back to Blighty and earn loads at summer schools?'

'A lot of them seem to,' agreed Scott. 'But we fancy staying here and...' He hesitated before adding, 'hanging around a bit.'

For some reason, he hadn't felt able to tell her about Uncle Ted and his challenge just yet. They'd not known her long, and besides, he felt was as if telling her would make it real, somehow, and then he would actually have to do the labours. As long as he didn't mention it, they could stay safely in the realm of the theoretical.

'Wish I could help, chaps,' she said breezily, 'but I probably earn less than you do.'

'We don't want money, Nessie – wouldn't dream of taking any money from you,' said Oliver. 'Got any ideas, though? It's only thirteen days before school shuts and we've got twelve weeks off with no salary. Maybe we could run events, tours and stuff?'

'We-e-ell, that's possible. I could ask the boss,' said Vanessa, trying and failing to look enthusiastic.

'Tours? You can't drive,' Scott pointed out.

'I've got a driving licence,' Oliver replied, pouring some water quite near to his glass but not quite in it.

'You also have, to the best of my knowledge, an HGV, forklift truck and pilot's licence, but that doesn't alter the fact that the only thing you've ever driven is a bumper car.'

'Fair point.'

Scott picked up a chip and dipped it in the tzatziki. He looked at Oliver and said, 'You could get your guitar out, do some busking, maybe even play in a bar.' Oliver had played the guitar since he was ten years old and was really good. He could also hold a tune and had the sort of voice you usually needed to dedicate a lifetime of smoking forty cigarettes and a downing a bottle of Jack Daniel's a day to cultivate. Somewhere between gravelly and dry-stone wall.

49

'Oh go on, why don't you?' added Vanessa.

Oliver shifted in his seat.

'Could do,' he said cautiously.

Much as he enjoyed playing and singing in front of mates, pissed, at the end of an evening, standing up sober in front of a group of strangers on his tod was not something he wanted to do if he could possibly avoid it.

Scott, guessing incorrectly the reason for his reticence, chipped in with: 'We could be a double act! I could have a go – you teach me a few chords and I'd be up for it.'

Oliver tried to look positive and failed miserably. In his view, if Scott had any hidden musical talent then it was buried twenty feet underground in a lead-lined bunker in the middle of a desert with a 'likely chance of death' sign on the door.

His scepticism was based on practical experience. They had tried to form a band at school. Oliver had been lead vocalist and rhythm guitar; a kid from his class had played bass due to the fact that his older brother had one; and another mate who sang in the choir provided backing vocals and could play the flute. That just left an opening for a drummer. They auditioned Scott, who borrowed a set of bongos from the music department for the occasion.

They set up a recording studio in the bassist's house and played a couple of cover versions into a tape. Scott was pretty pleased with his performance but even he had to admit, on listening back, that his timing was not the best. It sounded exactly like three fairly competent musicians trying their best to record a song while a guy locked in a cupboard was beating on the door to be let out.

'Could try that,' Oliver said tentatively and was mercifully saved from going any further by the owner, Taffos, who emerged from the kitchen and plonked himself down next to Scott.

Gregoris, to give him the name his parents had thought best suited their first-born, came from a wealthy family. In order to give him the best possible chance in life, his doting father arranged to send him to England at sixteen to study and learn the language. His father, a successful entrepreneur, had many sterling qualities – a shrewd head for business, eye for a bargain, an impressive facility for languages – but unfortunately no knowledge of geography whatsoever. Consequently, after two years of intensive study in Cardiff, young

Gregoris had returned to Volos having learned to speak English in a Welsh accent that could slice bread. On first meeting him Oliver had immediately rechristened him Taffos.

Their friendship had started off as a marriage of convenience. Taffos gave them a large number of free drinks and they provided him with introductions to a similarly large number of female English teachers who made up the surprisingly sizeable expat community. Although to their certain knowledge Taffos had never succeeded with any of the English girls, it didn't seem to bother him overmuch and you could not fail to be charmed by his relentless good nature in the face of constant rebuttals.

'Alright then boys, isn't it.'

'How's it going, Taffos,' said Oliver.

'Won't hear me grumble now, how are you, Vanessa love?'

'Very well, thank you, Gregoris.'

'Not out with Sarah tonight, then?'

Sarah was one of Vanessa's colleagues, to whom Taffos had taken something of a shine.

'Not tonight, she's off with some pals to…'

Vanessa suddenly realised that telling Taffos the exact whereabouts of Sarah and her friends would not endear her to the girls. 'Some bar,' she added vaguely.

'Pity, pity,' said Taffos. 'What you writing there, boyo?' he asked, pointing to Scott's scribbles.

'Just working out how we can make some cash this summer.'

'You might be in luck, Scotty boyo. Might have just the thing for you. You know Aussie Bob?'

'Heard of him – is he the guy that teaches windsurfing?'

'That's him, boy. He's selling up his stuff.' Taffos leant forward and adopted a conspiratorial expression. 'Between you and me, like, he needs to sell in a hurry. Take over his windsurfing business, you'll make a mint, look.'

'That's not a bad idea, Taffos mate.'

'Tidy. I'll give him a call.'

He disappeared for five minutes before easing himself back down at the table.

'Just spoken to him; 30,000 drachs and it's yours.'

'1000 quid,' said Oliver.

'For what exactly?' asked Scott.

'He's selling his windsurfing kit and a few other things. Tidy business that, tidy. He'll meet you tomorrow if you're interested.'

If all the world truly was a stage, then the final stage direction on Aussie Bob's Greek adventure would read, 'Exit stage left pursued by Immigration Control'. Hence his beach watersports business – consisting of four windsurf boards, two pedalos, a couple of canoes and a small dinghy with an outboard motor – was up for sale and he was in no position to drive a hard bargain. After some haggling, they got him down to £700, which, with their savings and Scott selling some shares his aunt had left him, they just about scraped together.

By the time July rolled around, they had decided on the location of their business, and they'd done it in the same way they hit on most things: with very little thought or planning, but plenty of mindless optimism. Taffos had suggested a venue and they'd gone along with it. It was five miles south of the city, along the coast, and on the face of it seemed a great place for the watersports business: an absurdly beautiful village at the foot of gently sloping olive groves, with a busy campsite and newly completed hotel – owned, inevitably, by cousins of Taffos, and in which, equally inevitably, he had an interest.

In exchange for cut-price access to their equipment for the patrons, they had the use of a small wooden shack on the beach and rent-free accommodation at the campsite. The setting of their windsurfing business was perfect in all respects bar one. The beach was long and golden, the sea blue with that peculiar blueness that screams of touched-up postcards but which in reality is the colour of the Aegean, the mountains that stretched into the distance … everything except a breath of wind.

Equipment, location and enthusiasm count for nothing if you don't have the right permits and qualifications, and the Port Police demanded an extraordinary amount of paperwork in exchange for the necessary safety permits. In this Oliver did not stint. By cunning use of a Thesaurus, a child's printing set, a candle, a coin and a ream of ivory premium linen paper, he came up with his usual creative solution. By the time he'd finished they were proud owners of matching certificates from the Captain Haddock Sailing Club, Torquay, stating they were advanced windsurf instructors and lifesavers. Each certificate was covered in quality legalese and had a number of wax seals of the Queen's head, which looked on closer inspection remarkably like fifty-pence pieces.

A week after they hung out the 'open for business' sign, things were not going entirely to plan. Even their most pessimistic calculations, based on Aussie Bob's assurances, had them clearing the equivalent of £50 a day. This was based on giving windsurf lessons at £8 per hour, renting out windsurf boards at £5 per hour, and whatever extra the pedalos and canoes brought in. Their plan was to reinvest any profits in more boards and maybe even a speedboat and some waterski equipment which would raise their income to around £100 per day by the time the season really hotted up. At that rate, raising the money they needed to buy a seaworthy sailing boat for the trip back to England and the inheritance would be easily possible.

The lack of wind rendered their calculations about as accurate as the Greek tax authorities', which traditionally was not very. The saving grace and the thing that kept them just about in food and bottled Amstel were the two pedalos, which were constantly in demand.

As a result, they had an assortment of watersports equipment that very rarely saw any water. In the case of the canoe, this was just as well, as its seagoing properties had resulted in it being christened Teabag.

While locking up the shed at the end of another slow August day, Scott made a conscious effort to focus on the positives. He had come a long way. If you had told him a year ago he would be teaching English in a Greek town, make loads of new friends and own a beach watersports business, he would have laughed in your face.

His Abi thing was still very much there and not getting any better or easier. The slowness of the days meant he saw her face far too often in random strangers dotted around the beach. What he needed was something to occupy his mind. It was time that he really got to grips with the labours.

Chapter 8

A few days had passed since the evening at the Blue Parrot, and Scott was sitting in his chair putting the finishing touches to the letter he was writing to his father. The belt hung proudly in his tent and he was pleased with the brief, heavily censored description of events and photographic evidence he had composed for his dad. He looked up as Oliver appeared from his tent, moaning.

'Will you look at that?'

'I'd rather not, mate,' said Scott wincing at the state of Oliver's face. 'It'll put me off my breakfast.'

After a night out with Taffos, Oliver had fallen into bed rather the worse for wear and had failed to zip himself in. An open tent was tantamount to sending out gilt-edged invitations and laying on champagne for the local mosquito population, who had turned up in good numbers, arrived early and stayed late.

'If I get reincarnated, I'm coming back as a frog to eat the little bastards.'

'That's what I used to be until that princess kissed me,' said Scott without looking up from his letter.

Oliver grinned tentatively, discovered it hurt, made a mental note not to find anything funny for the rest of the day and disappeared back inside his tent to rummage for a lighter. If there's one thing worse than having a hangover, a face covered in mosquito bites and being inside a hyper-heated tent, it is having all three while trying to find something that could be buried under any number or combination of items.

If, as someone once said, the face is the mirror of the soul, then it is equally true that you can learn a lot about a man from the cut of his tent. Scott's had a few random items scattered around; Oliver had his entire worldly possessions crammed into his. Partly this was due to his fascination with packing as many small things into as small a place as possible, and partly due to him having nowhere else to put it. Once they'd decided to move to the campsite for the summer, he'd given up the flat he'd rented during the academic year, which, given its size and location, was equivalent to giving up toothache. Rather than putting his stuff into storage, he had elected to lug it all with him. Security was not a great concern, as he owned nothing that wouldn't require him paying someone to take away.

There is an inverse correlation between the status of a hangover and the level of difficulty an otherwise simple task involves. Better and stronger men than Oliver have collapsed into broken sobs when, after a hard night out, they have snapped a shoelace while getting ready for work. At such times, rethreading it presents a task on a par with fitting a full central heating system with the help of a book from the library and a Swiss army penknife. Finding anything in his present condition was going to be a trial, and just at the point that he was considering adding 'the will to live' to the list of lost items, he stumbled across a box of matches. Seldom if ever has anyone camping found their matches behind an electric toaster, and certainly not one you could only see by moving a diving helmet.

Re-emerging from the depths, he lit the small gas stove and filled a pan with water from the bottle in the cold-box.

Their little campsite was at the top corner of the site, furthest away from all the amenities. Scott had a reasonably spacious two-man ridge tent and Oliver a palatial family number shaped like a giant caterpillar, which held his carefully arranged possessions with room to spare. They were pitched at forty-five-degree angles to each other, in the sparse shade of a pair of olive trees, between which was slung Oliver's hammock. Two small plastic chairs and a tiny folding plastic table occupied the area in front of the tents, in the space they referred to affectionately as 'the common'.

As Oliver handed him a cup of coffee, Scott put down his paper and examined his friend's face in more detail.

'Blimey, that looks like the pavement outside a kebab shop on a Sunday morning.'

'You should try being inside it.'

Scott nodded sympathetically. 'It's the noise they make that does my head in – that horrible whining sound you get next to your ear, and you can never see them. They've got a cloaking device, like that stealth technology stuff, they just disappear. Not unlike you at the first hint of heavy lifting, come to think of it.'

Oliver scowled but felt a reply was beneath his dignity.

Scott stood up, stretched and yawned. 'Better get on with it I suppose.'

'Getting on with it' involved a gentle stroll through the campsite, a brief burst of activity as they dragged the one functioning pedalo down to the water's edge, followed by a nice sit down in their deck chairs to await whatever delights the day had in store for them. Both the pedalos had been leaky from the start, but as this had got worse in recent days, Oliver had decided to fix them. He had filled in most of the cracks on one of them the night before and the Greek instructions seemed to suggest the filler needed twenty-four hours to dry. It was unusual for them to be busy enough for both boats to be out at the same time, so the loss was not likely to hit their meagre income stream.

They stared out over the sea.

'That Stealth Technology stuff,' said Oliver eventually.

After receiving no reply or acknowledgement for the next two minutes, he added, 'Urgent, requires answer.'

This was a device they had hit upon to keep conversation going. After a month of sitting in deck chairs doing very little, they had long ago exhausted most interesting threads of conversation and hence tended not to bother answering each other unless the 'Urgent, requires answer' card was played.

'What about it?'

'I wonder how they fuel the planes,' said Oliver. 'If they're invisible, the mechanic blokes'd be always walking into them. Barking their shins something chronic I shouldn't wonder.'

'Who knows?' replied Scott. 'And more to the point, who's interested?'

'And I bet they lose a lot of them. Forget where you parked it and you'd be buggered. They probably have special little hangars for them.'

'Might have something there,' Scott said nodding. 'Or perhaps they hang things on the wings so they stand out.' He looked round for something to illustrate his point. 'Towels, for example.'

Silence fell as they both digested this mental image. After a couple more minutes, Oliver said.

'Could just be the emperor's new clothes.'

'The towels?'

'No. How do we know there really are Stealth Bombers?'

'Ask people who've had bombs dropped on them?'

'Well, yes, there is that I suppose.'

Any further musings on the subject were mercifully curtailed by that rarity of rarities, a customer – or in this case, four of them. A rotund, balding man, standing next to his rotund wife and flanked by two plump children. Neither Oliver or Scott had got much beyond basic French, but the word *peddle-bot* and pointing suggested that they were German and wanted to hire a pedalo. It was a risk. It was the less leaky of the two but it still looked like the combined weight of the family of four would test its buoyancy to the limit. However, 3,000 drachs was 3,000 drachs whichever way you looked at it. They dragged the boat into the water and watched as the happy family climbed aboard, the pedalo settling ominously low in the water.

'Be lucky if we get that back without some underwater recovery vehicle,' said Oliver, watching them laboriously trundle out from the beach.

It was clearly going to be a day of surprises, because they were met at the shed by the second customer of the day. He was English and clearly something of an optimist as he wanted to rent a windsurf board.

Scott nodded with an expression of slight incredulity. 'A windsurf board?'

'Yes.'

Scott looked up at the little flag Oliver has rigged above the shed and saw to his surprise that it was gently fluttering.

Oliver, following his glance, stepped in.

'Smashing. There's enough breeze to get you out and you should find the wind picks up as you get out from the beach.' A bare-faced lie but one that sounded convincing. 'You done much before?'

'I've done it a few times.'

'You should be fine then,' said Oliver confidently and set about rigging a board and sail. He carried it to the water's edge and then watched as the customer stepped on the board and the sail filled enough to take him gently away from the shore.

Scott walked down to join him.

'Blimey, two hires in the first hour, that's twenty quid we're looking at there. Might be able to eat something more interesting than bread and tomatoes tonight.'

'If this wind keeps up, then we should be laughing,' said Oliver.

Chapter 9

Further down the beach, Vanessa was having a slightly less cheery morning. She was sitting at a beachside café flicking through the paper to the horoscope section, something to which she had an irrationally slavish devotion, rendered slightly pointless as the papers always arrived a day late in their little corner of Greece. Apparently, love had come yesterday in the form of the colour blue – which, looking around, didn't exactly narrow things down.

She was about to turn the page when a large shadow appeared over the table, attached to the stout figure of Mrs Collins.

Mrs Collins was blessed with a skin and stature that told of her Icelandic heritage, one that stemmed from a particularly active Viking some ten centuries previously who, when faced with a choice between rape or pillage, had opted for a minimalist attitude to material possessions (and who, incidentally, had given his name to the town we know today as Grimsby). These were facts of which Mrs Collins was, of course, blissfully ignorant. She was dragging along a sniffling lad who had been bitten by a jellyfish.

With an inward groan, Vanessa wondered to herself, not for the first time, how it had come to this.

Having inspected the rash on the hopping teenager and directed Mrs Collins to the chemist, she headed for Scott and Oliver's bench in the hope of hiding out for a while.

'Nessie, how's it going?' said Oliver, looking up from his chair.

'Oh my God! What's happened to your face?' Vanessa slipped into the vacant chair next to him.

He grimaced and absently scratched at one of the weeping sores on his chin. 'Mossies.'

'Have you put anything on them?'

Scott, who had been filling up an iced coffee with some water from the shed, reappeared and, catching Vanessa's eye, said, 'If only you had some kind of antiseptic cream, in – oh I don't know, some kind of medical kit.'

'Oh yes,' said Vanessa. 'You must have one in your survival kit! Go on, open it, go on … please!'

Oliver sniffed dismissively. 'Not a survival situation.'

Scott grinned at Nessie. As a teenager, Oliver had been given a book written by an ex-SAS instructor on how to survive in the wild, and it had become something of a Bible to him. It was a rare day when he wouldn't, if you gave him any kind of opportunity, happily tell you the intricacies of building a wild boar spear trap or creating a water filter out of an old sock and some charcoal. Linked to this was his tin. Oliver's survival tin was a standing joke between them and there was a running bet on which of them would get him to open it first.

If his tent was a masterpiece of intricate packaging, his survival tin was something an atomic physicist would have swooned at. Counting the odd neutron or mapping the trajectory of a proton was a doddle compared to extracting an object from the bottom of his tin. The survival kit had started life as a standard Golden Virginia tobacco tin into which he had managed to fit:

1m² tin foil
10 painkillers (strong ones from when his brother Pete broke his collarbone)
15m fishing line
10 fishing hooks
3 fishing flies
2 condoms
2 waterproof 'lifeboat' matches
12 Swan Vestas snapped in half and dipped in wax
wire saw
2 big keyring rings (for trap triggers and saw)
Guitar D string
Guitar B string
Bit of hexiblock (firelighter)
24 water purification tablets
Oxo cube
2 razor blades with tape on one edge
2 scalpel blades
3 Stanley knife blades

4 relighting birthday candles
10 split lead fishing weights
2 small lightsticks
magnetic strip glued on outside of lid
small polythene bag
sandpaper glued to inside of lid
5m dental floss
3 needles
5m black thread
5m darning yarn
sachet of petrol (Zippo refill)
sachet of WD40
a pen
swing bin liner
1 effervescent paracetamol/codeine
10 butterfly stitches
2 big plasters
miniature tube of Savlon
pocket Leatherman – pliers
small screwdriver
medium screwdriver
tin opener
bottle opener
file
6 multivitamins
3 small safety pins
1 nappy safety pin
1 diarrhoea sachet
3 2in nails
1 antiseptic wipe
credit card multitool taped on the outside of tin
5cm ruler
tin opener
awl
magnifying glass
4 spanners
butterfly screw opener
bottle opener

It really was a masterpiece of anal-retentiveness, and sadly, almost completely useless. To be of any practical help to anyone it would need to stand an outside chance of being used once in a while, but Oliver guarded his tin as fiercely as a lioness looks after her cubs. You could come to him – and Scott had, after an altercation with a broken beer bottle – with blood spurting from a gaping wound, begging for a bandage, only to be met by the Oliver Pond sneer. He would look at the injury suspiciously, like a nun face to face with a comedy penis, screw up his face, purse his lips and draw in his breath before pronouncing:

'Not a survival situation.'

And that would be that. No amount of pleading or blood loss could sway him. Only once in the last year had he removed an item – the diarrhoea sachet – on the grounds that failure to do so, although not leading directly to a potential death situation, would have resulted in his social and professional life effectively ending. On that occasion, the tin had taken him three hours to repack, and nothing since had persuaded him to do it again.

Vanessa slipped off her flip-flops and wriggled her toes luxuriously through the sand.

'Delighted to see you of course, Nessie, but aren't you supposed to be looking after a large number of pink delinquents?' asked Scott, sitting down with his back to the shed and stretching his legs out in the hot sand.

Vanessa smiled mischievously.

'Most of them are busy on the day's activity of fossil hunting.'

'Really?' said Oliver, sitting up and looking interested. 'There are fossils round here?'

'No, but it'll keep them busy looking,' said Vanessa.

'Nessie, I worship at the altar of your deviousness,' said Scott.

'So how's it going? Business any good with you chaps? Have either of you learned to windsurf yet?'

'It's been really slow, but maybe things are picking up. There's a little bit of wind today and we have actually hired out a windsurf board. As for learning to do it, we've tried a few times in the evening but there's never been enough wind,' said Scott.

'Is that him out there?' Vanessa picked up Oliver's binoculars. 'Golly, he's a long way out. Isn't that a bit dangerous?'

'Turn them round, Vanessa,' said Oliver.

'Oh, that's better. Don't think he's one of mine. He's not moving very fast, is he?'

Scott and Oliver both looked up at the flag above the shed, which was now barely moving.

'How're things with you?' Scott asked.

'Busy. They have me doing entertainment planning and we have to have two things going on every day, so I've spent most of my morning negotiating rates with someone offering alcoholic aerobics.'

'Sounds like my sort of exercise,' said Oliver. 'Talking of which, is it too early for a beer?'

'It is for me, but don't let me stop you.'

'So we're a bit skinter than we were hoping. We thought we'd be raking it in by now, but we're probably not even making as much as when we were teaching.' Scott shook his head. 'Never thought I'd miss that.'

'You both moan about it, but I'd love to be a teacher. You know teaching was one of the noblest professions that ancient Greece had to offer. Did you know that Socrates was a teacher?' said Vanessa.

'Was he?' asked Oliver.

'He was, and he taught Plato and Plato taught Aristotle and Aristotle taught Alexander the Great. And he taught the entire known world at the time a thing or two.'

Oliver scratched his head. 'So four of the most influential people in European history were all directly connected?'

'Weird, isn't it,' said Vanessa, taking a sip from a plastic cup of iced coffee. 'And another thing, while we're on the subject. The Greek word for teacher, pedagogue, comes from the word for boy and guide. It literally means someone who guides a pupil to knowledge.'

'I wouldn't mind taking the little bastards to school,' said Scott. 'Happy to drive the bus – it's just dealing with the sods once they get there that gets me down.' He took a swig of his beer before adding, 'Talking of Alexander the Great, did you ever hear the story of him and the Gordian knot?'

They both shook their heads.

'My Uncle Ted told me years ago. It's a belter. So there's this knot that's impossible to undo. Loads of people have tried and failed, and there's a myth that says the person who undoes it will be a great king.'

Vanessa leant forward. Oliver shifted in his chair.

'Then Alexander arrives with an army. He already has a bit of a reputation so they think he might be the guy. They take him to the knot to see if he can undo it. He looks at it, picks it up, turns it over, studies it for a few minutes then puts it down. He then takes out his sword, slashes it into two pieces and says, "There you go."'

'That's a great story!' said Vanessa. 'I love it.'

'Good, isn't it?'

'Wouldn't work with shoelaces,' said Oliver. 'Not unless you bought really long ones to start with … football bootlaces might do it.'

'Not sure you're meant to take it literally, mate. It's supposed to be the sign of a great king. Decisive action, thinking outside the box.'

Oliver considered this. 'So, the combined knowledge of Plato, Socrates and Aristotle comes down to: whenever you see a problem, you hit it with a bloody great sword?'

'I don't think that's the message you're supposed to draw from the story,' said Vanessa.

'Just saying,' said Oliver. 'Nice to know that when faced with some git giving it all that Socratic dialectic, if you disagree with his carefully constructed premise you can just punch him in the face.'

Vanessa rolled her eyes and Scott laughed.

'That's right – any lip from our customers, we can belt them round the head with a baseball bat and blame their finest philosophers.'

'Talking of which, I think your chap out there has fallen off. Look, he's waving at us.'

'Probably pleased to see you, Nessie.'

'He looks like he's trying to get your attention.'

'Really? How's the frappé? More sugar?'

'Are you sure he's alright?'

Scott sighed and glared out to sea. 'Hopefully he'll swim back in with the board, but it doesn't look likely.'

'What are you waiting for, then?' said Vanessa enthusiastically. 'Let's go and get him.' She strode purposefully towards the dinghy.

'Nessie, dear, did you ever read Thomas the Tank Engine as a small girl?'

'Practically brought up on it – why?'

'Because we are the proud owners of his cousin, Colin the Crap Engine, which has decided to reinvent itself as a large and ugly doorstop, which means we have a rescue boat that won't move and a spare pedalo that won't float. He either paddles it back himself or we have to evict that German family from the other pedalo to rescue him.'

'Ah. In that case, I think I'll just sit here and watch.'

Getting the family of happy Germans back on the shore and out of the pedalo took some doing. Oliver paddled out on one of the canoes, whereupon a fruitless conversation ensued as it transpired they were perhaps the only Germans in the world who didn't speak English. Eventually, by a flurry of pointing, pained facial expressions and throwing himself into the water, he convinced them that the pedalo was in danger of sinking, and he got them to paddle back to the beach where Vanessa was able, with the help of her A Level German, to placate them with a refund and a promise of a free hire later in the day.

That accomplished, Scott and Oliver pedalled out to sea. As they neared the stranded windsurfer, Oliver thought to himself that of all the dodgy scams he had prided himself on being involved in, running a watersports outfit without a functioning rescue boat was perhaps one of the least defensible.

They were both exhausted by the time they deposited their passenger back on the beach. Powering a pedalo was tiring work at the best of times and the various leaks ensured they were also carrying a large amount of seawater.

Back in their deck chair, Scott reviewed the morning.

'So, no money from the pedalo and only half an hour from the windsurfer. Not good.'

'At least you can have a break from it all tomorrow for a while,' said Vanessa.

'Tomorrow?' said Scott, looking vague.

'Don't tell me you've forgotten. Gregoris is taking us to see his place.'

'Taffos's place? Is that tomorrow?' asked Oliver.

'Yes.' Vanessa tapped her fingers on the arm of her deckchair in a show of mild irritation. 'He's picking us all up outside the bakery at twelve. Don't you ever remember anything?'

Taffos had invited the three of them to his family home for Sunday lunch, and Vanessa for one was looking forward to her first visit to a Greek family home. Scott, though, was experiencing the opposite. As soon as Vanessa mentioned it, his stomach did its familiar clenching and flipping at the thought of going somewhere new.

Chapter 10

They met the next day and Taffos picked them up in his Jeep. As they sped off, Vanessa found herself musing, not for the first time, about how the only thing Greeks did in a hurry was drive. Scott, sitting in the back next to Vanessa, concentrated on his breathing and fought against his rising panic.

'Are you okay?' she asked. 'You look a bit peaky.'

'I'm fine, just a bit of motion sickness. I'll be okay in a minute.'

'Ah, not far now boyo, be there in a jaffa.'

'Jiffy, Gregoris, I think you mean jiffy,' suggested Vanessa.

Scott looked down at the back of the driver's seat and concentrated on not looking out of the car. This was something that worked for him on car journeys: he could focus so hard on a small area of plastic seating that he would forget he was moving and get his panic under control. He consoled himself with the thought that at least Taffos must know the local roads, as they spun round yet another hairpin mountain bend over a dizzying sheer drop.

Oliver, as ever, nodded off and Nessie was too preoccupied with the breathtaking scenery to worry about anything else. After another ten minutes, which Scott calculated had cost him two years in terms of life expectancy, they pulled up outside an old stone-walled building. It was the original house of Taffos's grandparents, now used as a garage for the modern house attached to it.

As a barometer of the change in the family's fortunes, you couldn't have got a clearer indicator. The new house was built on one of the steepest parts of the mountain and spread itself over four levels. From the drive they walked into the third floor, where they were met by Ma Taffos, who had been watching their approach from one of the balconies.

She was a short woman, almost as wide as she was tall, with grey hair tied into a bun and a remarkable smile. It lit up her whole face and, as she seemed to find virtually everything hilarious, it was never far away. Taffos introduced them and they all received slobbery kisses on both cheeks, with the exception of Vanessa who got some additional pinching of cheeks and a stream of cooing sounds. Ma T leading the way, they were taken down two flights of stairs and onto the patio area of the ground floor, which looked down the mountain and over the sea.

'This is absolutely lovely,' said Nessie, smiling at Ma T and gesturing at the house and garden.

Ma T smiled back, nodded and directed a steam of Greek at Gregoris.

'She says it's all down to her hardworking son,' said Taffos.

Ma T glared at him and said, to their great surprise, in clear English, 'He is not a good boy. I say I show you round, you want to come?'

There was a lot to see, and Oliver for one was like a child in a sweetshop. There were chickens, donkeys, goats and ducks – and those were just the animals he could see from the patio. The only thing lacking from the garden, as far as he was concerned, was a herd of wildebeests and the occasional zebra. At the lowest point was a wooden shack that housed the four donkeys, and Oliver happily went to explore it, armed with apples and two sugar sachets he had been carrying in his pocket, in case of emergencies. Ma Taffos stood smiling approvingly as he scratched behind the ear of a grateful donkey.

'They like you,' she said, as she leant down and picked up a sack not much smaller than herself. She hoisted it onto her shoulder, ignoring Oliver's attempts to help, and wandered over to a scrubby patch of ground where the chickens lived. Oliver followed her and stood watching the chickens while Ma T took Nessie to meet the goats. Chickens, on account of having their eggs nicked daily, are understandably wary creatures, but these were smart enough to know that the sack almost certainly contained something they could eat. A group of them pressed against the low fence clucking hopefully in Oliver's direction. He bent down to lift the sack, with the intention of pouring some of the meal into their pen, but failed to lift it an inch off the ground. It weighed an absolute ton. He looked over at Ma Taffos, then back to the sack, and tried it again for just long enough to feel a muscle in his chest spasm into a ball of pain.

Meanwhile, over by the goats, it was becoming clear that Ma Taffos had decided that Nessie was the daughter she had never had, and Nessie was quite happy to be adopted.

'You have a boyfriend, Vanessa?'

'No, afraid not, not at the moment.'

'Hmm,' Ma T said, clearly unhappy about this state of affairs.

'I haven't found anyone special, I suppose.'

Ma T looked at her quizzically and said, 'Are you sure? I don't think you have to look too far.' She looked pointedly in the direction of Oliver, who was chasing a goat around the bottom of the garden.

Chapter 11

The brief flutter of wind from the previous day had disappeared and today even the pedalos seemed out of favour. They'd had no customers all morning.

It had reached lunchtime and Oliver was getting hungry. 'Cheese pie for lunch, then?'

'It'll have to be, I suppose.'

'Your round.'

'It always seems to be my round,' muttered Scott as he lifted himself out of his chair and strode off towards the bakery.

Cheese pies were cheap and filling, but after eating one and sometimes two for every meal for days on end, even Oliver, who would eat pretty much anything, was tiring of them.

They were seriously short of money and what little they had coming in was not covering their outgoings. Their chances of completing the labours and having enough cash left over to buy a sailing boat were diminishing with each passing day.

Scott's concern about the situation was growing, and while he was picking up the pies, something else occurred to him to add to those worries. He had an uncomfortable feeling the rent was due. Back at the shed, he handed Oliver his pie and asked, 'What day is it?'

There was a silence as Oliver battled to gather enough saliva to formulate an answer through a mouth full of filo pastry. The sound that eventually emerged sounded like 'Monday'.

'Doesn't feel like a Monday.'

'Ah, but it looks like Monday,' said Oliver, clearing his mouth with a swig of coffee.

'And what exactly does a Monday look like?'

'Well, you take your raw ingredients – a pale and flabby Englishman – you baste in lager for twelve hours and put on a moderate to high heat for eight hours, after which you'll be looking at something the colour of freshly cooked lobster. Now, the flights arrive on Saturday, and judging by the state of that lot down the beach, it is clearly Monday.'

Scott nodded, impressed.

'Why do you ask?'

'If it's Monday, then it's the first day of the month and we need to pay the rent.'

'Bollocks.'

Rent day meant facing Theo, Taffos's cousin and their landlord, or more properly their beachlord. In many ways a visionary, he was one of the first to spot the potential in hiring out clapped-out sheds to idiots. He gave them a cheap rent on the shed and had thrown in an old fridge, presumably in the hope they'd buy it.

'How much have we got?' asked Scott.

'Our operating capital, as I like to call it, is in the biscuit tin.'

'Better find out the worst, then.'

Getting to the far side of the shed was not easy. The floor was piled with a vast array of windsurfing paraphernalia, basically all the bits they couldn't work out how to attach. It was also sweltering. Balancing on a motorcycle helmet that Aussie Bob had somehow convinced them might come in useful, Oliver undid the two bolts holding up the side flap of the shed to let in some air.

'And get a couple of beers out of the fridge while you're there,' shouted Scott.

Oliver retrieved two cans from the dwindling supply in the fridge and balanced them on the ledge of the open side flap. Finally locating the tin under a spare sail, he squatted down and started counting.

Outside, Scott, rummaging in his bag for his notebook, became dimly aware of a figure standing next to the shed. He looked up as the man spoke.

'How much are those beers, pal?'

'I'm sorry, they're not for –' began Scott, just as Oliver, oblivious to the conversation outside, finished his money-box count and shouted out, '600 drachs.'

'Cheers, there you go, 1,200. You're alright, I don't need glasses,' he said, nodding at Scott and heading off down the beach with the beers. Scott was left staring after him, open-mouthed.

'Not loads, it has to be said,' said Oliver, reappearing from the shed. 'Where have those beers gone?'

'We've just sold them,' said a stunned Scott.

'What?'

'Two beers, 600 drachs, two quid,' Scott said dreamily.

'How much?'

'two quid. Each!'

'Each?'

Oliver was in his element. Hunched in the centre of a rapidly expanding circle of pages from his notebook weighed down with pebbles, he was allowing his creative inclinations full rein. Part of his charm was his unshakeable belief in his ability to do just about anything he turned his hand to, and as of an hour ago he'd decided those talents now encompassed architectural design and structural engineering.

Putting down his pencil with a look of triumph on his face, he said, '"Pond and Poole's Waterfront Bar".'

'Not the snappiest of names.'

'Granted, the name's shit but it will look nice.'

Scott took the paper and scrutinised it in much the same way a millionaire father might look at an impecunious art graduate to whom his daughter has just announced her engagement.

Under the new plans, the shed would be the centre of a much greater structure. Two of the panels were removed from the side to present an open bar area across three sides. In front and to the side were a series of pillars rising from the sand to support a roof, which seemed to be made of palm fronds.

'Hmm, the Parthenon meets Hawaiian beach culture – a little optimistic, don't you think?'

'Nope. All the ingredients we need are at hand. We just need to get hold of them.'

'We're not making a cake.'

'No, mate, we're making our fortune,' said Oliver, rubbing his hands together.

They started that evening. The advantage of living in a picturesque holiday resort is that there is always someone, somewhere, building something.

Greek building techniques had changed little over the years, and the main principle was simple. Do as little as possible in summer. A lot of hard physical work went into the construction of a house, and at the height of a Greek summer the only thing a sensible man would want to build up was a thirst. The other factor was time. With a paltry twenty-four hours in the day in which to part willing tourists from their cash, it was every available hand to the pumps during the season. The winter builders were all waiters, chefs, deckchair sellers or shop assistants, their building projects abandoned until October.

Scott spread out the list of materials they needed, all of which Oliver had located that afternoon during a leisurely stroll around the upper village. They were sitting on the common, enjoying the last fading light of the day and sharing a bottle of red that Oliver had just produced from his tent.

'Is this everything?'

'Yep, apart from some fishing net. We can get that tomorrow.'

'I thought you had some in your tin?'

Oliver chose to ignore this.

Scott pursed his lips. 'You don't think we're being a bit skanky about this, do you?'

'Skanky?'

'Well, not being trained in the legal profession I wouldn't like to say for sure, but wouldn't some people view this as theft?'

'Nah, this is more your borrowing,' said Oliver with conviction. 'Look, the way I see it, nothing we need is going to cost more than a few quid. And we only need it for the summer – they can have it back later.'

'And that's likely to happen, is it?'

'No, but that's not the point. We *could* give it back.'

'Absolutely. Just wanted to set the old conscience to rest,' said Scott.

The only thing left was to wait for darkness to fall in order to avoid any tricky questions from the locals.

They launched the raid at 2am, after the bars and nightclubs had closed and they'd got through another two bottles of wine. Consequently, what Oliver had planned as a commando operation of split-second timing and precision degenerated into a drunken mixture of sweating, giggling and swearing.

'Right, this is the place. Now we need four wooden beams.'

'Right, right you are. Right. Wooden beams, let me at the fuckers,' said Scott, shuffling sideways. 'I'll 'avealookoverhere.'

Oliver turned to see Scott stumbling away from the side of the house. 'Where the fuck are you off to? There's nothing over there.'

''Avinapiss. I'll see if there's...'

Quite what he intended to see was lost to the world as Scott suddenly and dramatically disappeared into a half-dug swimming pool.

Oliver turned the torch in the direction from which his voice had come and carefully made his way across the rubble.

'What you doing down there?'

'Dunno. Falleninahole.'

Being pissed had helped him bounce and avoid serious injury; the problem was how to get him out.

'Stay there, I'll get a ladder.' Fortunately, ladders are in plentiful supply on building sites and it was only a matter of minutes before Oliver returned with one to find an empty hole.

'Scott, mate, where are you?' he hissed into the darkness and nearly jumped out of his skin when a voice at his shoulder replied in true panto tradition: 'Behind you.'

'Woah! Fuck me, how did you get there?'

'Walked up shallowend,' Scott said, gesturing expansively towards the darkness and very nearly toppling in a second time.

'Come on, then, let's get going.'

By taking two lengths of wood in each hand, they managed all four in one trip and made it back to the common unspotted. A quick return secured a bag of concrete. Then it was just a matter of finding four industrial-sized olive tins. These were easy to come by. Practically every Greek house had ten or fifteen outside, usually full of geraniums, and by taking one each from four different households they figured no one was likely to notice.

The following day they made a start. Scott tried to look helpful while Oliver stared at his sketch of the plans for the bar.

'First thing we need is something to mix the cement on.'

'Like what?'

'Sheet of plastic would do.'

'I'll go and have a look for one,' said Scott.

It was a campsite and so it wasn't exactly hard to find bits of tarpaulin and plastic, but they generally tended to be attached to the things people slept in. His first port of call was the bins, as quite often people who had invested in very cheap tents would leave them behind when they left. Unfortunately, the rubbish had been collected the day before, so that drew a blank.

Scott realised he would have to go and see Theo, the campsite owner, and ask if he had anything they could use. He wasn't delighted about the prospect, as Theo, an unpredictable character, made him nervous at the best of times and there was a good chance he would remember that the rent was due. The best way to describe him was that he was nice as pie. Appropriate, since in Scott's experience, pies could range from the undeniably delicious spinach and feta to the day-old pasty of an indeterminate age sold at the railway station. One look told him that today Theo was having one of his railway-station days.

Theo looked up with a frown on his face and said. 'Fucking Italians! They fuck off and not pay.'

It transpired that a couple of young Italian backpackers had booked in for a week and were due to check out yesterday. Theo had assumed they were staying longer and had gone to find them that morning, only to discover their tent was empty and they were nowhere to be seen.

'Sorry to hear that,' said Scott cautiously. 'I need a small favour. Do you have a sheet of plastic, an old tarpaulin or something?'

Theo shook his head and then appeared to change his mind. He grinned, tilted his head as he considered something, made a decision and said, 'You have their fucking tent.'

Scott went to have a look at it. It was a very small two-man affair and would have been a snug fit for two reasonably-sized people. You can't exactly knock on a tent, so he scratched the side and said, 'Hello, anyone inside?'

There was no reply, so he pulled out the pegs and carried it back to the common.

Oliver had filled up their big water carrier and was back in his chair, contemplating his plan.

'Will this do the job?'

Oliver took the bundle of canvas he was holding and turned it over in his hands.

'Ideal,' he said.

He spread it out on the ground so that what would have been the groundsheet was facing upwards, and proceeded to make a pile of cement powder in the middle. To this he added water and stirred it in with a shovel they had borrowed from the guy who did the campsite gardening once a week.

He mixed the powder and water until the mixture met with his approval.

'Looks about right. Now you've got to climb up that tree,' he said.

'What?' said Scott.

'The tree. We need you to climb up it.'

'Oh "we" do, do "we"? I'm not climbing a bloody tree.'

'It's not very tall – you'll be fine. I'll give you a bunk up to reach the first branch.'

Eventually Scott gave in and, with a boost from Oliver, scrambled up and disappeared into the leaves. After a few seconds his head shot out the top.

Oliver passed up one of the long wooden beams they had 'liberated' from the building site and Scott grabbed hold of the end. Oliver then filled one of the olive oil tins with cement and put the other end of the beam in the mix. Scott leant his end against a branch and Oliver manoeuvred the tin until the beam was vertical. They repeated the process with a further three beams and Scott climbed down.

They spent the next three hours watching cement dry, which, given their normal daily activities, represented an exciting and welcome change.

When the cement had set, they carried each tin down to the beach. Oliver stood with his back to the bar and paced out five steps.

'X marks the spot. You need to dig a hole here.'

Scott looked aggrieved. 'Why is it me that has to do the digging and tree-climbing?'

'It's in the project plan. Can't argue with the plan,' said Oliver, tapping his piece of paper. He proceeded to pace out three more spots and then sat down in the deckchair, contentedly watching Scott wielding the shovel.

When Scott had finished, they dropped a tin in each hole, and when they were sure the beams were rising as near to vertical as they could gauge, filled the remaining space with sand. The result was four sturdy wooden beams appearing as if by magic from the sand in front of the shed.

A second evening trip to another half-built villa provided another four beams, which were then lashed and nailed horizontally to connect the tops of the vertical ones to each other and the bar to provide the structure for the roof. Over the top of this grid they spread out a fishing net, covered it in palm fronds, and put another net on top to stop them blowing away.

At the end of the second day, they were finished and the results were remarkable. They now had what looked very much like a bar and a large pile of dying geraniums.

All they needed was something to sell.

Chapter 12

'We'll have four crates of that one, a couple of trays of cans, and about five trays of assorted soft drinks.'

Taffos busily scribbled down the orders as Scott wandered round like a child in a sweetshop, or, more accurately given the circumstances, an alcoholic in a booze cash-and-carry. Taffos and a cousin, to no one's great surprise, owned the drinks warehouse that supplied all the bars in the village.

'And have you got any pork scratchings?'

'Not a great seller round here, Scott boyo.'

'Really? Oh well. A bottle of vodka, a bottle of gin, and a tray of tonics. That'll do for starters.'

'Right you are, let's see…' Taffos licked the end of his pencil and totted up the list. 'Fifty thousand drachmas, give or take, look.'

Scott took a deep breath and summoned up all the blagging skills at his disposal.

'Taffos, I was wondering if we could come to some mutually beneficial arrangement. The current fiscal situation being...'

'Thirty-two bottles of beer! Not the Queen Vic, are we? Couldn't you get any credit?' asked Oliver, deeply unimpressed.

'It seems that in addition to his Jeep, Taffos also drives a hard bargain,' said Scott, who was quite pleased with the gag.

Oliver, not to be deflected, looked morosely at the small number of beers.

Scott smiled brightly.

'Ah, but it's a start. The profit margin on each of these beers is 300 percent. That means that if we can sell these thirty-two, we'll be able to get ninety-six with the profit, and ... um … with that ninety-six, we'll get ... um …'

'Three hundred and eighty-four.' Oliver had an odd facility for maths.

They officially opened the bar for business at ten in the morning and sold their first beer at five past to an Austrian guy who was with his brother and two other mates. Although they were making a healthy profit on each drink, they were still quite a bit cheaper than the established restaurants and bars, a fact that did not go unnoticed by the Austrian. He and his friends liked a bargain almost as much as they liked a beer and between the four of them they accounted for a large chunk of the bar's initial stock. Within a couple of hours Scott was again knocking on Taffos's door.

'Alright, Scotty boyo, something wrong?'

'We need more beer, Taffos, we've sold out.'

'Tidy. That was quick, like. On to a good thing there you are.'

'Taffos, mate, I've been thinking. You know in September when all the new teachers arrive for the new year.'

'Yes.'

'Would you like me to personally introduce you to all the attractive female ones?'

Taffos thought for a very small amount of time.

'Tell you what, save you running up here every five minutes you can have a bit on credit and pay me later.'

Oliver was just helping a couple into a pedalo when Scott reappeared in Taffos's truck with a promising number of boxes in the back.

'Ten boxes of beer, five of water, orange juice, gin, vodka – blimey, mate, you've done well,' he said appreciatively.

'I would say we have something close to a fully functioning bar now. We can't go wrong.'

And, in true mindless optimist style, he was right. They sold a steady stream of beers and bottled water throughout the day and even developed a group of 'locals'.

The roofed area in front and to the side provided some welcome shade, and a number of souls who wanted a respite from the sun would sit there for hours at a time while their kids played in the shallows. Something about being on holiday breaks down barriers and encourages complete strangers to talk to each other, and soon there was a lively little community arguing good-naturedly, often about football.

One of their better ideas was the happy hour. Anyone who has ever had the pleasure of ordering food in a Greek restaurant will know that a Greek hour is uniquely flexible, and the cocktail hour became an event that could crop up at any time, based on which song was playing. For no other reason than it was a cracking tune, they hit on the idea of choosing 'The Mighty Quinn' by Manfred Mann as the precursor to 30 minutes of cheap drinks. With the three-CD changer set to random, there was no predicting when it might come on, and it being such a singalong number, all the locals would join in.

'Look at that – hard to believe, wouldn't you say?' said Scott. He and Oliver were standing just outside the bar, watching twenty comparative strangers all leaping up and down with their arms around each other, bellowing, 'Come on without, come on within' while the rest of the beach looked on.

'Great, isn't it?' said Oliver.

It became something more like a social club than a bar. If they had to go out in the pedalos to rescue a becalmed windsurfer, one of the locals would generally step in and serve drinks, or people would help themselves.

They were nowhere near as busy as the bar at the other end of the beach, but they were ticking over nicely and making nearly as much money as they'd hoped to bring in from the watersports equipment in their original plan.

The one problem with their newly constructed bar was that it was on the part of the beach where people tended to turn around. They'd be walking along, scuffing their feet at the water's edge, and realise the only thing to be gained from walking further was a strong possibility of bumping into naked Germans – and no one wants to do that on an empty stomach. Oliver had been so put off his breakfast one morning by a large couple standing unashamedly in front of him and demanding 'Eine *peddle-bot* bitte' that he'd put up a sign saying NO NAKED GERMANS, until Scott had spotted it and made him take it down. He had compromised and now their bar boasted a sign proudly proclaiming: LAST CHANCE OF A DRINK BEFORE SEEING NAKED GERMANS.

It raised a lot of laughs, and, to their credit, most German holidaymakers also found it funny. 'Germaning' had become an adjective, in the sense of 'Look, there's someone Germaning'. This had led to the lesser term of 'Austrianing', a reference to going topless or half-German.

Despite the considerable risk of seeing large naked people of a certain age, every day the plastic tables and chairs were soon filled and Oliver was intent on expanding their empire. Drawing on the experience of a holiday in Dahab in Egypt, he collected twenty hessian coffee sacks, filled them with sand so they resembled not-very-yielding pillows and laid them out on the beach in U shapes beside the bar. By covering them with the sort of cheap material every impoverished student in history has ever thrown over the top of a sofa from a skip, he managed to create a pleasantly bohemian lounging area. Its simplicity and effectiveness at no time prevented Scott from relentlessly taking the piss out of the 'Egyptian sofa' as he always referred to it.

As well as suffering from over-close proximity to potentially naked Germans, the bar was at the unfashionable end of the beach, a situation exacerbated by the popularity of the swanky bar at the posh end. In order to improve business, a few smart marketing ideas were urgently required. Scott duly came up with the Billy gambit. It was a complicated theory involving wind speed, sound waves and Billy's accordion. Get it right and his performances would drive punters out of sound range and into the waiting arms of their waterfront bar; get it wrong and you could hear the bastard. Although it initially yielded promising results, they made an executive decision to drop the tactic. The risk of a sudden gust of wind carrying the sound into the bar was just too high to take.

Chapter 13

There was one obvious way to improve business which they had briefly considered and then dismissed, and it took Vanessa to point it out again.

It was early evening and most of their customers had left the beach when she appeared at the bar for a drink on her way home. Scott was loading the fridge with beer cans and Oliver was counting the cash when her head popped through the hatch.

'Hello there, how are my favourite chaps then?'

'All good, Vanessa. Don't often see you at this time, everything all right?'

'Mystery caves day.'

Scott closed the fridge door and followed Oliver out of the bar.

'I've always meant to ask: why are they the "mystery caves"?'

'The mystery is that anyone would pay for a coach trip to see the bloody things,' said Vanessa, who had helped herself to Oliver's deckchair and now took the beer Scott was holding. 'Anyway, never mind about my day. I've had an idea for your next task. Have you got your list?'

'One sec,' said Scott. He ducked back into the bar for a replacement beer and reappeared with his bag. Once settled, he pulled out the list and spread it out on one of the plastic tables.

The labours of Hercules

1 Killed the Nemean lion
2 Killed a Hydra, a nine-headed snake
3 Captured a golden-horned reindeer
4 Brought back a bull from Crete
5 Captured the Erymanthian Boar
6 Cleaned the Augean stables in a single day
7 Chased away flesh-eating Stymphalian birds
8 Captured the horses of King Diomedes
9 ~~Got the belt of Hippolyta, Queen of the Amazons~~

10 Captured the cattle of Geryon, the three-headed, six-armed giant

11 Brought back the three golden apples from the Garden of Hesperides

12 Went into Hades and brought back the three-headed hound of hell

'What are you thinking?'

'Number six.'

Oliver scratched his head. 'Clean the Augean stables in a single day. Doesn't sound that heroic, doing a bit of cleaning.'

'Do you know anyone with some stables, then?' asked Scott.

Vanessa ignored the question and said, 'Are you as busy as the bar at the other end of the beach?'

'No.'

'Would you get more customers if your bar was near the only loo on the beach?'

It wasn't hard to see where she was going.

'No. No way, never. No,' said Scott.

'If you cleaned it out, I think you could claim it as number six and get more business. You should think about it,' she said.

Oliver, who was less squeamish than Scott, nodded.

'Let's go and take a look.'

It was about 30 metres further on down the beach from the bar, right on the edge of Naked German territory – an old concrete, flat-roofed building that had once been a beach facility but had become blocked up some years previously and fallen into disuse. Except that would be a misleading term. It was still being used, and used fairly regularly, by people desperate enough to crap on the floor of somewhere with crap all over the floor.

Scott wasn't having any of it.

'Can't claim that as number six. It clearly states it has to be a stable. If Hercules had cleaned out an old bog, then fair do's, but he didn't.'

While Scott had a point in that it didn't exactly fit the bill, as far as Oliver was concerned, anyone who could crap in the old toilet block in its current state could safely be described as an animal. Also, given the size of some of the deposits. it did not seem impossible that a few random horses had wandered in and crapped on the floor.

Oliver was grinning in a way that Scott had come to fear.

'You've had one of your ideas, haven't you?'

'Might have.'

Scott also knew from past experience that no amount of questioning would get Oliver to reveal what he had up his sleeve.

The next morning, Oliver excused himself from the daily tasks and went off in search of Taffos. He found him drinking coffee and munching pastries at a café in the village.

'Taffos, mate, how's it going?'

'Tidy, Oliver boyo, tidy. Take a seat. You after some more stock?' He shifted along to the next stool to make room.

'Thanks, but I need to get moving, I'm after your mother.'

Ma Taffos lived just a couple of miles up the mountainside, and if she was surprised to find Oliver on her doorstep asking to borrow one of her donkeys, she didn't show it. The donkeys remembered him and ambled over in the hope of sugar and ear-scratching. She picked out the oldest female, who was called Ariadne.

'They like you,' she said, nodding approvingly. This cemented Oliver's position in her good books and she helped him coax the donkey into the horsebox and hooked it up to Taffos's truck. Oliver promised to have Ariadne back before nightfall and they set off back to the beach.

'What the fuck have you got there?' asked Scott, somewhat unnecessarily.

'A donkey,' said Oliver.

'I can see that. I mean, where did you get it?'

'Ma Taffos's.'

'Why?'

'Your old man needs to see some evidence of a stable being cleaned out. Well, put a donkey in the bog and you've got a believable situation there.'

Scott went to say something, found no words would come out and so just stared, open-mouthed.

'She's got to be home after teatime so we've only got her for a while. It's all set – Nessie's coming to film it about six-ish. Thought we'd get started when it's a bit cooler and less people about.'

Scott shrugged resignedly and thought really hard about how good it would be to own his own club, in the hope it would help convince him this was a good idea. It wasn't working.

'Say hello to Mildred,' said Oliver, scratching the donkey's back.

'Mildred? Not very Greek, is it?'

'Couldn't pronounce her real name so I thought Mildred suited her.'

Scott moved his hand towards Mildred's nose, only for her to jerk her head back and bare her teeth at him.

'Woah, she tried to bite me!'

'Nah, she likes you, mate. Sign of affection, that, in donkeys. There's some hay for her round the side. Be back in an hour. Taffos is waiting.'

'Wait! You can't just leave me with …'

'See you in a bit,' said Oliver over his shoulder as he disappeared off down the beach, leaving Scott holding the rope that was attached to Mildred's collar. Scott glared at his retreating back and then turned to look for something to tie her to. He settled for one of one of the supporting beams and looped the rope around it while Mildred watched him implacably. She was in the shade of the netting and palm fronds, and seemed reasonably content as long as Scott didn't get too near, so he left her to it and continued with getting the bar ready.

After about ten minutes, he found himself warming to Mildred. She had already drawn quite a crowd and she was happily submitting to being stroked and poked by small children while Scott sold drinks to their parents. He was beginning to think that a small petting zoo might be the way to make some serious cash.

After a while, the kids got bored and went back to playing in the sand and jumping in the water, leaving Scott and Mildred to it. When it had quietened down, Mildred slowly turned round to face him before raising her head and braying in what he took to be a meaningful manner. Deducing that she might be hungry, he went round the back of the bar to look for the hay Oliver had left. It was baled up with twine and a tentative pull revealed it to be very heavy.

85

Scott's working motto had always been to avoid any heavy lifting if at all possible, so rather than risk putting his back out, it seemed sensible to take Mildred to her food rather than the other way round.

He undid the rope and pulled her gently in the direction of the straw, only to discover Mildred had other ideas. She had decided that although it was quite shady where she was standing, it looked a lot cooler inside the bar. As he leant to pull her, she shifted her weight in a surprisingly nimble manoeuvre and headed in the opposite direction. Scott lost his footing in the sand and the rope slipped from his hands long enough for Mildred to carry out her plan. There was just enough room for her to get through the door but not enough room to turn around once inside. Not that she had any intention of doing so, as the first thing she came across was a sack filled with bread rolls on the floor by the fridge. A few days previously, they had managed to cadge an old sandwich-maker off Taffos and had branched out into toasted cheese and ham rolls. They had proved very popular, so earlier that morning Scott had bought fifty from the local baker. Mildred approved. She had her head in the bag as she munched her way through the rolls, with her rear at the other end, blocking the door. Scott tried to squeeze past her to get into the bar but she shifted her weight to block him and raised one of her hind legs in a menacing fashion.

As long as she had shade and bread rolls, she was not moving, and Scott was at a loss as to how to shift her. He sat down to plan his next move when a couple arrived.

'Hi, can we get some drinks?'

'Sorry, we're temporarily closed …'

At that moment, Mildred revealed herself to have perfect comic timing by raising her head and peeking over the edge of the hatch at the voices.

'There's a donkey in your bar.'

'Yes, there is,' agreed Scott. 'That's why we're temporarily closed. We've been the victims of an equine coup.'

'You what?'

'There's a donkey stuck in my bar and I can't get him out,' explained Scott.

'Ooh, I love donkeys,' said the woman, and headed over to say hello to Mildred.

Mildred took a break from the bread rolls to have her ears and back scratched a bit more. 'What's her name?'

'We call her Mildred,' said Scott. 'Although I think Winnalot would suit her more,' he muttered under his breath.

'Why do you keep her in the bar? Not very hygienic, is it?' asked the man.

'Look, mate, health and safety is the least of my worries right now. I have a donkey in my bar, eating its way through my stock, and I can't get in to sell any drinks.'

'Well, you shouldn't keep her in there,' the man retorted.

Scott gave up.

'Thanks for the advice. You are absolutely right and I apologise for not thinking about that before. Going forward, I promise not to keep a donkey in my bar. Now, sorry I can't help you but I don't have anything to sell you right now. I recommend the bar at the other end of the beach which has a strong no-donkey policy.'

After they had left, he leant into the bar and tried to get her interested in handfuls of hay, without any success. Mildred, it seemed, was full. So he reverted to a brute force approach. He fed the rope back behind her through the open door and stood as close as he could to her back end, without risking a kick, and heaved on the rope. As he strained against her weight, Mildred decided she would make a movement. A bowel movement. Whether it was down to the strange situation or the new diet was a moot point, but the result was she had a dodgy tummy, the contents of which were sprayed all over Scott's bare legs and feet.

He dropped the rope and looked down at himself. He was covered in slimy brown shit from the waist down.

Scott walked briskly away from the main bar towards the no-man's land between holidaymakers and naked Germans, where he ran into the sea. As he waded out, a watery brown cloud surrounded him, forcing him to walk as fast as he could into deeper water. He swam out until he felt confident he was clear of donkey diarrhoea and then swam parallel to the beach before heading back in towards the bar.

He was met by Oliver, who had returned with a box and a couple of shovels.

'What are you doing pissing about there? I promised Ma T we'd look after her donkey. While you've been swimming, she's only gone and got into the bar.'

Scott proceeded to swear, and in between his many swear words he conveyed a brief précis of his recent adventures, at which Oliver laughed and laughed and then laughed a bit more. When he had finished laughing, he went up to the bar and, by means of standing at the door waving sachets of sugar, got Mildred to obediently back out of the bar and submit to being tied up where he had left her.

After using one of the shovels to move the sand that had soaked up the small amount of donkey shit which had not landed on Scott, Oliver opened the box. In addition to the shovels, he had somehow managed to rustle up a couple of full white body suits as worn by crime scene investigators, plus boots and some seriously thick rubber gloves.

They reopened for business, and after a number of cold beers Scott had calmed down to a point where, although he wasn't exactly seeing the funny side, he could acknowledge that somewhere, just out of reach over the horizon, there was one.

Chapter 14

Later in the afternoon, Vanessa arrived with her camera. They shut down the bar and headed the short distance along the beach with Mildred in tow.

'Anything we need to know about this one, Nessie?' asked Oliver.

'By anything, you mean what Hercules did, where he did it and what happened next – in other words, everything, I presume?'

'That would be nice, yes.'

'It all took place in Elis, which in ancient Greece was an independent state in the Peloponnese near Olympia.'

'Always fancied going to Olympia – it's supposed to be good. Can't we go there and find a nice small stable that isn't too grubby?' said Scott.

'We could, but as we're here now, I suggest you get on with it,' she replied as they came to a halt on the sand outside the old toilet block.

'Can't understand how this got in. Bit of cleaning, not exactly heroic is it?' said Oliver.

'It was quite an impressive feat, you know,' replied Vanessa. 'The king of those parts was called Augeas, which, you'll be interested to know, meant "bright" in ancient Greek.'

'Not that interested, to be honest, Vanessa,' said Scott, who was determined to play the role of the moody teenager throughout.

'It didn't exactly suit him, as you will see if you listen,' she said firmly.

Scott bowed his head and scuffed at some sand with his flip-flop.

'His father had inadvisably bequeathed him a very large number of cattle. Inadvisable as Augeas had no interest whatsoever in farming and, given the choice between swanning around wearing a crown or mucking out cowsheds, had sensibly opted for the former.'

'A bit lazy, then?'

'On the nail, Oliver dear. When Hercules turned up on his doorstep one day, offering to clean his stables out, he was as pleased as punch. They hadn't been cleaned for thirty years and he had to keep relocating his palace to keep out of range of the smell. They struck a deal whereby Hercules would get one-tenth of the cattle if he could accomplish the task in one day.'

'Wouldn't mind so much if we were getting something out of this,' said Scott, who was refusing to be anything but relentlessly negative about the whole affair. Vanessa chose to ignore him and continue with her story.

'So, the following day Hercules set about the job and took Augeas's son with him to witness the work. He noticed that the stables were flanked by two rivers, the Alpheus and the Peneus, and his idea was to let the water do the work for him. He started by ripping big holes in the front and back walls of the stables. From the back wall he dug a trench to the Alpheus, and then he dug another out the front to the Peneus. He then diverted the flow of water through the stables and back into the river to take all the crap away.'

'He got the water to flow into the Peneus? Bet that made his eyes water,' said Scott.

'Thank you, Mr Puerile,' said Vanessa.

'So, nice clean stable and all done in a day. It doesn't sound that dramatic,' said Oliver.

'Well, yes, so far so good. But then he returned to tell Augeas the good news and collect his reward, only to find him refusing to pay up on the grounds that he didn't want to and there was no proof of their deal.'

Scott was becoming interested despite himself.

'Double-crossing on a deal with the hardest man in the classical world? See what you mean about his name.'

'Yes, not the brightest of actions. Anyway, they went to court to settle the argument and the king's son testified that his father had indeed promised to pay Hercules one-tenth of the cattle and Hercules had performed the task within the specified day. The court found in favour of Hercules and the king had to pay up. But afterwards he banished Hercules and his own son from the kingdom.'

'So that was that, then?' said Oliver.

'Yes, although after Hercules had completed his twelve labours, he made a point of returning to make his point with Augeas with what I can only assume was something very pointy.'

Unfortunately, unlike Hercules, they had no means of washing out all the crap with a diverted river, or even a power-hose come to that, without depositing a slurry of sewage on the beach. This was a job for shovels and the thickest refuse sacks they could find.

Vanessa held her nose and took some photos of the inside of the toilet block by way of scene-setting, and Oliver performed his donkey-whispering trick to get Mildred to back into the doorway far enough for a shot of her looking out the door. Having established the vague illusion that this was a stable, they got to work. They started by putting on the white overalls and discovered that they had been designed for the slightly smaller figure. Scott's was a snug fit and Oliver's only reached to just below his knees and elbows. The suits also made them look from a distance like Morris dancers. Welly boots and gloves completed the look.

The smell was so bad inside that they were forced to hold their breath, run in, shovel some shit into a bag and run out again, gasping for clean air. After five minutes of this approach they were both seeing stars and were on the verge of fainting. Clearly this tactic was not going to work.

'What about your diving helmet?' asked Scott.

'Nah, won't work. You'd need the suit to screw it onto to keep it airtight,' replied Oliver. 'Although ...' He paused for a moment as the thought formulated itself in his brain. 'Got an idea, be back in a minute.'

Thus it was that ten minutes later Scott found himself wearing a swimming mask and snorkel with a length of hosepipe attached to it with gaffer tape. A Morris dancer wearing a snorkel attached to a hosepipe is an inherently amusing sight, and Vanessa was finding it hard to hold the camera still while giggling.

The hosepipe was long enough to reach outside while Scott was inside, breathing clean but slightly rubbery air. Shovelling was hard work, and he was breathing heavily until suddenly he wasn't breathing at all. Mildred had put a hoof down square on the hosepipe. He pulled out the snorkel and took a heaving breath of the foulest air that had ever entered his lungs, then raced out. In the meantime,

Mildred had repositioned her feet and looked at him innocently as he staggered, gasping, onto the sand.

Oliver took the next shift while Scott tested his snorkel, which now seemed fine. After they had each done a few five-minute shifts and filled a few bags with shit, they hit on a more efficient way of working. One of them would do the shovelling while the other filled the bag. Oliver was at the coal face, so to speak, scooping up crap and then swivelling at the waist to shove it off the end of the shovel behind him. Scott would then put this big pile into bags ready for disposal.

They made good progress, and after 30 minutes Oliver was down to the last few shovelfuls when Scott's already bad day took a turn for the worse. Communication is not the strong suite of the male species, and wearing snorkels made it virtually impossible. In hindsight, Scott should have made more of an effort to convey that he was bending down to scoop up some shit just when Oliver was about to swivel round. The edge of the shovel smashed firmly into the face mask of Scott's snorkel, throwing him flat on his back. For the second time that day, Scott found himself covered in shit as the contents of Oliver's shovel hit him squarely in the bits of his face not covered by the mask.

Enough, he decided, was enough. He crawled outside, stripped off his crime scene outfit and once again plunged into the sea, rubbing shit off his face. He waited until he was sure Oliver had finished before deciding it was safe to come out of the water.

The final tally was ten bags of crap, which they loaded into the back of Taffos's truck and took to the waste disposal site on the edge of the village before returning Mildred to Ma Taffos.

Later that evening, with a glow of alcohol making everything seem better and secure in the knowledge he was that bit closer to his dream, Scott took out his list of labours and firmly put a line through number six.

Chapter 15

They were now two labours to the good and over the next few days their takings on the bar were up. Having a functioning toilet on the beach had improved trade but not as much as they were hoping. Things were looking rosier, but even so, the lack of windsurfing hires was biting into their profit projections and it was still going to take some effort if they were to buy the boat they needed to sail back to gain the inheritance. It was essential they grabbed every possible cash-generating opportunity, and, if there weren't any, to invent them.

Hence, a couple of days after the shit-shovelling nightmare, Oliver was hard at work on his latest wheeze when Vanessa appeared for an early-morning coffee and chat.

'What are you up to now?' She nodded to Oliver, who was hunched over a large pile of smooth pebbles, holding a paintbrush.

'Well, now you're asking. This is the Great Green Stone Hunt, Nessie!' he said while dabbing luminous green paint on a small rock.

'Okay, what is the Great Stone Hunt?'

'The Great *Green* Stone Hunt. It's all in the detail,' added Scott.

'Sorry, Great Green Stone Hunt,'

'Oliver there is painting stones green. We then gather large numbers of keen scuba divers, drop the stones in the sea and offer a free Amstel to anyone who returns with one.'

'Right … I see,' said Vanessa, who clearly didn't. 'So this new money-making scheme involves – giving away free beers?'

'You say that,' said Oliver, rising to reveal a pile of bright green stones, 'but you've got to consider the corrosive effects of salt water on watercolour paint.'

'How marvellously devious.'

'Isn't it! We're getting Billy to knock up a few posters, get a crowd of would-be pearl divers poised on the beach and watch them drown their sorrows when they return empty-handed.'

'Of course,' added Scott, 'it's just the sort of event Sunny Sunshine tour reps would probably like to support.'

'Oh no it isn't, Mr Pond, it's just the sort of unethical swizz that Sunny Sunshine tour reps are there to prevent,' said Nessie sternly.

'Dinner at Plazzo's?'

'And free cocktails at the Blue Parrot, of course,' added Vanessa.

'Done,' they said in unison.

Vanessa did her work well. On the Wednesday of the Great Green Stone Hunt, or Big Wednesday as it had been christened, there was a boisterous crowd of candidates and onlookers swamping the bar. Oliver had elected himself Master of Ceremonies, and was showing off dreadfully. He was standing on a pedalo, facing the crowd, with a bulging sack at his feet. In true 'Club Rep' style, he was endeavouring to whip his audience into a frenzy of anticipation with the sole device of crude sexual innuendo.

'Who'd like to see my sack?' he bellowed above the hubbub.

Scott turned to look ruefully at Vanessa, who was shaking her head. It got a laugh and a number of poor-quality heckles. It turned out to be the peak of his repartee, as he followed up with, 'You all seem pleased to see me, or are those snorkels I can see?'

'Get on with it for fuck's sake,' shouted Scott to rousing cheers.

'Okay! For those of you who don't know the rules, I'll be distributing stones from my sack.'

'First time for everything, you jaffa!' shouted a wag from the bar.

Vanessa looked at Scott with raised eyebrows. 'Jaffa?'

'Someone who fires blanks, no pips.'

'Ah,' she said, not much wiser, and turned back to hear Oliver tell his heckler he was banned.

'I'll be dropping these stones in the water. There will then be a waiting period of four minutes to let them settle, and then it's a free Amstel for any you find and bring back.'

Oliver sank onto the seat of the pedalo and pedalled out to a depth of about four metres. Making sure he was above the rocks, he stood up and delved in his bag, theatrically pulling out a bright green pebble to more cheers from the beach. Holding it like a dart, he carefully threw it into the water. To an amateur, it would seem his mistake lay in not letting go, but to anyone with an appreciation of the value of slapstick, it was superb. His flailing left arm as he overbalanced was the pièce de résistance. He resurfaced, grinning, to the gratifying sound of raucous laughter. Climbing back on, he proceeded to distribute the remaining nineteen stones in a wide circle around the pedalo.

Four minutes later, it was like a scene from a Bond movie when the baddie has just tossed a lackey into the piranha pool. The water was packed with increasingly puzzled snorkellers and some lucky winners. (To prevent a potential riot, they'd had the wit to paint five of the stones with water-resistant paint, and these were soon retrieved by a few proud winners.)

By the time they closed the shutters early that evening, they had taken the equivalent of nearly £150, their best day so far. Putting on events was obviously the way forward, and as the average tourist only stayed for a week, they agreed they should repeat the stone hunt every Wednesday. They just needed to think up some more events, preferably without asking Billy to play or sing.

Scott broached the subject with Vanessa when they all met up for the promised dinner a few nights later.

They were sitting at their usual table, the one right on the beach, and had been chatting to Moe about business. His job in the evenings was to hang around on the edge of the tables and encourage passers-by to sit down and eat. He was good at it, and had managed to snag two couples and a family of four in the time it had taken them to eat their pizza. Oliver took a swig of beer to wash down his last slice and cleared his throat.

'Nessie, of the events you put on, which ones get the most interest?'

'God, the tackier they are the more people love them. The foam party is always a winner.'

'Could we make some foam?' Scott asked Oliver.

'Could have a go. An old washing machine and a load of washing-up liquid might work,' said Oliver, reaching across and collecting the pizza crusts from Scott's plate.

Vanessa pushed her plate in his direction so that he could pick off the last remnants.

'The key feature of said foam party is that you get to roll around all soapy on a slippery surface. Don't think sand would work quite as well.'

'Could sell it as a full-body exfoliation session,' said Scott.

'You could try. Spa treatments are actually quite popular. We have a chap who comes once a week with toe-nibbling fish, and that's always packed.'

'Toe-nibbling fish?'

'"Fish foot spa pedicure" is what we advertise it as.'

'How does that work?'

Nessie shrugged. 'Goodness knows.'

There proceeded a burst of unintelligible noises from Oliver, accompanied by pizza crumbs. The both raised their eyebrows and waited for him to swallow the remains of their respective meals.

'Garra rufa fish,' he finally said, which did not make a lot more sense than the sounds he'd made with his mouth full of dry pizza.

'Get a what a fish?' asked Scott.

'Garra rufa fish – it's a toothless Turkish carp. You get your garra rufa fish, put your feet in a pool of them and they eat all the dead skin tissue off your feet.'

'How do you even know stuff like that?' asked Nessie.

Oliver shrugged and grinned. 'Read about them somewhere.'

'My dad's got some carp in his garden. They're bloody huge – they could take your leg off,' said Scott.

'These are little lads, about an inch long if that.'

'Would your average punter know what a garra rufa fish looked like?'

'Probably not,' said Vanessa.

First thing the next day saw Scott and Oliver out with their fishing nets in the shallows, scooping up as many small fish as they could find. After they had filled a couple of buckets, Oliver knocked up a sign offering:

'Drink & Foot Spa. One thousand drachmas.'

A wise man once said you never get poor by underestimating the intelligence of the general public, and the first idiot arrived about half an hour after the sign went up. It was actually a couple of idiots, and they were deciding what to go for.

'What d'you reckon?'

'I think you should. We're on holiday, love – if you fancy it, have a go.'

'I think I will.'

'Go on then.'

'Right.'

The male half of the conversation turned to Scott and said, 'We'll have one beer, a Diet Coke, and we'd like a foot spa please.'

'Certainly, sir. Here you are, if you'd like to take a seat we'll be right over.'

They took their drinks and had just sat down when Oliver appeared with a bucket in each hand. They had toyed with the idea of a getting a kids' paddling pool, but, on the grounds that you have to walk before you can run, elected to start with a bucket for each foot.

'Morning. Who's for the foot spa?' Oliver said.

'That's me,' said the female half of the equation, looking uneasily at the buckets. 'I thought you'd have some kind of tank. When I saw it on the telly, they had a tank.'

'Ah, very unhygienic, your tank,' said Oliver. 'Get a load of different feet in and it becomes a breeding ground for infections. Latest research suggests you should have an individual approach and change the water each time.'

'That makes sense, Maureen, he knows what he's talking about, him.'

Maureen did not take a lot of convincing, and she settled a foot into each bucket.

'Ooh, Brian, they tickle!' she said as numerous small fish brushed against her bare feet.

'That's what you want. That'll be them at work, cleaning up your skin. Right you are, I'll just leave you there. Ten minutes should be about right,' said Oliver. He headed back to the bar, leaving her contentedly sipping a Diet Coke with each foot in a bucket.

After ten minutes he returned.

'You should be done now – how was that for you?'

'Lovely,' said Maureen. 'Very relaxing, thank you.'

She took her feet out of the bucket and examined them with some satisfaction. In fact the only difference was that her feet felt a bit cooler, but she was happy to convince herself that her money had been well spent.

'Look at that, Brian, my feet feel ten years younger! Hey, you don't want to put your head in it, do you love?'

'I could put something else in it that could do with feeling a bit younger!'

'Ooh, Brian, you'll make me blush,' said Maureen, cackling. When she had finished, she turned to Oliver.

'Thank you very much, young man, we'll be sure to recommend you.' And with that they headed off back to their sunbed, leaving Oliver and Scott rubbing their hands.

'This is great!' said Scott. 'one thousand drachmas a pop for ten minutes, this could really change our fortunes.'

By the end of the day, they had serviced three more clients and were congratulating themselves on a good day's business when the last customers of the day appeared at the bar. They were a couple in their early twenties and they made a handsome pair. Scott leapt up from his chair and appeared behind the bar.

'Good afternoon, how can I help you?' he asked with a friendly smile.

'The campsite man, he said you have our tent,' said the young man with an unmistakably Italian accent.

A couple of hours later, back in the taverna with Vanessa, they reviewed the day.

'So, we're ten thousand drachmas down for a new tent and have two buckets of dead fish. Fucking great.'

'Life deals us some harsh blows,' agreed Oliver.

There was a lengthy pause as they brooded. Vanessa broke the silence.

'I can't believe you did that foot spa thing. What were you thinking? What if someone found out? I'm sure it's fraud or something.'

'Everyone went away happy, Nessie,' said Scott defensively, while pouring out water into three glasses. 'They had a lovely, cooling foot experience, and who's to say that the fish didn't do the odd verruca a bit of damage.'

'Remember when you tried to catch my verruca?' said Oliver.

Scott nodded and took a sip of water. 'It's burnt on my memory. I had to join the swimming team for a term because of that.'

Vanessa looked from one to the other.

'Part of me really, really doesn't want to know, but I'm going to have to ask,' she said, picking up her wineglass.

Scott grimaced at the memory.

'If you had a verruca, you got excused from swimming, and our school had an outdoor unheated swimming pool. Git-face there didn't have to freeze his bollocks off on account of his verruca, so he offered to let you catch it for two quid a time.'

'Only charged you a quid, fair's fair,' said Oliver, reaching across and helping himself to a glass of the wine Vanessa had ordered.

'Anyway, I started off by wearing his socks for a day, but that didn't work so I was rubbing my toe against his when the games teacher came in and caught us at it. He made me go swimming every day for six weeks. Bastard.'

'I had to do rugby practice,' said Oliver.

'Which you did anyway!'' pointed out Scott.

Vanessa shook her head. 'Well, that's an image that's going to cost some money at a decent therapist to get rid of. Thank you for that. But you know, I think this tent thing is karma.'

'Karma?' said Oliver.

'Yes. You kill bucketloads of innocent tiddlers, diddle people out of their cash and you lose money. That's karma.'

Scott nodded. 'I'm inclined to agree with you, Nessie.'

Oliver was not overly convinced by the cosmic nature of the situation, but he did feel a bit uncomfortable about the fish.

'We'll just have to come up with something else to make some cash,' he said.

'Something will turn up,' Agreed Scott.

'Bound to.' Oliver nodded.

'I reckon you should focus on the next labour,' said Vanessa. 'Let's have a look.'

Scott dipped into his bag and moved the carafe of wine and two bottles of beer to make room.

The labours of Hercules

1 Killed the Nemean lion

2 Killed a Hydra, a nine-headed snake

3 Captured a golden-horned reindeer

4 Brought back a bull from Crete

5 Captured the Erymanthian Boar

6 ~~Cleaned the Augean stables in a single day~~

7 Chased away flesh-eating Stymphalian birds

8 Captured the horses of King Diomedes

9 ~~Got the belt of Hippolyta, Queen of the Amazons~~

10 Captured the cattle of Geryon, the three-headed, six-armed giant

11 Brought back the three golden apples from the Garden of Hesperides

12 Went into Hades and brought back the three-headed hound of hell

Oliver pulled his reading glasses out of his breast pocket, gave them a polish with a spare napkin and focused his attention on the list.

'Hmm. Don't fancy our chances with the lion.'

'That's off limits. Uncle Ted was a vegetarian, he wouldn't want me killing anything.'

'Well, that's number two out as well. We'd have to find a zoo to get near a reindeer.'

'There's a zoo in Thessaloniki,' said Vanessa.

'I love a zoo, me – reckon they'd have reindeer?'

'I'd say it was unlikely,' said Scott.

'Bet they have bulls in Crete, though. Fancied going to Crete since Whatsername told us about it.'

'Whatsername?' said Vanessa. 'Who would that be?'

'Do you mean Samantha? Girl who lives with Su and we played bridge with?' asked Scott.

'That's the girl.'

Vanessa nodded. 'Sam, she lived in Crete, didn't she? She loved it, she's always waxing lyrical about it.'

'Thought that was singing while carrying out a bit of exfoliation-based female hygiene,' said Oliver.

Vanessa grimaced. 'Why do I put up with you, Oliver, and more worryingly, why do I find your puerile sense of humour funny?'

'We can't go to Crete,' Scott pointed out. 'What'll happen to the bar and the kit?'

'You could, you know,' said Vanessa. 'After all, you don't actually do a lot, do you? All you need is someone to serve a few drinks and occasionally move a pedalo about. There's lots who would do that for a week. Maybe one of your teacher mates. Carl – he'd do it. You could pay him a cut of the profits.'

'Carl?' asked Oliver.

'I saw him yesterday handing out flyers for restaurants and hotels at the harbour. He'd jump at the chance to run your place for a while.'

Scott could feel the irrational panic of old rising as the conversation moved forward. He'd got used to Volos – the beach was only a short bus journey from town – but Crete? That was far, and it would involve buses and trains and ferries. He tried to keep his face neutral while desperately thinking of convincing reasons not to go.

'Can we afford it?' he asked. 'Got to cost a lot to get to Crete.'

'We've got enough, and it'll do us good to get away for a few days.'

'I don't know. I think we need to think about this for a while. We're just getting the business going – is this a good time to leave?'

'Don't see why not, mate. We'll still be making some money while we're away. Sounds good to me.'

The conversation continued in this vein, with Scott presenting objections that were gently rebutted by Oliver or Vanessa until he could think of nothing more to say and reluctantly found himself agreeing to the idea of heading off in the next couple of days.

Chapter 16

After a couple of days of checking train times and ferries, they were all set. The evening before they due to leave, Vanessa found Scott waiting for her as she came out of her office.

'Hello gorge, what are you doing lurking around here?'

'Can I speak to you?'

Something in his tone of voice made Vanessa drop her jokey tone. She nodded.

'Sure, let's go and grab a coffee.'

They settled down at a table in the back of the café, away from the sea. Vanessa waited as Scott fiddled with the sugar sachets and aligned and then realigned the paper square his coffee was sitting on.

'Is everything okay?'

'I'm scared, Nessie.'

'What are you scared of?'

'I don't want to go to Crete. I don't want to go anywhere and I just don't know why.'

'Is this just now?'

'No, I've always had it, as long as I can remember. My Uncle Ted understood it, I think. I'm pretty sure that is why he sent me here, to try to beat it. Local trips aren't too bad, but I really don't think I can do this.'

Vanessa nodded and reached across to pat his hand.

'We all get anxious sometimes. I get it when I have to meet new people. I go all clammy and can't get my words out. I forget to breathe and can't speak. What is it that's worrying you?'

It all poured out. Scott had never told anyone before of his fears, and once he started, he couldn't stop. He talked about how hard it had been to get to Greece, how hard the first days had been, how he had got used to it and thought with the move to the campsite he was getting over it. Now it felt like he was crashing back to earth again. He just couldn't face it.

Vanessa took it all in. 'I sometimes feel like that, you know – I think most people do a bit,' she said at length. 'What I do when I'm having a bad day is take it in five-minute chunks. Promise yourself that after each five minutes you can stop it and go back.'

'I've tried that, but then I have to get on a boat or a train or a bus or a plane, and you know that you can't get off for hours. I can't stop thinking about it.'

'I had a friend who had something similar. She was terrified of flying. What she did was imagine that something she really wanted was waiting for her at the end of the journey. It deffo worked for her.'

Scott thought about this.

'I'll try it. Thanks, Nessie.'

'The other thing she said is that each time you do it, it becomes a bit easier.'

'Thanks. I'll give it a go.'

Lying in bed in his tent, Scott tried Vanessa's idea. He thought about Abi. He imagined her face, her green-grey eyes, the way her face lit up when she smiled, her long naturally curly hair, and saw her standing at the bus station in Athens, waiting for him. She ran up to him and threw her arms around him. He, at this point, got his arm caught in the strap of the rucksack, as there would obviously be some way in which he would arse it up. He held the vision and found that the knot in his stomach and the ache in his jaw began to recede. He dropped off to sleep with the idea fixed in his head that tomorrow morning he just had to sit on a train and then he'd see Abi again.

Scott awoke with a feeling of positivity, like something good was going to happen. His brain then clicked into gear, but before he could focus on the bus journey, he skipped ahead to the vision of Abi at the bus station and he actually found himself smiling. This could work.

The bus to Athens took around four hours, which was a cue for Oliver to perform his normal trick of instantly falling asleep and remaining so for the duration. Looking at him, with his head lolling against the window and his jaw hanging open, Scott mused on the whole business of 'travelling'. When people say they are 'going travelling' it's generally assumed to be a life-enriching and rewarding experience. In Oliver's case you'd have to call it 'going arriving', as all he ever saw during the travelling stage was the inside of his own eyelids. Although, when Scott came to think about it, and right now he had nothing else to do, it was probably true of most people. 'I'm going travelling in Australia'. What that meant in reality was, 'I'm going to see the interior of a variety of aircraft, trains and buses, and when I stop travelling I'm going to look at things.'

Scott had never really liked the expression anyway. As well as his fear of the act itself, in his view most people who used it gave it a weight and gravitas entirely at odds with the reality. People who said 'yeah, I've been travelling for a year' tended to adopt the same tone as someone saying, 'Yeah, I've invented a cure of malaria and built an orphanage this year.' After all they'd only been on a bleeding holiday, so why the big deal.

He nudged Oliver to see if he wanted a cheese pie and was rewarded with a non-committal grunt, which he took to mean no. So he carried on staring out of the window as Greece trundled by at a steady fifty miles per hour.

When they arrived at the central bus station, there was of course no Abi to throw her arms around Scott, but he'd thought this out. In his mind he picked her up and carefully moved her to the port side, in front of the ferry they were due to get on. She'd be waiting for him there; he just needed to get across town to see her.

From the station they took a cab to the Athens port of Piraeus and found their ferry. Abi now got moved to a picturesque port in Crete, where she'd be waiting for him when the ferry docked, and they made their way onto the small city that doubled as the ferry to Crete. It had five bars, two dancefloors, live music and a casino, to name just the obvious attractions. After wandering around for thirty minutes they discovered that all it lacked for a top cheesy night out was a kebab shop. It probably had one of those, too, but they figured if they needed it they'd stumble across it.

To save a bit of cash they'd opted for tickets only, rather than booking a cabin, and they established a base in one of the lounges before throwing themselves into the evening's entertainment. Oliver, now wide awake and bushy-tailed, insisted they carry out one of his experiments. He reasoned, quite lucidly, that if they got staggering drunk then their natural tendency to totter on their feet would counteract the natural movement of the boat. This should, in theory, give them the appearance and sensation of sobriety while under normal circumstances they'd be falling-down pissed.

What he hadn't factored in was the possibility that your body might be lurching to the right at the same time as the boat. By midnight they had to accept that the plan was deeply flawed and the only safe course of action was to go to sleep. At 2 am, they agreed they'd have just one more for the road. At 2.30, Scott, ever the pedant, pointed out that they should really have had one more for the sea lane, so they did.

After finally making it back to the lounge, Oliver decided that fresh air was what was urgently required. He'd recently purchased a hammock and felt, with that certainty only possessed of the truly pissed, that this was the ideal time to christen it. Scott left him to it and passed out in a chair.

Out on deck it was quite cold, but in his inebriated state Oliver was oblivious to everything but battling with his hammock. After much fumbling and swearing, he finally managed to tie it between two poles. Within minutes he was sound asleep and snoring happily, blissfully unaware that the rope had gradually started to slip down the pole at the head end. By the time gravity had decided it had done enough, the hammock had reached a forty-five-degree angle and his head was three feet below his ankles. If Scott had woken him any later, he would almost certainly have been made it onto the Darwinian lists of idiots who improved the future of humanity by accidentally killing themselves before their genes could pollute the pool. As it was, his head had turned bright red and grown to twice its normal size, and the veins in his forehead looked like hosepipes.

'You all right? You look like someone's put a space hopper on your head.'

'Feeling a bit light-footed, actually, not much going on below my neck.'

'Novel reversal of the norm, then,' said Scott, handing him a bag of long-life chocolate-filled croissants. 'We've arrived.'

There's nothing quite like arriving at a place by boat, and Chania was looking particularly welcoming in the morning sunlight. Scott looked out at the town and the little ant-like figures scurrying around at the rapidly approaching port. He focused on one that in his mind was Abi and then moved her into the town, and, as he was a practical as well as a romantic man, into a café that was serving breakfast.

Oliver, with uncharacteristic forethought, had brought a map.

'Any idea what side up it goes?' asked Scott, turning away from the boat rail. 'A scale would be nice.'

'Do, re, mi, fa, so …'

'Too early, too early,' said Scott, wincing. He turned the thing over in his hands. 'Not one to knock a bit of initiative, as well you know, but it's a bit useless, isn't it?'

Oliver looked hurt. 'It's got a lot going for it. Simple, easy to read, too heavy to blow away …' He stared at it for inspiration. 'Easy-grip carrying handle, colourful.'

'And doubles up as beach tennis bat.'

'Exactly, multi-purpose. Besides, there can't be that many roads here, it's an island.'

What Oliver was unaware of was that Crete was rather a big island, the biggest in Greece and previously home to the Minoans, one of the oldest civilisations in history. Three thousand years ago they had running water in their houses, sewers and quality earthenware. Historians believe that a thriving trading culture existed between Crete and the island of Thera, 100 miles north. As well as the high-class tableware so beloved of the Minoan man in the well-drained street, Thera also provided the Minoans with a particularly fine firework display, swiftly followed by a free delivery of molten lava. They wouldn't have had too long to think about what to do before the tsunami hit, washing away the lava and the Minoans with it.

Blokes with terrible haircuts and bad sweaters have calculated that the volcanic eruption that ripped the heart out of the island we now know as Santorini threw a column of burning stuff 30 miles into the sky. They still routinely find fossils of crabs and whatnot on the highest Cretan mountains. That much may be true, but no archaeologist has yet created a plausible hypothesis as to why on earth the Minoans decided to worship bulls. Admittedly, legend has it that they bred a pretty impressive type of bull in Crete: the minotaur, half man half bull, which was either incredibly scary or incredibly silly, depending on which half was which.

As he disembarked from the ferry, Scott was feeling tentatively ok. He didn't want to push it, but apart from the plane journey, when he had been a bit pissed anyway, he had just travelled further and on more means of transport than he had for as long as he could remember. The vision of Abi as his goal was working and he was also feeling stronger for having done it.

They found a café and Oliver ordered himself an omelette while Scott furthered his research into the spinach and cheese pies called *spanokopittas*, which was the Greek for spinach and the Greek for pie. He had first had one the day after arriving, and it had been love at first bite. Since then he'd made a point of sampling one in every place he had visited in a quest to find the perfect pie. They ate with that intensity that comes only with a truly immense hangover, and didn't speak until the plates were empty and they were both on their second cup of coffee.

'Any good?' asked Oliver.

'Very nice – I'd say in the top five,' said Scott, dusting bits of filo pastry off his shirt. 'Bit light on the feta if anything.'

'Hmm.' Oliver sniffed. He had strong views on breakfast and felt that you could tell a lot about a nation from the quality of their morning fare. In his view, a breakfast should involve a plate with lots of stuff on it, and most if not all of that stuff should be fried.

'So, what's the set-up?'

'Find somewhere to stay, drop the bags off, have a shower and find a bull.'

'You ever seen a bull?'

'In the flesh? Not lately.'

'I've been chased by 'em down a street in Pamplona before, and they're big old fuckers.'

'Not easy to capture, is what you're saying?'

'Yes.'

'I've been thinking the same. I reckon we need to be a bit creative about this. The old man will be expecting something a bit leftfield.'

Oliver thought for a while.

'Hmm, bull, bull … We could get a pit bull dog, that would do it.'

'It would, you know. That could be the first good idea you've ever had, Mr Pond,' said Scott.

With renewed purpose they paid the bill and received directions to a tourist office, which in turn directed them to a couple of cheap rooms in the old part of town. A few hours later, they were walking around the town looking for dogs.

The idea seemed promising but ultimately drew a blank. The good people of Chania out walking their dogs did not seem to favour the particular breed they were after. It was a bitter blow. Despite their best attempts at asking locals, with the help of Scott's battered Greek dictionary and a phrase book, all they had elicited was baffled, bemused or downright frightened looks from the locals.

Part of this was due to their peculiar way of dealing with the Greek language. Oliver was pretty good at verbs and Scott had an equal facility for nouns. Consequently, their Greek conversations were a bizarre double act. A typical example would be:

Oliver: 'Excuse me, could you tell me where the...'

Scott: 'Bus...'

Oliver: 'Leaves from?'

The other thing dogging their progress, pun fully intended, was the erratic translations of their dictionary. Unknown to them, 'pit' was translated as 'big hole or tomb' and 'bull' was the slang interpretation of the word. Hence the recoil of the locals was not an entirely unreasonable reaction to being asked: 'Excuse me, could you tell me where to buy a grave falsehood?' After a day spent watching people edging, and in one case actually running, away, they'd decided that they needed to try a different approach.

Chania, being a slightly upmarket place, was not the cheapest and if their money was to last they needed to find somewhere a bit cheaper to stay. After a brief return visit to the tourist office the next day, they were soon on the bus to a beach resort on the other side of the Island. It all seemed to be getting easier. Scott used his Abi technique again but part of him was also thinking that, now he'd been through Athens and on a ferry, a short bus journey was nothing to be scared of.

What they needed was economy, and in the rather ugly shape of Malia, Crete had just the place. The First World War poet Rupert Brooke once movingly said, 'There's some corner of a foreign field that is for ever England'. And it's equally true to say that there is a part of Greece that is forever Blackpool. It was horrible and they loved it. It even had a McDonald's. There could be no better or more effective way of reminding the homesick Englishman of all he was not missing.

On the second night, they were sitting outside 'Dazzlers' with a couple of bottles of beer, the only thing served in the whole town that didn't come with five sparklers and assorted furniture sitting in the glass, when a party of inebriated bright red youths streamed past. The group consisted of five schoolgirls, three schoolboys, two nuns, and a gorilla.

'That's something you don't see every day,' said Oliver, whose attention was fixed on the most attractive of the schoolgirls.

'Hmm,' murmured Scott, who had a faraway expression on his face and was doing his 'cat's arse mouth' thing. He was having a eureka moment. An expression made famous by Archimedes who shouted it while having a bath, and which is actually a bad English translation of the Greek for 'I have found it!' What Archimedes had found was the answer to a particularly tricky question concerning the king's crown. The king had wanted to know whether it was solid gold or had other metals mixed in, a question that had him and the finest minds of the time stumped. Until, that is, the fateful day Archimedes found himself lying in the bath contemplating his very own crown jewels and realised the amount of water they displaced would help ascertain the weight of the king's and therefore the amount of gold contained therein.

Scott punctuated his eureka moment by muttering the word 'cow' and saying, 'Have you got the dictionary?', which lacked the same punch and was unlikely to be quoted in 2,000 years' time.

Oliver handed over the battered blue pocket-sized book.

'Panther, panties, pantomime … ah, I thought so! The Greek for pantomime is "pantomime".'

''Thieving bastards!' exclaimed Oliver.

'You don't think, given that on the one side you have Pericles, Sophocles and the Greek tragedians, while on the other you've got Tim Rice, Ray Clooney and "Whoops where are my pyjamas?", that they might have got there first?'

'Fair point,' accepted Oliver.

'Be back in a minute.' Scott slipped off his seat and followed the menagerie into the next bar, leaving a nonplussed Oliver wondering what he was up to. He returned ten minutes later looking delighted with himself – as well he might, since he had just secured the loan of a pantomime cow outfit.

In order to put on their weekly fancy-dress pub-crawl, the tour company had invested in a job lot of costumes, most of which had seen a fair amount of use. The likes of the Pirate, Elvis, Schoolgirl, Nun and even Charles the First were looking a bit threadbare, but the cow outfit was pristine. Not surprisingly, given that the only reason for being on such a holiday is to shag as many people as possible, Mr Cow had seen very little use. It's not easy to cop off with someone while wearing a cow outfit, and if you did, would you really want to shag someone who wanted to shag a cow? Consequently, the offer of two thousand drachmas to borrow the outfit for a couple of days had fallen on receptive, if slightly incredulous, ears.

Now they just needed someone stupid enough to be the back end of a customised panto cow in 30-degree heat.

Pete collected glasses at the Pink Lady. He had arrived in Malia six weeks previously and had managed to get so pissed on his final night that he'd missed the flight home. Skint and denied his usual income stream, which was knocking out pills in a Birmingham nightclub, he viewed the chance of sticking his head up Oliver's arse as a positive career move. Given his previous work experience, there was a good chance that he'd list the role on his CV. If he had been any less intelligent, he would have needed watering twice a day,

They all met up at ten the following morning for a pre-manoeuvres briefing before getting the bus to the archaeological site of the minotaur legend.

'So – Oliver's got the outfit in his bag, we go in, find the centre of the palace, you both slip into it and I lead you out. All clear?'

'Do I have any lines, like?' asked Pete.

Oliver rolled his eyes.

'Pete, mate, have you ever met a cow that could speak out of its arse?'

'Alright, just trying to, you know, get my motivation.'

110

'Your motivation is five hundred drachmas.'

'Fair enough.'

They arrived at the palace of Knossos at around three, paid the entrance fee and wandered in behind a tour party of Scandinavians.

'Lucky they didn't search the bags,' whispered Pete.

'And why would they search the bags of someone entering an archaeological sight?' Scott was finding Pete heavy going.

'Bombs and that, like.'

'He's got a point, mate, you wouldn't want a mad bomber reducing all these ruins to rubble,' Oliver added, grinning.

Knossos was a pretty impressive sight but suffered from having been discovered in the days when the only qualification needed to be an archaeologist was to be posh, own a trowel and wear a tweed suit.

Sir Arthur Evans, who qualified on all three counts, had adopted a somewhat cavalier approach to historical accuracy and had routinely moved things that didn't make sense to places where, he thought, they did. Finding a thing like a throne on its own, he had promptly had it moved to the grandest room and had announced he'd discovered the throne room. This seemed the obvious place for Scott to 'capture' the bull and lead it out of the palace.

Dropping behind the Scandinavian party, who were now having the niceties of the throne room explained, they sprang into action. Oliver and Pete wriggled into their respective ends of the cow while Scott, taking the lens cap off the camera, spotted a snag. He needed evidence of him mastering the 'bull' but had no one to operate the camera. Cursing his stupidity, he was just attempting to balance the camera on a wall when a couple of straggling Scandinavians wandered around the corner. Composing his face as if it were the most natural question in the world, he said,

'Excuse me, would you mind filming me and this bull for a couple of minutes?'

If you were looking for someone unlikely to be fazed by such a question, you could do a lot worse than find a Norwegian.

'Sure, what am I doing?' the male half of the couple asked without a flicker of surprise.

Scott explained the workings of the camera while Oliver and Pete, beginning to enjoy their starring roles, performed a reasonable attempt at a comedy dance routine. Timing is everything, and it was perhaps unfortunate that a walkie-talkie-toting security guard chose that moment to appear. Judging from his expression, he considered two halfwits in a panto cow outfit to be a slur on the archaeological integrity of Knossos and consequently an insult to all things Cretan. Within seconds the area was crawling with unamused uniformed staff, none of whom were inclined to believe Scott's claims that he was filming a BBC documentary encouraging viewers to visit Crete, particularly as his Greek attempt at explanation came out as: 'We are filming a...' while the muffled word 'documentary' came from the interior of the cow.

Outside the site, they reappraised the situation.

'Banned from an archaeological site, that's got to be a first.'

The two Norwegians smiled at Oliver and introduced themselves as OddRane and Rikke.

'That was real fun,' said Rikke, who didn't seem in the least upset that she and her boyfriend had also been thrown out.

'I think we owe you two a drink.'

Running across the 'Royal Ted', with its large sign advertising Guinness, softened the blow considerably.

In OddRane and Rikke they found kindred spirits. OddRane was wearing an alarming safari shirt and obviously shared Oliver's thoughts on the subject of leg apparel. They both subscribed to the 'bigger is best' theory and favoured clownishly baggy linen trousers.

He and Rikke were planning to get married and his pride in his fiancée was evident. It therefore came as something of a surprise when, as he watched her glide to the bar, he raised his beer and said, 'The first time I am seeing her, I knew she was the one. She looked absolutely minging.'

Timing again. Given the choice, Scott probably wouldn't have had a mouthful of beer at this moment. When he'd mopped up the table and could bring himself to speak, he patted OddRane weakly on the shoulder and asked, 'OddRane, mate, where did you learn that word?'

'Some English guys told me my shirt was minging. I am thinking it means cool and beautiful.'

'And that'd be the shirt, would it?' asked Scott, pointing to the safari aberration.

OddRane nodded.

'How can I put this – what's the worst thing you can imagine?'

OddRane wrinkled his brow before stating decisively, 'Sweden!'

'Well, in that case Sweden, is minging,' explained Oliver.

OddRane's huge frame shook as he threw back his head and bellowed with laughter.

'Sweden is minging! Very good.' He slapped his thigh as tears appeared in his eyes. 'And my shirt is like Sweden. And, and Rikke...' By now he was having trouble speaking. 'Rikke is like Sweden!'

Watching him was not dissimilar to watching Thera erupting, but a good deal better-natured. They had both fallen in love with Greece and plied the boys with questions about what it was like.

'We want to buy an old place and build it again.'

'Renovate it' Added Rikke

'Well, there's plenty of wrecked old places on the mountain near where we live, you should come and visit and check a few out.' Said Scott, 'Is that what you do, building?'

'No, my brother is a builder, I am just a, how do you say, Do It Yourselfer'.

'He's very good, he built me a treehouse'. Added Rikke.

'A treehouse'? Oliver was intrigued.

It transpired he had fancied Rikke for years and had been too shy to do anything about it so he had built her a tree-house. He explained this as if it was the most natural thing in the world. His brother had helped him out, but basically for pretty much every weekend for a year he had driven into the forest and cut, sawed, hammered and fiddled until at the end he had built a palatial tree house complete with a wood-burning stove. He had carved Rikke's name on the door and then plucked up the courage to ask her if she would like to take a walk in the woods.

'Then what'? Asked Oliver

'We walk and chat for about an hour then we get to this lake and start to walk around it and he say, 'look, there's something over there'. Said Rikke.

'So we go over and there is this thing in the tree and a ladder, he say to me, go up the ladder and see, and at the top there is a door and it had 'Rikke' wrote on it.'

Oliver clapped OddRane on the back. 'Every credit mate.'

Scott, clinked his glass in a toast and said, 'So why do you want to look at houses? don't you just want us to find a nice tree that you can live in?'

OddRane grinned.

'Only once, never am I doing that again. Unless I need a new girlfriend of course!' Which brought a gentle punch from Rikke.

'It's a nice place to live but the Winters aren't great, I'm told it gets pretty cold and there's not much to do.' Said Scott, in an unaccustomed role of the voice of reason.

Neither OddSvien nor Rikke were unduly impressed with the threat of 'a bit cold'. Living in a place which dips to minus twenty degrees on a bad day and is never much above zero on a good one for three months of the year, they felt confident of their ability to deal with anything Greece might throw at them. They did agree, however, that it would make sense to come back in January or February for a week to have another look round and to see what life was like it a Greek winter.

They spent the rest of the evening together until OddRane and Rikke decided it was time to head off. They were planning to travel round Greece for a couple of months, so Oliver gave them his address and made them promise to visit when they got to the mainland.

After a couple more pints and a few games of pool, they moved on to the dartboard. It was an unequal match, Oliver had the twin advantage of possessing incredibly long arms and playing against a man, in Scott, who would have trouble hitting the back end of their costume with a banjo. Scott, having scored his second-highest score of thirty to get his score down to 306, watched as Oliver, needing seventy-five to win, hit a five and a twenty, leaving himself fifty to win with his last dart.

'Fifty to win, all I've got to do is hit the...'

They looked at each other and said in unison: 'Bull.'

Later that evening, Barry was wiping down the bar with a wet cloth and trying to pin down the nagging feeling that he'd forgotten something. He'd started his shift an hour ago, had bottled up, cleaned all the ashtrays and wiped down the tables, but he couldn't rid himself of the feeling that something was missing. He stared into space, mentally ticking off the list of tasks, frowning in concentration, oblivious to the fact that he was staring directly at the space where the dartboard used to be.

A swift return to Knossos the following day, where they disguised themselves by the simple expedient of wrapping bandanas round their heads, secured the necessary photographic evidence of Scott clutching the dartboard in the throne room, and that was the third labour under wraps. It was time to bid farewell to Crete and head for home.

With Abi waiting for him at each leg of the journey, and knowing he had managed it all once already, Scott found that he was able to cope in a way he could never have previously imagined. He still had a wobble or two on the ferry, but compared to the crippling sense of fear he had lived with for so long, this really felt like a new beginning.

Chapter 17

Scott looked across the restaurant at the newly installed dartboard and smiled to himself. He'd given it to Taffos, who placed it in a position of honour, above a picture of the Acropolis. They had just told Vanessa about their trip and the completion of the latest labour.

Oliver wandered off to talk to Taffos about something, leaving Scott and Vanessa alone.

'So how are you feeling now?' she asked.

'Better. So much better. Thinking of someone, I mean something, positive at the end of each bit of the journey really worked for me.'

'I'm really pleased.'

'I think I can do this now. I've been to Crete and back, so maybe I can go anywhere.'

'Maybe you should try another trip soon.'

'Like riding a bike?' said Scott.

'I was thinking of a horse, but yes, exactly.'

At this point Oliver reappeared and sat down at the table. 'Someone going horse riding? Smashing, I'm well up for that.'

'After my experience with that bloody donkey, no way, never again.'

'Fair enough. You going to eat those chips?'

Vanessa pushed her plate towards Oliver. 'So let's see the list, then – what's next?'

Scott delved into his bag and pulled out the list.

The labours of Hercules

1 Killed the Nemean lion
2 Killed a Hydra, a nine-headed snake
3 Captured a golden-horned reindeer
4 ~~Brought back a bull from Crete~~
5 Captured the Erymanthian Boar
6 ~~Cleaned the Augean stables in a single day~~
7 Chased away flesh-eating Stymphalian birds

8 Captured the horses of King Diomedes

~~**9** Got the belt of Hippolyta, Queen of the Amazons~~

10 Captured the cattle of Geryon, the three-headed, six-armed giant

11 Brought back the three golden apples from the Garden of Hesperides

12 Went into Hades and brought back the three-headed hound of hell

'What about number eleven?' said Oliver. 'I love an apple, me.'

'Anyone know where Hesperides is?' asked Scott.

They both looked at Vanessa. 'Anyone?' she echoed. 'Just me, then.'

Hesperides was a mythical place, described only as being a far western corner of the world.

'Doesn't give us a lot to go on,' said Oliver.

'It's all in the interpretation,' said Scott. 'For example, "far" for you is the end of the beach and back. All we need is some apples on a corner that we approach with a brisk walk from an easterly direction.'

'I can see that,' nodded Oliver.

'So, on his way to Hesperides, he ran across a chap called Prometheus.'

'I know all about him – he was the fire man,' said Oliver smugly and speared an olive with a cocktail stick.

'Very good!' said Vanessa.

Scott looked confused.

'I didn't know they had firemen back then.'

'Not *fireman,*' said Vanessa. 'The man who gave the gift of fire to mortals.'

'It's your classic survival situation. You need a fire, your man Prometheus was a dab hand with the tinderbox and rubbing sticks, could knock one up in no time.'

Vanessa ignored Oliver's contribution and continued.

'Up until then, fire had been the sole preserve of the gods. Prometheus was a minor god who felt sorry for the mortals – that's us, by the way – and showed man how to make fire.'

'Good of him.'

'Yes, but it didn't do him any good. Zeus…'

'Head of the gods,' interrupted Scott, keen to show off his limited knowledge and to trump Oliver's Prometheus.

'…as you say, head of the gods, was livid. As a punishment he chained Prometheus to a rock and every day sent an eagle to eat his liver. Every day it grew back and got eaten again the next day.'

'Sort of Groundhog Day meets Reservoir Dogs?' said Scott.

'You could put it like that. Anyway, Hercules rescued him and then continued on his way to Hesperides. When he arrived, he discovered Atlas holding up the sky on his back.'

'Odd,' said Scott.

'Not really. Atlas was the father of the Hesperides nymphs who guarded the golden apple, together with a dragon called Ladon. Hercules knew Atlas would be able to get past his own daughters without any bother, so he did a deal with him. He offered to give him a break from carrying the sky if he got the apples.'

'Bet he jumped at it.'

'He did. What's more, when he came back with the apples, he double-crossed Hercules by saying he was going to take the apples and Hercules could carry on holding up the sky.'

'Sneaky,' said Scott.

'So Hercules pretended to agree, but asked if Atlas could just take the sky for a second while he adjusted his cloak to pad his shoulders. Then, of course, he left him to it.'

'Not the brightest, your gods, are they,' said Oliver.

'So we're looking for a garden with some apples, and three nymphs guarded by a dragon.'

'With a bloke carrying the sky on his back round the corner,' added Scott.

The local mayor had an apple tree, a really annoying wife and three daughters who went like the clappers. It would have to do.

The operation took place the next Saturday night. Oliver had been sent ahead to take his position outside the wall of the mayor's garden. Scott and Nessie, who had her camera to record events, followed twenty minutes later.

They arrived as planned to find Oliver holding a large geography book on which was balanced a satellite dish he had found in a skip.

Scott whispered, 'Can I hold up that Sky dish for you while you get me some apples?'

They swapped places and Oliver hauled himself over the wall, dropping to the other side.

It was at this point that things started to unravel.

Scott's optimistic assumption that the sign on the wall said 'This is where the mayor lives' turned out to be a fairly crucial mistake, which he would not have made had he known the words for 'guard', 'dog' and 'beware'. This, coupled with the surprise discovery of a water feature directly below the wall, were both unexpected obstacles. The whole operation hinged on speed and silence, but the latter was compromised by the shout of 'Fuck!' echoing around neighbouring buildings as Oliver, dropping onto what he expected to be the ground, found himself waist-deep in water.

Struggling out, he made his way to the apple tree when he heard barks heading speedily in his direction. Thrusting an apple into each pocket, he sprinted for the wall and was just pulling himself up when a set of jaws clamped on his left calf. Kicking out with his right leg, he forced the hound to slightly release its grip and he was able to scramble over, leaving it with just a chunk of denim to satisfy its territorial instincts.

After hobbling back to their tents and surveying the damage, they realised he was going to need medical attention that was beyond the scope of his tin.

At the hospital, the language problem reared its head for the second time that night. The word *xenos* in Greek means 'foreign' – as in xenophobia, a fear of foreigners – but unfortunately it also means 'stray', as in dog. Consequently, on being asked if the dog was *xenos*, Oliver, after rummaging in his pocket dictionary, was able to tell the nurse he'd been bitten by a man from Germany who was working as a shepherd.

Four stitches, a tetanus injection, and a lot of bemused looks later, they were able, with a certain satisfaction, to cross out labour number eleven.

Chapter 18

Business at the watersports shack tended to come, appropriately enough, in waves, leaving lengthy periods of inactivity in the trusty deckchairs. The mornings were often quiet, with trade building up around lunchtime. The days also made a difference. Most of the package holidays ran from Saturday to Saturday, which meant that day was their quietest of the week.

This particular Saturday morning, Oliver was still snoring away in his tent as it was Scott's turn to be on 'earlies'. Having got all the kit out and opened the bar, he found himself glaring at their dinghy. The Robin Reliant of ocean-going craft, it had an outboard motor more temperamental than a Hollywood diva.

As the least practical or mechanically-minded person you were ever likely to meet, Scott had a theory that if you snuck up on machinery, you could catch it unawares and get it to work. His general ineptness and lack of practicality had seen a previous girlfriend describe him as 'practically useless', which he had felt was harsh but probably fair.

He got up and sauntered towards the sea, whistling, before hopping, catlike, into the boat, where he seized the starter cord and gave it a purposeful tug. The engine coughed encouragingly, started up, ran for a few seconds and then died. After a further ten attempts to coax it into life, each more desultory than the last, he lost his patience and kicked it. An unwise move at the best of times, and frankly stupid when wearing flip-flops. Clutching his foot and hopping back from the boat, he became aware of two sunbathing girls who had taken in the whole performance.

Smiling ruefully at them, he shrugged his shoulders and said by way of explanation, 'Having trouble with the motor.'

The one on the left looked up from her book and said, 'Sounds like a collapsed primer bulb. You've probably got a vacuum forming inside the fuel tank, cutting off the fuel supply to the engine. You'll need to loosen the vent screws to allow some ventilation and then pump the primer bulb until it hardens up.'

Her friend nodded and, looking up from doing her nails, added, 'Yep, that sounds like the problem. But before you do that I'd suggest checking the kill switch. It can sometimes get pulled out by accident. Check to see if it's out, and if it is, disengage it.'

Scott stood stock still while his brain attempted to compute this most unexpected stream of information. He finally managed to say, 'Collapsed primer bulb, eh? Why didn't I think of that! Thanks very much.'

'You're welcome.' she replied before returning to her book.

Scott hobbled back to the bar, where he sat and rubbed his throbbing toe until Oliver arrived.

'All right?'

'Hurt my toe a bit on the engine, but I think I know what's wrong with it now. It's got a primer bulb somewhere and could need vacuuming.'

Oliver, who was slightly more practically-minded, found this unlikely and commented, 'You sure? That sounds like bollocks.'

'Go and ask them,' said Scott, gesturing at the two girls. 'It was something like that.'

Oliver looked at the two girls lying on the sunbeds. The one on the right was sitting up painting her nails while her friend had her head in a glossy magazine. They were both wearing big, stylish and no doubt expensive sunglasses and had large handbags next to their sun loungers. He turned back to Scott and said, 'Those two?'

'Unlikely, I agree, but they seem to be experts on engines. They were very convincing.'

Oliver walked over and introduced himself. The one who had spoken first was called Tonia and her friend was Natalie. Patiently they repeated the advice they had given Scott.

Oliver looked thoughtful.

'Well, it's not the kill switch – I've checked that – so it probably is the primer bulb, thanks. Can I offer you a drink?'

They both accepted the offer of iced coffees and he headed back to the bar to rustle some up. A few minutes later, they came up to collect them at the bar, where Scott was still nursing his foot.

'How's the toe?' Tonia asked.

'Fine, thanks,' said Scott through gritted teeth. 'Having a nice time here?'

It transpired they were indeed having a nice time. They'd arrived two days earlier and were booked for a two-week stay. Tonia was a dental nurse, information which led to Scott pursing his lips into a reasonable impression of a cat's arse. He was not particularly proud of his teeth, as a combination of strong coffee and red wine had taken a toll, and from then on he attempted to speak without opening his mouth more than half an inch. As for Tonia, her teeth would have been the envy of a Hollywood A-lister, and the rest of her face gleamed with health and vitality.

Natalie was dark-skinned with an afro and worked as an investment manager. Like the boys, they had been friends since their schooldays in a small Devon sea-side resort and now shared a flat together in Exeter.

Scott had visited their home village on a family holiday, which helped the conversation along, and they sat chatting at the bar while drinking their coffees, in no hurry to leave. The two women were in fact suffering from the same level of over-familiarity as the boys. Having been in each other's company for forty-eight hours straight, they were both craving alternative conversation.

'So what does an investment manager do then?'

'It's not very interesting,' Natalie replied.

'Try me?' said Oliver.

'Well, I look at companies and businesses and decide if they're good opportunities for investments. If they are, I recommend them to our clients, or we may invest ourselves.'

Oliver waved his arm, taking in the bar and the windsurfing equipment.

'What d'you reckon? Worth a punt?'

Natalie laughed.

'You've put me on the spot! I'd need to look at your cash flow and profits, but ultimately we tend to look most at the people running the business and decide if we want to invest in them.'

'That's us fucked then,' said Oliver.

Natalie looked back at him and said, 'Oh, I wouldn't say that,' raising one eyebrow.

Oliver found himself blushing as Tonia said 'Natalie!' and then laughed. He got up to try to disguise his red face and said, 'Another coffee?'

The both declined and wandered back to their sunloungers, leaving the boys to carry on with their daily chores, which meant sitting down and playing backgammon. They were in the middle of an epic series of games, the running score of which had recently tilted in Scott's favour. After a couple of hours, they'd reached a crucial point in the game when their attention was drawn by a lone customer hovering at the bar, politely trying to get their attention. It was Natalie.

'Hi again, can I get a bottle of water?'

Scott stood up, but she waved him back to his seat and said, 'Don't stop your game. I can help myself if you don't mind.'

'Okay, thanks. They're in the fridge at the back.'

'And grab us a bottle while you're there,' added Oliver. Trying his luck.

It worked and she did. What's more, while she was doing it, she served two other people with beers from the fridge.

Tonia, who was watching her, got up and joined in. The pair of them spent a half-hour in the bar leaning out of the side flap to serve customers, while Scott and Oliver merely had to sit on their arses shouting out prices on demand.

'Think we've hit on something here, mate,' said Oliver, nodding towards the girls.

What they'd hit on was an improbably virtuous circle. Tonia and Natalie really liked hanging around the bar and serving drinks in between bouts of sunbathing and swimming, and their aesthetic appeal succeeding in making a lot of male holidaymakers more thirsty than Scott or Oliver had ever done. So, business improved, they had less to do and more fun doing it. It also allowed Oliver and Natalie to spend time together in close proximity, which culminated in them spending the night in her room in even closer proximity.

After the second time, they lay in a sweaty pool, her head resting on his chest.

'Do you know why I like you?' she said.

'Cause I'm handsome?'

'Oh pleeease. Nope, it's because when we told you how to fix your motor, you didn't ask us how we knew about that stuff.'

'Should I have done?'

'Most men would. They would look at us and see two girly girls and wonder how we knew big tattooed blokey stuff.'

'Got the same when I did the ballet dancing,' he said.

'Ballet?' She lifted her head to look at him. 'You did ballet?'

He raised an eyebrow and smiled and she hit him over the head with the pillow.

'I don't normally do this holiday fling stuff, you know,' she said.

'I'll take that as a compliment, then.'

'You should.'

Oliver raised his head as he heard the sound of a door opening and running water from the next room.

'Does Tonia mind me being here?'

'She's fine. She's getting married in three weeks' time.'

'Married? Blimey.'

'Yep. This is her hen do. Well, one of them – she does have more than one friend.'

Natalie snuggled her head into his chest and lay with her cheek on his left nipple.

'What about your mate Scott – is he alright? He looks worried a lot of the time.'

Oliver thought about this for a few moments.

'Wouldn't say he's worried as such. It's just money, really. We thought we'd be making more from the windsurfing.'

While they were talking, Natalie's hand had been slowly working itself downwards from his chest, and once it reached its destination, they decided the conversation had been going on long enough.

The next few days saw Natalie and Tonia hanging out with them pretty full-time. Tonia had worked in bars and nightclubs, so she really enjoyed the banter around the bar and spent a lot of her time helping out.

One morning she and Nat were serving some customers while Oliver pored over a hardbound book filled with pencilled numbers, with Scott standing nervously by his side. As Oliver also had his glasses on, this could only mean he was doing the accounts. After much furrowing of brow and bizarre scratching of various parts of his anatomy, he came up with a final figure, underlined it and passed it over.

Scott whistled through his teeth. 'That's not bad for a week.'

'That's since the start of the month, for the last three weeks.'

Scott looked pained.

'But that's ridiculous. We're busy enough all day, we're getting new supplies in from Taffos every other day – where's it all going?'

Oliver looked back at his figures.

'How much do we drink in a typical day?'

Scott thought about it. 'Well, now you're asking, a couple of beers around lunchtime, a few more in the afternoons...'

'Then there's the red wine around teatime.'

'Yes.'

'And cocktails in the evening before heading out for dinner, and also the freebies for anyone we like the look of.'

'I see what you're saying. We might have to cut down a bit.'

At this point, Natalie flopped down next to Oliver and demanded he rub some suntan lotion into her back.

Oliver reached over and began to massage the cream into her skin.

'Ohh, that's good ... who taught you to massage like that?'

'I learned it while travelling out east.'

'From a village elder in Norwich,' added Scot.

Natalie smiled. 'What were you two talking about? You looked dead serious.'

'We're a bit skint, and wishing we weren't,' said Scott.

'What's your turnover? Based on the last few days I'd say about fifty quid a day, that about right?'

'fifteen thousand drachs, so yes, about that,' said Oliver.

'And what's the margin on your sales?'

The both looked blank.

'How much more do you sell the stuff for than the price you buy it at?'

'Ah, that margin,' said Scott. 'We buy the beer for 125 and sell it for 600, and the same for the water.'

'Four hundred and eighty percent mark-up, can't see you going much higher. So you need to increase footfall or upsell. Upselling on drinks is not a viable option and your captive audience is pretty static, so footfall is problematic. Only one solution.'

Scott, not so much a fish out of water as a human in a fish tank, just smiled the smile of a genial idiot and nodded to encourage her to continue.

'You need to open in the evenings.'

He scratched his head. 'Not sure you've noticed, Natalie, but the beach is not exactly packed after sundown. What are we going to do? Tap shagging couples on the shoulder and ask if they'd like to break off for a quick lager?'

'You could organise evening events – music, dancing and stuff. Me and Tonia have done a bit of promoting before. We'll help.'

Oliver looked thoughtful. 'Could have something there. A traditional Greek night, maybe a bouzouki band, that could work.'

Chapter 19

While Oliver was thinking of bouzouki bands, Vanessa was thinking about him. She was about an hour away, heading up the mountain on a bus in which the air conditioning was either broken or, more likely, had never existed. Rivulets of moisture were forming on her forehead.

There was still another twenty kilometres to go along the winding mountain road to reach the gorge, and then ideally she'd be able to sit in the shade while the party wandered about, taking photos and buying tat. It was an easy day for her: all she really had to do was, rather like Tennyson's account of the Charge of the Light Brigade, count them out and count them in. Hopefully, unlike that battle, there would be the same amount coming back as had gone.

She'd learned not to take anything for granted, though, particularly after the affair of the boat trip the previous year. She'd taken thirty-two out and, after enjoying the hospitality of the captain, had failed to notice that she'd brought thirty-one back. Of all the places it's possible to spend a night locked in, the toilet of a Greek converted fishing boat is not the most luxurious – you might even describe it as your bog-standard bog – and the travel company had had to stump up £200 in compensation to keep the man in question quiet. Despite their best attempts, it had still made the press, but oddly had little effect on sales, which, if anything, had slightly improved. The explanation for this lay in the nature of the tourists that Sunny Sunshine Tours attracted. At their end of the market, people viewed a payment of £200 for a night locked in the loo as a stunningly good deal, and consequently on most trips Vanessa had to lever them out with a crowbar.

At least today's lot were slightly older than the usual group: families with kids looking for a break from the beach and a bit of local culture. At the thought of the beach, a little nagging pain went through Vanessa's stomach. In her mind's eye she kept seeing that girl – what was her name? Natalie? – with Oliver. The really annoying thing about it all was the fact that it annoyed her. She'd known Oliver for nearly a year now, and they'd always just been mates, and God knows how many times in that period she'd had to listen to him expounding about building wild boar spear traps or sucking water from leaves without seeing him as anything other than an amusing freak. So why did the sensation she had right now feel so much like jealousy?

In a conscious effort to turn her thoughts to other things, she opened her book and tried to remember where she'd got to. It wasn't easy. The title was Greek Mythology Simplified, and if its prose style was anything to go by, you'd need a doctorate to even think about picking up the advanced version. Reading it was akin to wading down a long corridor waist-deep in custard, but Vanessa had never yet failed to finish a book and was not about to be defeated by this one. Besides, despite its stilted style, it couldn't help but be interesting in parts because the stories themselves were so fascinating.

At the moment she was reading about Tiresias. He was renowned for being incredibly wise because he'd lived three times longer than any other man alive, and, according to legend, when he was a boy two enchanted snakes had turned him into a girl for a year before turning him back to a boy again. This was to come in handy, as one day Zeus and Hera got into an argument on whether it was easier to be a man or a woman. Failing to reach any agreement, they went to see Tiresias who was not only really clever, but had also dipped his toe in both camps, so to speak. Tiresias came down on Zeus's side, telling Hera it was nine times more pleasant to be a woman than it was to be a man. Hera didn't take this well, and in a fit of pique she blinded Tiresias. Zeus, feeling bad about his wife's action but unable to undo it, gave Tiresias the gift of prophecy, presumably on the basis he'd be able to predict which things he was going to bump into.

Vanessa let the book slip and gazed dreamily at the scenery flashing by the window. Nine times as pleasant to be a woman than a man? That needed some thinking about. If there was a man feeling nine times worse than her at this precise moment, then he had her unflagging sympathy.

The coach arrived and her party dispersed themselves all over the lower reaches of the twelve-mile-long gorge, their cameras snapping away furiously. For just three months in summer it was possible to walk the entire length of the gorge, but there was no danger of any of her lot getting that bright idea into their heads, particularly not in this heat. For those who liked that sort of thing, the best option was to take a bus to the top of the mountain to the springs that created the gorge and follow the path down. It started as a gentle trickle, but as you followed the steep path down it opened up into an increasingly high-walled canyon inducing claustrophobia in many an unwary rambler, or so the guidebook said.

The gorge trip was one of Vanessa's favourites, as it never failed to give her a sense of perspective. She wasn't in any way overly spiritual, but every now and then she had a feeling that some answer or insight was about to pop into her mind and it was just a case of waiting until it did. This afternoon was one of those times, and sure enough one duly arrived in the shape of a myopic bumblebee.

She was thumbing through the glossy guidebook of the gorge, marvelling once again at the steepness of the rock faces and the extraordinary wealth of vegetation it sustained, when a bee flew into the side of her head. Startled, she shot out a hand and knocked over the glass of water that had come with her coffee. It formed itself into a stream before marching down the slope of the table in its relentless desire to conform to the laws of gravity.

To Vanessa's eye, there was a message in the bloody-minded way the trickle of water went about its business. Everything in the book, everything she could see around her, had been created by water – all twelve miles of the gorge, made from small molecules of hydrogen and oxygen insisting on taking the path of least resistance. Biology GCSE had told her that the human body, her body, was ninety-six percent water, and by inference she was a woman who, given time, could, well, move mountains.

It was with a new sense of empowerment coursing through her veins that she climbed back on the bus that afternoon with a plan of action. She was going to see Ma Taffos.

Three hours later she was ensconced on the balcony overlooking the menagerie and the mountain sloping down to the sea. Vanessa raised the glass to her mouth, knocked back her third cloudy, homemade *tsipero* and reached for the bottle. Ma Taffos lit a cigarette, prompting a wheezy coughing fit before continuing:

'Oh yes, I remember the first time I saw him. I thought he was the most handsome man in the village. He had an eye, you see – oh, he could light cigarettes with those eyes. He can still.'

'Did he like you at first?' asked Vanessa, putting down her glass.

'At first? At first he didn't know I existed, he never took any notice of me. Never looked in my direction. Of course I was just a little girl to him. There were lots of us.'

'So what happened?'

Ma Taffos took another pull on her cigarette and spoke while exhaling a cloud of smoke.

'I watched him. Really watched him: watched what he drank, how he drank, what he ate, where he went, what he listened to, which friends he liked, which he didn't, what girls he spoke to, why he spoke to them. I was like a detective.'

She smiled at the memory, finished her glass and waited while Vanessa refilled it, spilling a good half-measure in the process.

'I saw that he liked attention. He was what we call *kamaki*.'

Nessie nodded. She knew the word.

'Fisherman, you say – he liked to catch girls. With him, it was a sport, though. After he'd caught them. he didn't want them. He'd throw them back and try to catch another one.'

'Sounds like a bastard,' said Vanessa.

'Oh, he was, Vanessa, he was, but then that's what we girls like, isn't it? A challenge?'

'A challenge,' echoed Vanessa, raising her glass, and spilling a bit more as they clinked.

'So what then?'

'I never let him see me watching him. Mirrors, reflections, the edge of the eye. Boys, you see, they are stupid. They look at you straight, they don't realise you can see just as much if you look to the side of someone and let the edge of your eye see. He never saw me looking at him and it killed him. As time went on, it drove him crazy, I was the only girl who never looked at him and more and more I could see him looking at me.'

Vanessa smiled.

'Brilliant. And he asked you out?'

'Not yet. It was the English classes. He had an uncle who lived in England – Bristol, I think. He went there in the holidays and he was speaking the best English of all the kids around. It was good to speak English. All the music we listened to was English and American, he could sing the Beatles. I learned English, too. I was a good student but shy. I learned at home from the radio and from the books. After exams I was put in the same class for English and we were the best two, him and me. More it was driving him crazy. This girl who never looked to him and was as good at English, and I was pretty then.' She stubbed out her cigarette and picked up the packet.

'I didn't smoke these then – I was one of the only ones not to – and one day after class he offered me a cigarette, and do you know what I said?'

Vanessa inclined her head.

Her shoulders started moving as a throaty chuckle developed into a full-grown belly laugh at the memory.

'I said, and I was so shy, I don't know what made me do it, I said, 'No, and you'd better to stop smoking or I won't let you kiss me.' Just like that! The first thing I'd ever said to him.'

'Fantastic!'

Ma Taffos pulled a white handkerchief from her sleeve and dabbed at the tears rolling down her cheeks. Slowly the laugh subsided and her breathing came back under control.

'Just like that! Of course he didn't know what to say at first, but then he started laughing and said he'd stop.' Her eyes shone at the memory.

'And he gave up?'

'Yes, he stopped and we got married two years later.'

'Such a lovely story,' said Vanessa, pouring herself another. 'Do you know, I always seem to, I don't know … it just never works for me.'

'You want to make someone see you? People like diamonds and gold. Why? They are hard to find. Make yourself difficult to find. If he thinks he can't have you, he'll do everything he can to get you.'

Vanessa smiled to herself as an idea began to take shape.

Chapter 20

It was a few days after Natalie had suggested the idea of the Greek night, and things had moved at pace.

'Are you sure they're any good, Taffos?'

'Michaili and the Athenians, quality, boyo, quality. Tidy band they are.'

'Well they're not cheap, that's the best part of sixty quid,' said Scott dubiously.

'Money well spent, mate,' added Oliver. 'We'll get Billy to knock up some flyers, bribe all the travel reps with free drinks – it'll be packed.'

Scott was still not convinced. Over the years he'd come to realise that anything Oliver was supremely confident about had a better-than-average chance of being a complete and utter balls-up. His misgivings were, however, useless in the face of the combined mindless optimism of Taffos, Natalie, Tonia and Oliver, so with a resigned shrug he went along with it. Taffos had managed at very short notice to come up with this band and Scott for one was keen to know where he'd found them and how good they were. The fact that Taffos's answers were suspiciously evasive, when pushed on the subject of what made them such a bargain at two hundred pounds, had led Scott to assume, from past experience, that they'd probably turn out to be distant members of the Taffos clan.

Word spread about their plans and Billy, having got wind that Scott and Oliver were putting on a music night, whipped himself into a frenzy of anticipation at the thought of playing. He was going through his morning set when Oliver came to find him. Tracking him down wasn't the hardest of tasks: all Oliver had to do was look for an expanse of beach strangely bereft of sunbathers, and sure enough, there was Billy manfully playing away in the middle, to an ever-increasing circle of emptiness.

'Billy boy, got a minute for a coffee?'

Billy, being the consummate pro, merely tipped his face upwards until he'd finished the final long-drawn-out 'ahh' of 'Doing the Lambeth Walk', and said, 'Right, okay, yes. Now?'

Oliver, noting Billy's state of barely suppressed excitement as they wandered off the beach, assumed his agitation was down to his legendary morning caffeine intake. Billy had a predilection for Greek coffee, the type served in tiny cups and brewed with the thick grains forming a muddy sludge in the bottom of the cup. Despite the enormous number of cups he'd got through, he was still not great at judging when it was prudent to stop sipping. Consequently, his next question came from teeth that looked like they belonged to a Victorian chimney-sweep ne'er-do-well.

'I hear you're having a music night?'

'Teeth, Billy,' said Oliver, offering him a bottle of water. 'Yes, that's right, next Friday, you free?'

Billy rolled both eyes high and to the left to indicate he was mentally scanning his packed social diary before concluding, 'Um, don't think I've anything planned.' He'd actually been planning his playlist ever since he'd heard about the music night, and had already revised it three times. He was wondering how to react to what Oliver was about to ask him. They were friends, but after all, he had his professional pride to think of. The Blue Parrot paid him the equivalent of £25 a night for his weekly slot – should he ask for the same, or offer a reduced rate? Perhaps a percentage of the takings would be fairer. Oliver interrupted his thoughts by saying, 'Excellent. We were hoping you could design us some posters and stuff to rustle up a few punters.'

Billy nodded. 'I've got the ones I use for the Parrot. I can just change the venue and the date.'

'Good thinking. The band is called Michaili and the Athenians.'

'The band?' repeated Billy.

'Yes, Michaili and the Athenians, some bouzouki band Taffos has sorted out. Twenty thousand drachmas, they'd better be good.' Oliver, at this point, was doing something men are notoriously incapable of doing. Multitasking. While half his brain was speaking, the other half was having an internal dialogue along the lines of, *What's wrong with his mouth? Looks like an arse that someone's just shoved a lemon up. Oh God, he was expecting to play, shit shit, oh, fuck it* – which culminated in him adding breezily, 'And of course we were hoping you could play, too.'

Billy beamed.

'Thanks, I'd love to. Um, about um, money – how much were you thinking?'

'Oh, that's alright, mate. Blimey, you're a mate after all, we wouldn't expect you to pay. Very kind of you to offer, much appreciated.' Wrongly attributing the stunned look of incomprehension on Billy's face to his extraordinary generosity, Oliver added, 'Tell you what, if you want to contribute to the night, just give us the posters and a few flyers in exchange for us putting you on.'

Billy nodded dumbly.

'Excellent. Well, best be off, catch up with you later.'

Billy's disappointment didn't last long. He loved having an audience, and in truth no one paid him much attention when he played at the Blue Parrot, so this was a good opportunity for him. But there was another reason that was keeping him in fine spirits. He had a date.

The following day he was due to meet a fellow English teacher, Briony, with whom he had been paired at an English-language testing centre the previous week. Their job had been to orally test students taking their English exams, which involved showing them pictures, listening to their descriptions and grading their use of English and pronunciation. Money for old rope, you might think. You would, however, have failed to appreciate the psychological damage inflicted by listening to literally hundreds of nervous sweaty teenagers repeating exactly the same lines they have been coached to say, regardless of what picture they were shown. There is a widely recognised condition called Stockholm syndrome whereby a kidnap victim develops a psychological attachment to his or her captor, often falling in love with them. There is not to be confused with the other Stockholm syndrome, a nasty condition that describes the feeling of impotent rage you get upon finding a key component missing from the box containing your flat-pack furniture.

After hearing 'I can clearly see an olive tree in the bottom left-hand corner,' and 'In my opinion the picture is very beautiful' for the hundredth time, Briony had found Billy steadily more attractive. By the end of the day, she would have shagged him in a broom cupboard if Billy had had the wit to notice. He was equally smitten, but in Billy's world, broom cupboards were strictly for brooms, and sex was rather like the Natural History Museum: he was aware it existed and had been there a few times before but didn't make a habit of it.

They had, however, arranged to meet the following week. Briony worked in a small town on the other side of Pelion, so they'd agreed to meet halfway in between, in a village called Tsagarada. It was on a particularly steeply sloping part of the mountain and as a result was effectively divided into two, imaginatively known as the lower and upper village. Both had a picturesque main square, charming traditional houses and fantastic views, but the upper village was the more renowned of the two, famous for housing the biggest tree on the mountain. It was a whopper, dominating the café and village square and drawing a surprisingly large number of visitors who would bask in its shade and enjoy the cheerful hospitality and stunning views from the café.

None of this provided any solace to Denis, the owner of the café in the lower village. He was a charming, friendly and hospitable bloke, and the views from his café were virtually indistinguishable from those of the upper village, but sadly his café lurked in the shade of a merely big tree. Size, in this situation, was everything, and being big was not enough when you were up against the biggest. The upper village's tree ate away at Denis like a festering sore, and there were occasions, after slow weekends, when he'd count his takings and find himself unconsciously turning to the tree-surgeon section of the local paper or wistfully reading through chainsaw catalogues.

The bus from Volos arrived twice a day during the week and four times at weekends, and the Sunday afternoon service had just arrived. Denis watched moodily as the majority of the passengers emerged from the bus and trooped up the path that led to the upper village square. All except one, a scrawny-looking fellow, who even at a distance of fifty metres was unmistakably English. There is some indefinable quality of a certain type of Englishman that makes him stand out like a face tattoo on a barrister, and the man standing by the side of the bus was no exception. He waited patiently while the driver reluctantly climbed out to retrieve from the luggage compartment a large black object, which the Englishman hoisted onto his shoulder before peering around the now deserted street.

Denis watched him walk towards the square and was surprised to realise he was carrying what looked like an accordion. It was siesta time and the square was deserted, apart from Denis who was sitting outside his café smoking a small cigar and reading the paper. Billy wandered over and said in heavily accented Greek, 'Goodnight.'

Denis nodded and smiled.

There was a flurry of activity as the accordion was placed carefully on the ground and a battered phrasebook was pulled out of a jacket pocket. When it came to Greek, Billy and grammar were barely nodding acquaintances, and he was about to make a small but crucial mistake. There are times when substituting the indefinite article 'a' for the definite article 'the' causes no confusion. Say, for example, you were ordering ice cream and asked for 'the ice cream' rather than 'an ice cream' – it's a safe bet that you'll still end up with what you wanted. Sadly, in this situation, getting it right was crucial. Billy straightened and asked, 'Is this a big tree?'

Denis looked at Billy, looked at the tree and thought to himself, 'Well, it's not small,' and replied, 'Yes, it is a big tree.'

Billy looked pleased and offered to buy the café.

Denis, interpreting this correctly as a request for a cup of coffee, wandered inside to do the necessary.

Left to his own devices, Billy looked nervously at his watch for the fifteenth time in the last twenty minutes.

He'd shaved twice, bought some aftershave and was wearing his best pullover. He had even rehearsed potential topics of conversation and should they flag, he always had the accordion to fall back on. She was, he mused, sure to appreciate a few specially played tunes. He had also casually put a few flyers for the music night under the ashtray. With most of his mind taken up with planning witty and interesting conversational gambits, he failed to heed the small, nagging voice in his head that was wondering why the square was deserted and why the 'biggest tree on the mountain' didn't seem much bigger than every other tree he'd ever seen.

Two hours later, he climbed disconsolately back on the bus, unaware that Briony had been sitting in the café fifty metres away in the upper village in the shade of Tsagarada's biggest tree. Her bus departed fifteen minutes after his and she appeared in the lower square just a few minutes after he had left.

She was less than happy at having been let down. She had been stood up before and had not pegged Billy for the standing-up type, and was therefore doubly annoyed. The weather was matching her mood. Conditions could change quickly on the mountain and what had been a glorious day of blue sky was now clouding over with a rising wind, indicating a downpour was on the way.

As she got to the bench by the bus stop, a particularly strong gust sent some sheets of paper skidding across the square, one of which landed by her feet. She put her foot on it to stop the wind moving it further and had the disconcerting first impression that she was looking at a picture of Billy wearing a top hat and grinning up at her. She picked it up and confirmed that it really was Billy and that he was playing a gig in four days' time. She looked back at the café from where the flyer had come and saw the owner wrestling with his awning in the wind. A brief conversation with the owner, involving her pointing to the image on the flyer, confirmed that Billy had been there but had left, and she had only just missed him.

Chapter 21

The day of the Greek music night had arrived and preparations were in full swing.

'And why haven't you finished that sign yet?' asked Scott, collapsing onto the sand in exhaustion. He'd just walked two-hundred metres from the far end of the beach carrying two crates of beer and was not in the best of moods. In addition to being knackered from the walk, he had still to forgive Oliver for agreeing to let Billy inflict himself on the evening.

'No time. Pond's Peach Punch is not going to make itself. Anyway, I can't spell bouzouki,' said Oliver, who was hunched over a food blender suffering from what looked like a nasty case of leprosy. He'd been experimenting with a variety of ingredients, most of which were peaches, and had managed to get a large amount of them all over his face, chest and arms.

'C.R.A.P. is the popular spelling and I believe in modern Greek the word "utterly" is often used as a prefix. Why not just write "traditional Greek music" instead?'

'Won't fit on the page, and I'm having trouble with me peaches.'

Ever eagle-eyed for a bargain, Oliver had wandered into the village to get some lemons and come back with ten kilos of cheap peaches, whose sell-by date was but a distant memory. He'd set his heart on turning them into a delicious fruit cocktail, but his early attempts had been less than successful. He'd been at it since eight in the morning and had so far succeeded in turning most of the bar into a very large petri dish.

'Nearly done, just finishing off this final experiment.'

'And what exactly would that experiment be?'

'Trying to neutralise the ingredient that makes it taste like shit. Not easy.'

'Have you tried taking out the peach?'

Oliver was spared the effort of replying by the appearance of two small children at the bar.

'Two Cokes, please.'

'Alright boys, we've got a special offer on peach juice today,' said Oliver with what he thought was a winning smile.

'Two Cokes, please,' they repeated.

'Suit yourself, there you are ... thanks.' He gave them their change. 'Hmm, perhaps I should knock up some posters announcing the new world premiere, trial period, special offer, today only: Peach Coke. What do you think?'

Scott was busy stacking beers in the fridge and didn't bother turning round to say, 'No.'

'Go on, no one would know.'

'No.'

'Life deals me some harsh blows.' Oliver scratched his head, which involved moving bits of peach peel about a bit, and took a speculative sip of the evil-looking concoction. What it needed, he felt, was a little extra zing.

Taffos was about to close for the afternoon when he heard the insistent hammering on the loading bay door. He muttered to himself as he dragged the door open again, but his round chubby face broke into a big grin when he saw it was Oliver standing there.

'Hello Oliver boyo, want to do something about that eczema, nasty that is.'

'That is not nasty, Taffos, that is peach,' said Oliver with quiet dignity.

'Right you are. What can I do you for?'

'Need something strong that'll go with peach.'

'Be my guest. There's a whole load of liqueurs out the back that might do the job, or ... I know what you need! I've got just the thing. Here you go.' Taffos proffered a dubious-looking bottle.

'Jock MacTavish Old Highland Malt?'

'Lovely drop of Scotch that is.'

'Lovely?'

'Well, cheap.'

'It says "produce of Turkey" on the back,' said Oliver, handling the bottle as if it were a live grenade.

'You haven't heard of Turkish whisky?'

139

'About as often as I've heard of Scottish carpets. Can you really drink this?'

Taffos looked serious and said, 'Had it sent for testing at a health laboratory.'

'And they said it was okay?'

'No, they said "your horse has chronic diabetes".' He broke into a grin.

'Sounds ideal.'

'Try some, tidy it is.' He unscrewed the lid and poured a measure into a plastic cup.

Oliver put it to his lips with a look of deep suspicion, hesitated for a moment then knocked it back.

'Ugh, you weren't joking – wow, that's terrible. You can't sell that!'

'Not even at 1000 drachmas a bottle?'

'I'll have two.'

'Like a man who knows a bargain when he sees one. Go lovely with peach, that will.'

Scott was still in the bar, organising their stock, when Oliver reappeared and put the two bottles on the bar.

'What's this stuff supposed to be?'

'The secret ingredient that's going to turn Pond's Peach Punch into a world-beater.'

'What's this on the label? It looks like …'

'A set of bagpipes, rampant against a sporran backdrop?'

'Strangely enough, yes.'

'Top-quality Turkish whisky.'

'Oh joy. Well, you'd better get it finished and I'll make sure everything else is ready. People will be turning up in a few hours and this place looks like your punch tastes.'

Two hours later and the final preparations were nearing completion. Oliver had finally stopped experimenting and was looking, appropriately enough, as pleased as punch.

'There we are, Pond's surprise,' he announced proudly, offering a glass to Tonia.

'What's in it?' she asked, sniffing it suspiciously.

'A delicate blend of delicious ingredients, the exact recipe of which is an old Caribbean secret, handed down through the mists of time and known only to a select few of the elders of St Lucia's Island.'

'How do you know about it, then?'

'He found it written on the back of an old shampoo bottle,' said Scott. 'A fact that would have led most to assume that it was shampoo. But not Mr Pond.'

Scott was standing outside the bar with his head on one side, checking the final preparations.

'Natalie, can you give me a hand here?'

'On condition I'm excused from tasting the punch.'

'Is this straight?'

Natalie stood back to survey the sign advertising the fabulous bouzouki experience of Michaili and the Athenians.

'D'you know, I think the sign is okay. It's the shed that's not straight.'

'Bar, Natalie, please. Not shed. Bar. Well, not much we can do about that. Now all we need are some punters,' said Oliver, rubbing his hands with enthusiasm.

Scott stood back and, despite his misgivings, he had to admit it was looking good. They had strung lights all around the roof and sides of the bar and had erected a small stage to the left by borrowing four pallets from Taffos's cash'n'carry. Billy had brought his portable PA system, which provided a bit of amplification, but the music would be essentially acoustic.

In fact, the only concern Scott had was Billy himself, who was clearly lacking his usual enthusiasm. With the prospect of an audience he was normally a hyperactive bundle of energy, offering to help with anything and everything. As it was, he had spent most of the afternoon sitting on his PA, staring into space.

'You alright, Billy?'

'Um, what? Ah, yes, I'm okay.'

'You don't sound it, mate. You sure everything's alright?'

'Yes, fine thanks,' he said, sounding anything but.

'Shall we do a sound check, do you think?'

Billy nodded and started fiddling with various knobs and microphone levels before saying a couple of unenthusiastic 'one-two, one-two's and getting a thumbs-up from Natalie in the bar.

Oliver wandered down the beach to join Scott.

'It's not bad, is it?'

Oliver winked at him. 'Just need a little faith. It'll be blinding. I've got Billy down to twenty-five minutes and have vetted his song list, and Taffos reckons the band are, as he put it, tidy.'

'I'm a bit worried about Billy. Looks like his dog has just died or something.'

'Probably nerves. I'm sure he'll be fine.'

'All set, then?'

'Yep. Not seen Vanessa, though, thought she'd be here early.' Raising his voice, Oliver shouted, 'Hey, Billy boy, seen Nessie around?'

Billy looked up from the area of sand he had been studying.

'Sorry, what?'

'Seen Nessie recently?'

'Oh, um, yes, I forgot to say: she told me to tell you that she might make it later but can't promise. She has a date and they'll try to come later.'

'What do you mean, *a date?*' demanded Oliver.

'I would imagine it means she's out with a bloke, mate', Scott explained.

'But – but –' Oliver struggled to process the information. 'Right, a date, hmm.'

'Italian guy, I think she said. Or could have, um, been Spanish.'

Scott looked at Oliver closely. 'You alright, mate?'

Oliver looked back at him blankly before adding vaguely, 'Fine, yes, yes, why?'

'Just looks like someone has shit in your best hat, that's all.'

Oliver dragged his face back into a semblance of nonchalance and said, 'Thought she'd be bringing a load of her tourists along tonight, that's all.' And wandered off to fiddle with the lighting.

It wasn't long before the first of the evening's customers arrived. Oliver, Scott and Tonia were in place behind the bar to greet them Natalie's job was to wander around the crowd, taking orders.

'Evening ladies, the first glass of punch is on the house,' said Oliver.

'Ta very much.'

'Ooh, that's nice that is,' said one of the girls, knocking back her glass. 'I'll have another one of them.'

Scott turned away to avoid the smug grin he knew would be coming his way and focused on four guys ambling up the beach. One of them, a tall, wasted-looking guy with sideburns, sidled up to the bar.

''Ow do,' he said in a strong northern accent. 'Where's the boss?'

'You're looking at him.'

''Ow do,' said the other three in unison.

'Can I get you a glass of punch? "Traditional Greek Surprise".'

'I could butcher a beer, me, but we'd best set up first. I'm Mike and this 'ere is the Mancunians – I mean the Athenians.'

Scott swallowed and silently mouthed 'Michaeli and the Athenians'. Shaking his head, he whimpered, 'You're not Greek, then?'

The main man wrinkled his brow.

'Barry's stepdad was Turkish, weren't he, Baz?'

'Aye.'

'What sort of music is it?' asked Scott, doing well to keep his voice under some semblance of control.

'Covers and the like, you know. Beatles, Oasis an' that.'

'Taffos, you useless fucking bastard,' said Scott to no one in particular.

Oliver put his arm around Scott's shoulder and said, 'It's alright mate, leave it to me.' And, taking Mike by the arm, he led him and the 'Athenians' away towards the temporary stage.

Scott watched their retreating backs and wondered why he'd ever agreed to it. Fortunately, he didn't have long to think, as a steady stream of customers kept him, Tonia and Natalie busy. The punch was proving a surprising winner, and had almost run out by the time Oliver returned.

'About time, I've been rushed off my feet. Can you knock up a bit more punch?'

'Sure. I've sorted out the band. Think they'll go down well,' said Oliver with a mischievous grin. 'Billy's just about to start up.'

As Billy took the stage, a ragged and unconvincing cheer went up from what was now a packed beach. He didn't look like the most inspiring of acts. His shoulders were slumped and he stood fiddling with his microphone before saying 'Good evening all' with the enthusiasm of an auditor. He looked out over the audience and his eyes snapped back to a vision in tie-dyed blouse and skirt, who was standing five back in the centre. Briony smiled at him and gave him the thumbs-up.

The effect on Billy was electric. His body straightened, his shoulders went back and the nervous, fidgety bloke on stage was transformed into something between Tim Buckley and Mick Jagger – a Tigger, if you will. He started singing like he had had never sung before. He belted them out and had the audience in his palm. Thirty-five minutes of singing along and dancing later, he was being cheered off after his second encore.

Watching from the bar, Scott was impressed by Billy's efforts, but couldn't help being struck by the fragile relationship between artistic appreciation and alcohol. He shook his head in baffled incomprehension and mused aloud, 'There really is no accounting for taste, is there?'

'The amount this lot are drinking, he could play Doris Day covers and go down a storm.'

'They're not going to be so happy when they discover we've stitched them up over the bouzouki band, though.'

Smiling, Oliver said, 'You might be surprised.' Then he disappeared behind the shed, re-emerging with five litres of punch from the back fridge to deal with the interval rush.

Tonia, wrestling with a bottle of wine, shouted above the CD on the sound system, 'This corkscrew's bent.'

'Of course it's bent. It's a corkscrew. If it wasn't bent, it would be a nail.'

Scott raised his eyebrows and in spite of himself, found himself chuckling.

Which was more than could be said for Vanessa. Not only was her date, Antonio, proving to be a sleazy nightmare, she also really wanted to be at the bar watching Billy and the bouzouki band. However, she had no doubt that the plan Ma Taffos had hatched would eventually bear fruit and she was in a 'no pain, no gain' situation.

She had agreed to go out with Antonio solely because he was due to fly back to Rome the following day. She hadn't, however, reckoned on it being quite as painful as unanaesthetised childbirth. They were sitting in a romantically lit taverna, suffering from an acute failure to understand each other. He was assuming that with under twelve hours to go in Greece, it was about time he got into her pants; she was trying to persuade him that he really wanted to spend a proportion of that twelve hours listening to traditional Greek music on a beach with hundreds of other tourists. Not so much a breakdown in communication as a multi-vehicle pile-up.

It took a while, but eventually Antonio realised that the only possible way of achieving his evening's ambitions lay in going along with Vanessa's. They arrived just as Oliver took to the stage. The music gradually faded out and the crowd turned expectantly towards him. Grabbing the stage mic, he announced: 'Ladies and gentlemen, welcome to the Waterfront Bar bouzouki sessions!' He let the surprisingly loud cheer drown out before continuing. 'And now, the moment we've all been waiting for. All the way from Athens – put your hands together and give a warm welcome to the fabulous Michaili and the Athenians!'

Mike stepped forward, adjusted his guitar and began:

'One, two, a-one two three four. Hey Judos, dontos make it bados, take a sados songos and make it bederos ...'

You'd have to say that only a pissed-up crowd of predominantly British sun-stroke sufferers overdosing on alcoholic peach would fall for this, which was handy.

Oliver was standing by the bar, revelling in the success of the evening, when he found himself eye to eye with an annoyingly handsome man. Attached to the handsome one was Vanessa, who said a breezy, 'Hi Oliver, great show – this is Antonio.'

Oliver smiled unconvincingly and held out his hand.

'Antonio, pleased to meet you.'

'Very nice night,' replied Antonio.

I bloody hope it isn't for you, Oliver thought to himself as they shook hands.

Vanessa leant up and kissed Antonio on the cheek, taking his hand in hers before saying, 'Yes, we've had a lovely time. We had a really romantic meal in the taverna and then came along to see how it was going.'

'Nice,' said Oliver. 'Well, great to see you and thanks for coming. I'd better get on and serve a few drinks I guess.'

Vanessa watched him go, and smiled to herself.

Chapter 22

The dust had settled since the Greek evening. They'd said their goodbyes to Tonia and Natalie, who had flown home amidst lots of hugs, kisses and promises to keep in touch. Summer, at least in terms of tourism, was drawing to a close. The next few days saw fewer people on the beach and business was tailing off. Scott returned from the lunchtime bakery trip to find Oliver hunched over, writing in a card of some sort.

'What are you doing there?' he asked.

After a pause which, had it been pregnant, would have matched the gestation period of an elephant, he added, 'Urgent, requires answer.'

'Eh?' replied Oliver.

'I asked what you were doing,' said Scott.

Oliver waved an envelope at him. 'Me parents' anniversary, thirty years, sending them a card.'

'Thirty years? My word. What do they talk about? I've known you since we were eleven, spent all day every day with you for the last eight weeks, and I pretty much know everything there is to know about you. Not saying you're boring, mate, but you really have nothing left to give.'

'Might have hidden depths.'

'You haven't, though, have you. Some might describe you as deeply shallow.'

'Nice,' said Oliver. 'Mind you I reckon there is stuff about me you don't know.'

'Come on then,' said Scott. He proceeded to rummage in his bag and pulled out a pen and notebook that he handed to Oliver. 'I bet I can guess your favourite curries to start with.'

'Top five?'

'Yes.'

'Starters and sundries included?'

'Go on then.'

'You're on,' said Oliver, taking the notepad, 'I'll write 'em down. If you guess right, I buy the pizza tonight.'

He sucked on the end of the pen for a few minutes before writing down:

Jal Frezi
Methi Chicken
Peshwari Nan
Cobra
Hot towel

He neatly folded the paper and wrote 'My favourite curries' on the other side.

The hot towel was a bit leftfield and would never ordinarily have made the top five, whereas Sag Aloo certainly would have done, but there was a pizza up for grabs and he thought it would catch Scott out.

Scott also found an envelope in his bag, into which he placed Oliver's folded list and solemnly declared it to be the 'envelope of truth'.

The game filled up an otherwise dull couple of hours. Scott guessed the first three pretty quickly. It took him a while to get the beer, and the fifth left him completely flummoxed.

'Those little mints you get at the end?'

'Nope.'

'Doing a runner?'

'Nope again,' replied Oliver.

'Well, while I'm thinking, I'll write down mine and I bet you won't get them.'

They discovered that this was something they could extend over a range of topics and had a stab at favourite girlfriends, drinks, TV shows, things they missed about England and various others. Over the next couple of days, periods of quiet were broken by one or other of them randomly saying 'Bombay Sapphire' and receiving either a nod or a shake of the head.

Scott was also aware that it kept Oliver from brooding, which he had done quite a lot of since the recent departure of Natalie and Tonia. His normal cheerfulness had deserted him and Scott assumed he was pining for Natalie. As they sat down in 'the common' outside their tents one evening, he was looking particularly glum.

'Life's rich tapestry, mate!' said Scott, trying to add some cheer into the gloom. Oliver scowled at this while disconsolately whittling a stick.

'Still, plenty more fish and all that,' Scott offered breezily, before realising from Oliver's expression that he'd failed to hit quite the right note.

'What I mean is, we've got a bit of cash and sitting round here won't do us any good, so I vote we get our arses into gear and crack into the next task.'

This sounded like a great idea to Oliver, but for an entirely different reason to the one Scott had assumed. Since the Greek night he had not been able to stop thinking about Vanessa. He had been shocked at his reaction to seeing her with Antonio, and as they hadn't seen her since, he kept imagining her shacked up in her apartment, screaming Antonio's name in ecstasy every couple of hours. He needed something to take his mind off things.

So it was agreed that they would close down for a few days and attempt their next Herculean enterprise. They decided to have a go at the eighth.

The labours of Hercules

1 Killed the Nemean lion
2 Killed a Hydra, a nine-headed snake
3 Captured a golden-horned reindeer
4 ~~Brought back a bull from Crete~~
5 Captured the Erymanthian Boar
6 ~~Cleaned the Augean stables in a single day~~
7 Chased away flesh-eating Stymphalian birds
8 Captured the horses of King Diomedes
9 ~~Got the belt of Hippolyta, Queen of the Amazons~~
10 Captured the cattle of Geryon, the three-headed, six-armed giant
11 ~~Brought back the three golden apples from the Garden of Hesperides~~

12 Went into Hades and brought back the three-headed hound of hell

The action had taken place in a place called Abdera which was close to the city of Xanthi. Oliver suggested that they should do a bit of what he called 'real camping' while they were there. This would involve finding a deserted beach or suchlike and spending a couple of days in what he called 'survival mode'.

Since the success of the Crete expedition, Scott felt he had overcome a number of internal barriers, and although he was apprehensive about the trip it was nothing to the all-encompassing fear he would have felt before. That said, he was still sufficiently nervous about getting to their destination and back without the added thought of being stuck on a deserted beach, miles from civilisation. He consoled himself with the thought that he would almost certainly be able to find a local taverna or something while Oliver tried to skin some roadkill.

In many ways, Oliver was something of a contradiction. His love of the great outdoors and the idea of surviving in the wild was matched only by his desire to sit on his arse in a nice comfy chair, staring into space with a big fat joint in his hand.

The Greek attitude to drug use had seen that particular avenue closed off as the penalties that ensued were draconian – an appropriate word as it came from a Greek, more specifically the first official legislator of the Greek state in the seventh century BC. Draco was a bit of a stickler and his penalties for any misdemeanour pretty much all resulted in death or slavery. Owe someone some money and miss a payment – slavery. Steal a cabbage – death. Oddly, this seemed to make him quite popular, presumably with whoever was left alive and wasn't a slave.

His own death was somewhat unusual and managed to combine the theatrical elements of comedy and tragedy in one impressive performance. He was on stage speaking in front of an audience who were so pleased to see him that they showed their appreciation in the traditional Greek way: by showering his head with hats, shirts and cloaks, which had the unfortunate side effect of suffocating him. Presumably they were all immediately put to death afterwards, although that's not mentioned in the history books.

The spirit of Draco was alive and well in the modern Greek view of drug use, and the combination of not knowing the local ne'er-do-wells and Oliver's aversion to sharing a six-man cell with a load of hairy-arsed Greek crims had forced him to forego his previous habit. It did mean he was a bit more productive and got out and about a lot more, and he was very much looking forward to spending a few days hunting stuff and building shelters.

In the eighth labour, Hercules had been sent to capture four horses owned by a particularly nasty king named Diomedes. The king's favourite trick was to kill his rivals, or anyone that looked at him in a funny way for that matter, and feed them to his horses. The horses, having gained a taste for humans, would attack and munch their way through anyone they could get their teeth into, and hence were a fierce proposition for Hercules.

Chapter 23

A train to Thessaloniki and the vision of Abi got Scott safely over the first leg, and then an hour hanging around at the station for the train to Xanthi, in the north-east of the country, saw them with plenty of time to while away with their new hobby. On the first leg of the journey, they covered favourite sitcoms, least-liked nationalities, favourite nationalities and least-desired diseases. The last one saw a group of Americans switching seats after uneasily listening to a conversation that consisted of:

'Pleurisy?'

'Nope.'

'Smallpox?'

'Nope.'

'Malaria?'

'Yes.'

Which had the benefit of letting them spread out a bit. They had taken Scott's tent to save cash on accommodation and satisfy Oliver's insistence on trying a bit of wild camping. He had been reading up on survival techniques in his book and had intimated that he might even be prepared to open his tin, should the situation require it. They planned to stay for a few days and beyond that had no real idea of what to do. 'Camp on a beach, steal a horse, go home' was the somewhat loose plan they had concocted on route.

Their journey took them past the city of Drama, famous throughout the world as the birthplace of precocious middle-class children. Scott had borrowed Vanessa's book on mythology and, on the approach to the city of Xanthi, was filling Oliver in on the details of the story.

'So, after capturing the Cretan Bull, Hercules was sent to get the man-eating mares of Diomedes, which were owned by the king of a Thracian tribe called the Bistones, and bring them back. Apparently, Hercules sailed with a band of volunteers across the Aegean to Bistonia.'

'I reckon if Hercules asked you to volunteer, you probably did,' added Oliver. 'Wouldn't want to get on the wrong side.'

'Not surprisingly, he and his mates overpowered the grooms who were tending the horses, and took them towards the sea.'

'We haven't got to take this horse back on a ferry, have we?'

'Let's worry about that later. On the way they were attacked by the Bistones, who had realised what had happened, and tried to recapture the animals. To free himself to fight, Hercules entrusted the mares to a youth named Abderos. Unfortunately, the mares killed him.'

'And ate him?'

'Doesn't say. Let's assume so. Meanwhile, Hercules fought the Bistones, killed Diomedes and, in honour of Abderos, he founded the city of Abdera which is now an archaeological site twenty kilometres from Xanthi.'

'Nice. So what's Xanthi like, then?'

An hour later, Oliver was finding out for himself during a ten-minute taxi ride from the station to the central square.

The town was an interesting mix of Greek and Turkish influences and quite different from other places they had been to. For a start, all the *kafenios* or cafés hosted a large number of old men playing chess, rather the ubiquitous backgammon they were used to. They found one called Diomedes, which seemed like a good omen, and sat at a table overlooking the central square. All the other tables were accommodating old guys with worry beads hunched over chessboards or smoking and talking in loud voices. Their attempts to gain directions to a tourist information office were met with shrugs that expressed something between incomprehension and indifference from the clientele. When the café owner came over with their coffees, he looked pointedly at them both and said 'English?' as he put down the drinks.

They nodded and looked at each other ominously as he immediately disappeared, only to pop back carrying a tray holding three brandies.

'Fin n handy!' he said as he placed them down on the table, smiling broadly.

Assuming it was some local variation of 'cheers', they both repeated, 'Fin n handy!' and raised their glasses.

He nodded at their bags and said, 'Long time on Flog n Towd?'

They both nodded carefully, which seemed to please him, as he pulled up a seat and sat down. He then proceeded to tell them in fast, fluent but terrible English that he had worked as a chef in London for ten years. Most of what he said was incomprehensible until Oliver picked up on the fact he was peppering his language with cockney rhyming slang.

Oliver swirled his glass and said, 'Fine and dandy – brandy!' To which Kostas, as he had introduced himself, grinned and repeated, 'Fin n handy.' They subsequently learned that Kostas enjoyed the currant bun and didn't miss the hell for leather but would murder for a decent Ruby Murray.

Pulling out his map, Oliver pointed to a deserted stretch of coastline just beyond a small village about twenty miles away, which he thought would be good for a bit of off-grid camping.

'Kostas, how can we get here?' he asked.

Kostas turned to consult with one of his customers and there ensued that typical conversation between two Greek men of a certain age. It was the one in which they are politely asking each other if they would like another sugar in their tea but which sounds like they were about to come to blows over a festering fifty-year-old family scandal. After five minutes of raised voices, angry exclamations and twirling arms, Kostas returned and told them that there was one bus a day on the frog and toad to the place they were heading for, and it left in an hour.

If they were going to be camping out on a deserted beach for a couple of nights, they would need some provisions. To save lugging their bags around, they took turns to shop, with one staying behind at the café to look after their things while the other went to get the necessary stuff.

Before long they were bumping along an increasingly pot-holed road adjacent to a beautiful coastline. There was lots to see – or in Oliver's case, peer at short-sightedly – and in just over an hour they arrived at their destination. He and Scott had a fundamental difference of opinion in what they were looking for when it came to outdoor adventure. Scott was after a cosy taverna that closed late and opened nice and early for breakfast, while Oliver was after deserted spaces with no one but the occasional crazed hermit or ancient fisherman knocking around. For this trip, Scott had been sold on the idea by Oliver pointing out that it would be in the spirit of Hercules to rough it a bit for a couple of nights, and he had set off fired up with images of Herculean feats to be completed.

They arrived in the small village, made their way down to the seashore and started walking. They had walked about a mile when Oliver found a place on the beach he decided was suitable.

'This looks good. Bit of shelter there from the sand dune, some trees for wood, ideal.'

'Thank fuck for that. This bag weighs a ton,' said Scott, throwing off his backpack and dropping onto the sand. He lay on his back looking up at the perfect blue sky.

'If I were Hercules, I reckon I would probably be having a beer right now. Can we start drinking yet?'

'Got to get the camp set up first,' said Oliver. 'Shelter and fuel for the fire. I'll put the tent up, you go and get some wood.'

Scott wandered off and started to collect driftwood from the beach. There was a lot of it and pretty soon he had made an impressive pile. Oliver, meanwhile, had put the tent up and was unpacking his kit bag.

'Seems a shame to burn all this when we could be making artful driftwood mirrors out of the stuff,' said Scott, nodding to his pile of wood. 'Which we could then sell and live in a nice comfortable house with running water and heating. Rather than burning it and living in a tent,' he added, just in case Oliver had somehow missed his point. Which he had, because he wasn't listening.

'Need to focus on the essentials in a survival situation. Survive and thrive, that's the key. I'll get the fire going.'

'I'm looking forward to the thriving. I could murder some chips.' Scott watched as Oliver produced a knife and started whittling a stick to create a pile of small shavings. When he had a decent-sized pile, he pulled out some cotton wool and a magnifying glass.

'If you've forgotten your glasses, the wood is over there,' Scott said helpfully.

Ignoring him, Oliver bent down with the magnifying glass just over the kindling. He had it smoking within a minute and blew into it until a flame appeared, which he then fed with small twigs. In spite of himself, Scott was impressed.

'Nice. I thought we'd be rubbing sticks together for hours before giving up and getting the Zippo out.'

As the fire got established, they made a ring of large stones and sat companionably around it, poking it with sticks. Scott picked up Oliver's survival book and flicked through it.

'It says here the key to survival is to learn from how the local people live and copy them. Sounds like a piece of piss, this. We just need to sit outside a taverna playing backgammon all day.'

'That's your local tribes. You copy their hunting techniques and stuff.'

'Well, I could happily hunt myself a beer right now.'

Oliver looked around and was pleased with what he saw. The tent they would be sharing was all set up. Outside it was a tarpaulin where he'd placed his tools. He had a set of cooking pots that fitted together like Russian dolls, a couple of plates, fold-up cutlery and some utensils for stirring and stabbing whatever they cooked.

'Fire, shelter, cooking stuff – reckon we deserve one,' he said.

They had split the job of buying provisions so that one had bought a bag containing beer, water and snacks and the other bought one containing bread, tins and meat to cook on the fire.

They both went to their respective bags and pulled out two beers.

There was a pause. They looked at each other as the implication sunk in.

'You bought beers?' said Scott.

'That's what we agreed,' said Oliver.

'No, we agreed I would buy the beers and you'd bring the food.'

'Not how I remember it.'

'Well, what did you buy then?'

They had sixteen bottles of lager, two packets of cheesy wotsits, two packets of spicy crisps, a half-eaten bar of chocolate and two large packs of gummy bears.

'Probably got the calories to get us through a couple of days,' said Oliver.

'We've got enough e-numbers to fuel a primary school day trip. We should build ourselves a soft-play area or have a game of hide and seek,' said Scott. 'I don't even like cheesy fucking wotsits. We'll have to go back to the village – they're bound to have a shop or something.'

They got back to their feet and walked back the way they had come a mile along the beach. It was easier going without their bags, but walking on sand sapped their energy and they were both pleased to reach the narrow road into the village. They were less pleased to find it was completely deserted. The only shop and the only taverna were both shut and looked ominously unlike they were planning to open any time soon.

'Where is everybody? It's like a ghost town.'

'Siesta time,' said Oliver. 'Probably all having a kip. We'll just have to come back later.'

As there was really no other option, they headed back to their camp along the beach for a third time. After a couple of beers and half a pack of gummy bears, they figured siesta time would be over and wandered back to the village. There was no change. It was like everyone had left for the day, which in fact they had. Right that minute the shop owner's daughter was saying the Greek equivalent of 'I do' to the son of an accountant from Athens, and the whole village had gone off to see it happen. The wedding was taking place in a church in the upper village, about five miles up the mountain, and the reception party was happening in the restaurant near the church.

Oliver and Scott, of course, had no way of knowing this, and they just assumed that they were a bit early and the shop or taverna would open later. So back they went to the camp. Three beers, the other half of the gummy bears and two packets of crisps later, they wove their way rather unsteadily back to the village, found everything still locked up and deserted, and trudged back to the camp.

'So, we're twenty miles from the nearest town, the next bus is in fifteen hours, and we've got one pack of gummy bears, two packets of cheesy wotsits, some water and six bottles of beer. At least we've got some sunglasses.'

'Not ideal,' agreed Oliver.

'Come on then, you're the survival expert – what are we going to do? More to the point, what would Hercules have done?'

Oliver scratched his head and looked around.

'Could set up a wild boar spear trap, but don't have high hopes. We could try some fishing.'

'Right you are, let's give it a go,' said Scott.

An hour later, as the sun dipped behind the mountain, the lengthening shadows fell on what would have been an idyllic beach scene were it not for two trouserless men standing up to their pants in the water, morosely holding fishing lines and peering down.

'This is pointless and it's getting dark now,' said Scott. 'I won't even see if I get a bite.'

Oliver agreed and they waded back to the shore, where they sat drying themselves in front of the fire. Oliver was still quite upbeat, partly because he just loved being outdoors and partly because he knew Scott didn't like cheesy wotsits. Scott was less happy but not particularly surprised. From countless experiences over the years he had learned that anything organised by Oliver Pond was likely to end in disaster, farce or some form of incarceration, so this situation was about par for the course.

'This is rubbish. I could be sitting in a nice taverna right now, tucking into a nice moussaka, bottle of red wine in front of me, plate of chips to the side, before heading off to a club.'

'Ah, but you get to see the stars, sit by a fire, smell the fresh air. You need a bit of this in your life every now and then,' said Oliver, tossing another lump of driftwood onto the fire.

Scott consoled himself by opening a beer and taking a handful of gummy bears.

'Could be worse, I suppose,' he said.

That was when it started to rain. Scott lay in the tent, staring at the roof, listening to the drumming of the rain and the rhythmic crunching of Oliver popping cheesy wotsits into his face, and wondered if Hercules hadn't had it easy.

'Not exactly thriving are we?'

'I dunno. These cheesy wotsits are great and I've got another beer. Could be worse.'

Eventually Scott must have fallen asleep as he woke up in the morning with a terrible dehydrated hangover next to a contentedly snoring Oliver. It was still raining and the fire was out. They packed up their wet stuff and walked back to the village, which, to their no great surprise, was still empty, it being full of similarly hungover people all busily sleeping off the excesses of the previous day. They were both now soaking but at least their bags, minus the beers and water, were a bit lighter. They found the bus stop and settled down on the little bench to wait the two hours before it arrived.

They got off at a stop just outside Xanthi that was next to an official campsite, with showers and shops and a taverna down the road. It was in the same type of dusty olive grove as theirs and had a toilet block and a little shop that sold essential food supplies for prices that would make a rich man blink at on the Champs-Élysées. They bought a few bags of long-life croissants, which they inhaled while putting the tent up and hanging their wet stuff out to dry. That done, they took the short walk along the road to the nearest taverna, which was just opening for lunch.

The food was incredible, and after silently working their way through the first two dishes of starters, they began to sit back and pay some attention to their whereabouts. On the bar there was a stack of brochures advertising days out and holiday services in multiple languages. Scott grabbed a handful and returned to their table.

'Now we're back in civilisation, let's see what there is to do round here,' he said, handing half the pile to Oliver. For a moment there was silence as they flicked through the leaflets. Scott finally waved one over the plate of dolmades. 'If we're going to make a holiday of it, how do you fancy the "caves and mountain village trip"?' he asked.

'Not much, might involve walking.'

'What's wrong with walking? You love the great outdoors, surviving on nature's bounty and all that.'

'Other walkers, or "hikers". Can't stand 'em. They wear those trousers that unzip at the knee and talk about Wales a lot.'

'Fair enough.'

'I'd prefer the "dolphins and hidden island trip", me.'

'Don't like dolphins,' replied Scott.

'What do you mean? Everyone likes dolphins!'

'Not me,' said Scott. 'I think they get too much of a good deal. You get all that "dolphin-friendly tuna" stuff on tins but no one gives a toss about the tuna, do they? Just because tuna can't balance a beach ball on their noses or make stupid squeaking noises, they can happily be netted in their millions and eaten on toast.'

'Ah, but they're a lot smarter than tuna. Very intelligent animal, your dolphin,' said Oliver.

'Allegedly,' said Scott. 'People are always claiming they're really smart, but put it this way: I first played Monopoly when I was five. Not seen a dolphin do that, despite all the training they get.'

'Be hard for them to roll the dice,' offered Oliver.

'Tell you what, though, if they could play Monopoly they'd insist on being the bank and make sure they slipped themselves the odd £500. Sneaky bastards the lot of them.'

'Right, that's a no to dolphins. What else?'

Scott flipped through a few other brochures, dismissing them, until he came to one he held up in the air with a flourish.

'This is what we do tomorrow,' he said, opening the brochure on the table. It had pictures of lots of horses and smiling happy people in horse-riders' hats, and said on the front: 'Spend a day hose riding at the Xanthi Hose Rider School!'

'Hose riding? That some kind of specialist publication? Birds with fireman?'

'Almost certainly,' replied Scott, 'This, however, is a badly spelled horse riding school brochure and therefore somewhere we can get a horse.'

'And then?'

Oliver's question was still in the air the following morning when they found themselves at the horse riding school, signing up for a day of lessons and trotting around in fields. They were shown to their respective mounts, both quite small by horse standards but bloody huge to Scott, who was still partly traumatised by his experience with Mildred. He was not too good with animals in general and really didn't fancy getting on a horse.

Oliver walked confidently up to the slightly larger of the two horses, rubbed its nose, scratched behind its ear and was greeted with a whinny of welcome. Scott watched carefully and adopted what he thought was a confident swagger as he approached his horse. He reached out his hand to the horse's nose and it bit him. Animals are said to be able to smell fear, and Scott's previous experience with Mildred had removed any vague feelings of confidence he might have been able to muster. As far as his horse was concerned, he might have been a man-sized lump of overripe scared Gorgonzola, and the last thing he wanted on his back.

Meanwhile, Oliver had pulled an apple and a sachet of sugar from his pocket, and he and his horse were well on the way to being best buddies. After the instructor had found a plaster for Scott's bleeding finger and assured him that this was very unusual, usually such a good-natured animal, never any trouble … they were ready to mount up. An assistant brought some little wooden steps, which Oliver didn't need; he put his foot in the stirrup and swung himself up. Scott climbed the steps and put his leg over just as his horse shuffled sideways towards him, causing him to slide gracefully straight off the other side. Eventually they got him in place, balanced precariously, clinging onto the reins as his horse took every available opportunity to turn its head and attempt to nip at his legs.

After two hours of being led around the fields, Scott had been thrown off three times and had decided that he never wanted to see a horse again in his life.

Once they'd handed in their gear, they stood together at the stables, Scott rubbing his back and grimacing.

'Fuck that – no way am I having anything to do with one of those animals. We'll chalk this one off as a miss. I'd sooner go camping with you again than try to head off with one of those fuckers.'

'Granted, yours was a bit lively, but they're lovely animals once you get to know them. That said, I don't fancy nicking one.'

That decided, they agreed to head back to Xanthi. After a few hours of sight-seeing they found themselves back in the main square at Kosta's café.

For many weeks all they had really walked on was sand and their feet, unused to hard, unyielding paving stones, ached like bastards. Actually Scott couldn't really tell whether his feet hurt or not, since his whole body was a dull, throbbing ache following the morning's activities.

Kostas delivered them two cold glasses and bottles of 'bigs ears', which they sipped as they looked across the square.

'Fancy a game?' asked Oliver. 'Urgent requires answer,' he added two minutes into the subsequent silence.

'Game of what?' said Scott, who had been miles away dreaming of investing in a knackers' yard and glue factory, not that they probably made glue out of horses these days.

'Chess,' replied Oliver, nodding towards the other tables full of old men thoughtfully moving their pieces around the board.

'Go on then.'

Oliver took a set from the pile that was sitting on a table just inside the café and brought it back to their table.

He hadn't played for years and he vaguely recalled that Scott might have been in the chess club at school, so he was not feeling overly confident. It turned out he was right. From the start Scott moved his pieces in a brisk confident manner, as if he had a plan, and Oliver found himself hemmed in with no obvious moves. Scott had pinned two of his pieces and he was dithering as to which of the bad moves on offer was the least bad. After he had prevaricated for five minutes, Scott said, 'Look, mate, you're going to lose a bishop or a knight. Which one's it going to be?'

Oliver frowned and moved the knight away to safety. 'Go on then, you can have me bishop. I'm keeping me horses, they're useful.'

This statement was met with a long pause before they both looked slowly up from the board and grinned at each other.

Twenty minutes later, Scott had forced checkmate and during the process had, with no little ceremony, taken the black knights, which were now nestling in his pocket. They paid the bill, leaving a tip that they estimated was large enough to buy a replacement chess set for the one now missing two pieces, and headed back to the campsite to pack up and leave.

Chapter 24

'So, the conquering heroes return!' Vanessa stood up and hugged Scott and Oliver in turn before they all settled down at the restaurant table. In her hug with Oliver, neither of them fully committed, and they ended up in a sort of half-arsed clinch which made them both blush.

'How's it going, Nessie?' said Scott. 'Still seeing that Italian stallion of yours?'

'Oh, he's long gone. We might keep in touch, but I doubt it. You know how these things are.' She was quick to note the smile of relief that flashed across Oliver's face as she spoke.

They were meeting back in Volos, the boys having got off the train that morning. Scott was seizing the chance to stay in his flat and enjoy a night in a comfortable bed. Oliver, though, was keen to get back to the campsite, and planned to catch the bus later.

They told her all about their trip and Scott proudly produced his two chess pieces, which were quite literally the horses of Diomedes.

Vanessa particularly liked Scott's description of the camping experience.

'Don't suppose he got his tin out?' she asked.

'Nope, not a chance. Mind you, the only way it would have been any use was if it had doubled up as a Christmas hamper. Never want to see another gummy bear for as long as I live.'

Oliver grinned and took another slice of pizza.

Vanessa looked at the list that he'd put on the table.

The labours of Hercules

1 Killed the Nemean lion
2 Killed a Hydra, a nine-headed snake
3 Captured a golden-horned reindeer
4 ~~Brought back a bull from Crete~~
5 Captured the Erymanthian Boar
6 ~~Cleaned the Augean stables in a single day~~

7 Chased away flesh-eating Stymphalian birds

8 ~~Captured the horses of King Diomedes~~

9 ~~Got the belt of Hippolyta, Queen of the Amazons~~

10 Captured the cattle of Geryon, the three-headed, six-armed giant

11 ~~Brought back the three golden apples from the Garden of Hesperides~~

12 Went into Hades and brought back the three-headed hound of hell

'So, five down already. What next then, chaps?'

Oliver put down his slice of pizza and said, 'I reckon we find a really tall bloke with some cows and have a bash at number ten.'

'Capturing the cattle of Geryon, the giant,' said Vanessa.

Scott couldn't help himself.

'Yes, we could rustle up that one ... I say rustle up ...'

Vanessa sighed and looked pained. 'I do so hate to be the voice of doom, but Geryon also had three heads and six arms, and a two-headed dog,' she added.

'Two-faced bitch,' said Scott.

'I'm sorry?'

'The dog, Vanessa.'

'Moving on. To get there, Hercules crossed the Libyan desert and got so angry in the heat he shot an arrow at the sun. Helios, the sun god, was impressed with his bravery and gave him a golden cup that somehow enabled him to sail across the sea to his destination.'

'A golden cup?' repeated Oliver.

There was a pause as they all considered this.

'Are either of you seeing that teacup that small kids sit in at the fair, on the little roundabout with the racing car and the jet?' he asked.

'Yes ... The story isn't particularly forthcoming about how he got there in a cup, but he seems to have managed it,' continued Vanessa. 'On arrival, he clubs the dog to death, shoots Geryon in the head with an arrow dipped in the blood of a Lernaean Hydra, and makes off with the cattle.'

'Put me down for making the bow and arrow. Always fancied having a go at that,' said Oliver.

'So, what we're looking for is a farmer, with terrible acne, who owns a lot of guns and a bipolar dog,' said Scott.

'Guns?' queried Vanessa.

'Six arms – arms – armaments.'

'It's a bit tenuous, even for you boys, isn't it?'

'Can't say I'm altogether enthused by the prospect of stealing anything from a heavily armed peasant, now you come to mention it,' Oliver added.

'Or clubbing a dog to death. Perhaps we'll pass on that,' said Scott as he got up from the table and headed for the loo.

Oliver and Vanessa, left alone for the first time since the evening of the Greek night at the bar, both toyed with their wineglasses before simultaneously looking up and saying:

'So, what are you …'

'Have you decided …'

They both laughed nervously and Oliver said, 'Go ahead'.

'I was going to ask what you're planning to do about your flat. Have you found a new place?'

'Not as such, no. Alkis, the boss, has a place I can use for a while but it's not the best. Haven't had much chance to look around yet. You?'

Vanessa looked down at the table. 'I'm going back to England. I haven't seen my family for yonks and my sister's getting married in a month's time.'

'Oh,' said Oliver. 'Going for long?'

'Well, my pay stops next week and I really can't face bar work, so it'll probably be until next summer. Depends how things go back there.'

'When are you going?'

'I'm actually leaving tomorrow; I get the bus for Athens at seven in the morning.'

Oliver's face did one thing while his voice did another. He looked like a man who had just run over his own puppy, but he managed to say breezily, 'Lovely, be great to see your friends and that I guess.'

'Yes, but I will miss …'

Quite what Vanessa was going to miss was smothered by Scott landing on the table. He hadn't spotted her handbag next to his chair, got his foot caught in the handle and staggered into the table, knocking glasses, an ashtray and a plate onto the floor.

Taffos and the waiter, Dimitris, were immediately on the scene, mopping things up and rearranging the table. Vanessa's wine had dropped into her lap and Dimitris hovered hopefully with a cloth.

'Don't even think about it,' said Vanessa as she took the cloth from him and dabbed at her skirt.

'Damn. Sorry about that, didn't see your bag there,' said Scott when the table had been reset and they were sitting again.

'Don't worry,' said Vanessa. 'Although I think I'd better be going. I need to soak this skirt and I still haven't packed.'

'Going somewhere?' asked Scott.

Vanessa explained that she was heading back to England for a while, probably until the new year.

'Well, that's a shame, we'll miss you,' said Scott. 'If we capture the cattle while you're away, I'll let you know.'

Vanessa smiled and stood up.

'Right then – best of luck – see you both soon,' she said, hugging them in turn, and lingering a bit longer than was strictly necessary in her clinch with Oliver. Then she was gone.

Oliver sat down and drained his glass of beer before motioning to Dimitris for another. Scott looked at him quizzically.

'Are you alright, mate?'

'Think I fancy Vanessa.'

'Ah.'

'A lot.'

'Clearly I'm no expert in the relationship stakes, but shouldn't you be telling her this rather than me?'

'Was going to, been working myself up to it, hadn't reckoned on her leaving.'

'Write her a note. Tell her how you feel, and then when she comes back you'll be able to, well, you know.'

'Not a bad idea, mate. Give me your notebook.'

Scott handed him some paper and got Taffos to dig out an envelope. Oliver stared into space for a while, looking pained.

'Keep it simple if I were you, mate,' said Scott.

Oliver nodded and swiftly wrote:

Dear Vanessa

I wanted to speak to you before you left but missed my chance. I will miss you and hope we can see more of each other when you return.

I will miss you.

Love

Oliver xx

He folded it and put it in the envelope.

Since Scott was going back to his flat below Vanessa's place, he offered to post it through her door so she would find it in the morning before leaving. They finished their drinks, paid the bill and went their separate ways.

The next morning, Vanessa got up at 6am and walked around her small apartment, grabbing any last-minute things that might be useful for her trip. She was still debating which books to take when the buzzer went, announcing the arrival of her taxi. As she locked the door, she noticed an envelope on the floor and, assuming it was a note from her landlord, shoved it in her bag to read later.

Somewhere above Italy, cruising at 30,000 feet, she remembered the envelope and pulled it out of her bag. It contained a folded piece of paper. Her heart skipped a beat as she recognised Oliver's handwriting and read the words.

Things I miss

Smiling, she took a moment to consider what it would be about her he most liked and would miss. Her hair? The smell of her skin? The way she smiled ...?

Unfolding the page, she read:

Pickled eggs
Cryptic crosswords
Pork pies
Whitstable Brewery IPA
Marks and Spencer's pants

Thirty thousand feet below, back in Volos, Scott slept on, oblivious to the fact that the note Oliver had written was sitting under a pile of papers on his table amongst lists of favourite curries, top American comedy shows and most disliked lead singers (groups, not solo artists).

Chapter 25

At least Oliver didn't have much time to brood on Vanessa's departure. The business of packing up the bar and watersport gear and preparing for the new school term took most of their time. As the summer season came to an end, the locals drew a collective sigh of relief and bid farewell to sixteen-hour days and sharing their village with bright red strangers driving on the wrong side of the road.

At the final reckoning, done as ever by a bespectacled Oliver squinting at tiny calculations he'd made in the margins, they'd made enough for half a sailing boat. Unbelievably, they were on course to satisfy the requirements of Uncle Ted's will. They cleared out the bar for the winter after disposing of all surplus stock by the simple expedient of drinking it, and then it was the start of a new term at the school.

They each taught kids between the ages of twelve and seventeen, as the children were organised according to ability rather than age. The Greek state school day was designed to maximise resources, so children were divided into two groups: one that started school at eight and finished at one, and another that started at two and went through to seven. It was a pretty good system, as it meant the limited resources could be used for double the number of children. Those who were on the later roster came to the private schools to learn in the morning and those in the morning came later in the evening, Some unlucky ones, whose parents had them attending extra classes in maths, English, French and goodness knows what else, had to come straight from their school at seven in the evening to start their additional English lessons. For Oliver and Scott, this meant that the morning classes were often filled with sleepy grumpy teenagers who hadn't properly woken up and the evening classes with tired grumpy teenagers who'd already had a full school day under their belts.

The period running up to the start of the school term was always a nervous time for the language school owners. Each year, it seemed, more schools opened and the competition for students became stiffer. This year, Alkis was leaving nothing to chance and had pinned his hopes on a radio advertising campaign. His nephew, who worked for the local radio station, had been roped in and had written a script, which would require an English native speaker.

The sound test consisted of Scott, Oliver and Carl saying, 'Learn English with English professionals at the Volos school of English.' They all tried four or five times, with varying degrees of failure on the side of Carl and Oliver. Scott, though, unexpectedly revealed himself as a natural, delivering his lines excellently, but then also spiralling off into an ad-libbed monologue about the school, which they kept in the final version. Having a good face for radio helped, of course, but the production staff were all impressed with his modulation, tone and diction, which up until then he'd assumed were a legal firm.

While Scott was recording in the sound booth, Oliver shared a beer with a bloke he knew well from the summer, Surfing Yianni, who, it turned out, also worked as a DJ for the radio station. Yianni was with the station producer, Christina, and when the final recording had been wrapped up, the three of them together with Carl and Scott headed off for a quick drink, which turned into a *tsipero*-fest.

As the fourth glass arrived, Scott, his face already a telltale red, turned his attention to Christina and Yianni.

'So, do you know any ancient Greek?'

Yianni nodded. 'Oh, yes. We do it at school but no one remembers much really.'

'A bit like Shakespeare then?'

'I guess,' agreed Christina.

'The thing about Greek philosophers, as I understand it,' Scott continued, 'was that they were always pissed.'

'You mean angry?'

'No, that's American pissed. I mean English pissed, you know, drunk.'

'Ah, yes – they certainly used wine, to, how do you say, free their ideas?' said Christina.

'Now my dad knows a bit about all this,' said Scott. 'He used to study the classics, that's Greek and Latin and a bit of history. I don't really take after him, as you might be able to tell.' Scott paused in a failed attempt to suppress a burp.

'Take after?' asked Yianni.

'Means he's not similar to his father,' explained Oliver, who after a year was getting the hang of the English teaching malarkey.

'Exactly, well put mate. Now, the old man …'

'His father.'

'… once tried to interest me in Socrates by telling me about how Socrates and Plato and their mates would sit around getting drunk and having a natter about life and stuff. Now, I may be wrong, but wasn't Socrates considered the cleverest man in Athens because he knew that he knew nothing?'

Christina and Yianni nodded.

'So, as I see it, there's Socrates sitting there, on a park bench, clutching a tin of Tennents Super …'

'Strong beer.'

'… screaming, "I don't know anything" and "Has anyone seen my dolphin?" Right? Now, you get a couple of Athenians-about-town strolling past and one of them says to the other, "Oh that Socrates is off his trolley again." And the other says, "He says he doesn't know anything, you know that's really quite profound, darling" and they go home, tell the neighbours and the word spreads that Socrates has discovered a philosophical truth, that he knows he knows nothing. When in actual fact he's slumped on a bench, smelling of piss, mumbling that he doesn't know his name, where his house keys are, where he lives, what's living in his beard. Nothing.'

Scott paused to drink more *tsipero*.

'And another thing. You take his mate, Zeno I think his name was. Started the Stoic movement. Know why? Because he was a Premier League tight-fist.'

'Didn't like spending money,' added Oliver helpfully.

'Thank you. So anyway, he wanders down to the market one day and sees all this stuff there, loads of stalls, food, nick-nacks, perhaps a whelk stall or two …'

'Tell you later,' said Oliver to Yianni and Christina's bemused looks.

'So, he's a miserable tight sod and he can see Mrs Zeno itching to splash out and buy, I don't know, a jug or a kilo of olives or maybe a statue of the Parthenon for the front room, so to stop her getting the cash out he says, "My, my, what a lot of things I don't need." Now there's a group of chaps loafing about nearby who hate shopping and

171

who, on a Saturday afternoon, just want to watch the wrestling. So they hear him and say "That Zeno's a genius, that's just what we've been thinking," and they all get together, join a club and call themselves the Stoics. Couple of thousand years later, you get people like my dad reading about the Stoics' denial of personal pleasures and the consumer society, when you're really talking about a bunch of tight blokes who hated putting up shelves.'

Oliver grinned at the laughing Christina and Yianni and said, 'He gets like this every now and then, there's no stopping him.'

'And another thing, your national costume. Forgive me if I'm wrong, but this is based on the uniform of a typical soldier around 2,000 years ago?'

Yianni, guessing what was coming next but smiling so much his cheeks hurt, could only nod weakly.

'Thought so. What's all that about? Dresses, tights, and slippers with little pompoms on the end. Now as I see it, what you're talking about here is an inspired early use of psychological warfare. Put yourself in the position of the Persians, or the Spartans or whoever. There you are, army with a bit of a reputation and you turn up at Thermopylae intent on a bit of extreme violence, and you step ashore to be faced by a thousand transvestites. What are you going to think? I'll tell you what you're going to think: you're going to say to yourself that anyone prepared to leave the house dressed like that has got to be bloody hard, psychotic and probably both. Add to that your reputation. Get routed and thrown into the sea by a well-armed, well-trained army and you limp home to a hero's welcome, place in history assured as gallant and plucky losers. Limp home duffed up by a load of hairy-arsed bearded fellas wearing dresses and slippers, and it's not going to play too well with the waiting crowds.'

After a few more drinks' worth of the gospel according to Scott Poole, two unexpected things had occurred. Christina had proved, against all probability, that it was possible to look attractive while laughing so much things are coming out of your nose, and Scott had been offered a weekly radio show.

172

Chapter 26

Two weeks later and he was on.

The red light went on and Scott was off and running.

'Hello, this is London calling, your weekly radio show about what's on in London this week. We'll be going to our on-the-spot reporter for a rundown of what's hip and what's happening. Plus, we'll be talking about English-speaking events in Volos and much more, after this.' The music kicked in and Scott, taking a swig of water, looked through the glass partition to where Christina was grinning and giving him the thumbs-up. 'Piece of piss, this', he thought to himself.

The format of the show consisted of a running phone-in between songs. That evening, the question for debate was: how are the English thought of in Greece? This inevitably sparked some lively views on the Elgin marbles and some rude comments on English football fans and drunkenness. Most of the callers on the latter subjects sounded suspiciously familiar and were clearly his students winding him up. The main feature of the show was an interview with 'the station's man in London'.

'Hi, Alfie! What's happening?'

A familiar voice came on the line. 'Oh hello, mate, hang on a moment, the Time Out's in the bog, back in a sec.'

'Thanks for that, Alfie, ha ha ha, that crazy English sense of humour, oh I've missed it. It's good to speak to you *live* on air, ha ha!'

'Live? You mean now? Bugger me.'

'Ha ha, you're breaking up, Alfie, we'll call you back.'

It became a minor cult hit overnight. The show went out once a week and soon drew a loyal audience of mostly, it had to be said, students who tuned in hoping to hear Scott or 'Alfie' say something rude by mistake. Chaos being an everyday condition for anyone spending time around Oliver, Scott was used to it and remained unflappable as the world disintegrated around him, which somehow gave the illusion that he had planned it all. Oliver's increasingly eccentric reports as 'Alfie', the London correspondent, certainly helped.

'Now we pass over again to London for our regular check-up on what's happening in the UK with the station's very own special correspondent, Alfie. Hello, Alfie!'

'Hello, Scott, yes I'm talking to you from a small bar in Piccadilly Circus here in the heart of London,' replied Alfie, from the phone booth in the Volos post office.

'Can you tell us what's happening over there in the club scene this week? What are people wearing and what are they listening to?'

'Well, Scott, the vogue here is for shapeless trousers and big, baggy cotton shirts. They're calling it beach chic. The girls here are really going for guys in big trousers.'

'Interesting. What are people listening to?'

'There's a new and massively growing underground scene that, I have to tell you, is so exclusive that only a very few of the music press have picked up on it.'

'So, and I'm guessing here, what you are saying is that it's very unlikely we'll hear about this in the papers, magazines or TV?'

'Exactly.'

'Probably just from you, in fact.'

'Yep, this is really cutting edge.'

'So, what is this new music phenomenon?'

'It's being called 'A Triple F', and you're quite right to call it a phenomenon for that's what it is. 'A Triple F' is, of course, Accordion Folk Funk Fusion!'

'Of course it is. Perhaps we could hear a sample?'

'As I said, it's not widely available in record shops yet, but I do happen to be in the company of one of the leading proponents of the style, who is going to play you his latest hit.'

The listeners were then entertained by a whispered two-way conversation:

'Go on then.'

'What, now?'

'Yes.'

'But we're in the post office.'

'Just start playing, for fuck's sake.'

Then came the unmistakeable sound of Billy singing 'Papa Was a Rolling Stone', accompanied by his accordion and a drum machine, booming out over the airwaves. He finished to a stunned silence before Scott recovered himself and said, 'Well, that was great – and who was that?'

'That was Billy Funk and the Irony. They are to 'A Triple F' what the Sex Pistols were to punk.'

'Can we buy their album in the charts?'

'No, Billy Funk scorns the mainstream. Their CDs are only available to select friends and the hippest club faces. But with my contacts I should be able to get a few copies over to you for your listeners.'

'Thanks, Alfie, and we'll speak to you again next week. Well, something of a scoop there, listeners, we'll be watching out for Billy Funk and the Irony in the weeks and months to come. Now let's hear some U2 before the first part of our new series: The Rules of Cricket.'

Chapter 27

The radio show and Oliver's creation of the Alfie character had started out as an interesting and fun sideline, but ended up making quite a big difference to their day jobs. The first year of teaching had been hard, and much of the time had been spent on crowd control in the hope that the school principal wouldn't hear the children shouting. The rest of the time had been spent desperately trying to get them to remember something that might help them to pass an exam at the end of the year.

Now that Scott and Oliver were a couple of months into the new term, there had been something of a transformation, with a combination of factors making their lives much easier. The fact that they had stayed around for longer than one year was unusual, and the children seemed more relaxed as they didn't have to 'break in' a new teacher. More importantly, they had both become 'cool' in the eyes of their students, firstly for owning a beach bar and watersports business but predominantly for Scott's radio show and Oliver's regular guest slot appearances. As a result, theirs were the classes that all the children wanted to be in, and so they made sure they behaved themselves. The other knock-on effect of their newfound popularity was that the teenage girls, pretty much en masse, developed crushes on them.

This presented something of a problem when they were out and about in the evening, as many of the local bars were pretty lax about asking for IDs. Greek teenagers, unlike their English counterparts, had very little interest in drinking alcohol, and hence were often found sipping iced coffees or soft drinks in the same café-bars as Oliver and Scott. That the girls in particular tended to look and dress a good five years older than their age provided a potential minefield that they were careful to avoid.

It was weird and slightly unnerving to be sitting at a bar with a number of very attractive girls desperately trying to catch your attention and flirting outrageously when they did, all the while knowing that they still had fluffy toys attached to their school bags.

The one good aspect of the situation was the looks of envy and confusion that they generated from the male clientele, who wondered what on earth these two scruffy English guys had that drove the women crazy.

The boys in the classes spent most of their time trying to get them to say which of the big Greek football teams they supported, and then taking the piss if they came up with the wrong name.

As autumn began to stretch out towards winter, the days grew cooler and the cafés on the waterfront moved their tables inside. Scott was enjoying a last warm Sunday at one of the few bars that still had its wicker chairs and cushions out, doing some marking while he waited for Oliver to turn up. He had a big pile of books in front of him and the obligatory table of moonstruck teenagers sitting at one nearby, gazing at him. After an hour of ploughing through the homework exercises, he broke the monotony by writing down a couple of new entries in his book of student bloopers. He'd asked his new junior class to write some dialogue between a shopkeeper and a customer. This had generated two classics for his book. Eleni, a lively eleven-year-old, had written:

Customer: 'Have you got the new singly song record?'

Shopkeeper: 'One moment, I think it is in Stoke.'

And he had a fourteen-year-old Dimitri who had come up with:

Customer: 'I was hungry and wanted some meat so I entered the butcher.'

He was chuckling about the latter example when Oliver arrived.

'Alright?'

'Just doing some marking.'

Oliver looked around and took in the youngsters at the nearby table, spotting a couple of his students.

'Alright Vivi, Zoe?

'Hello, Mr Oliver,' they chorused delightedly before breaking into giggles.

Picking up Dimitri's exercise book from Scott's table, he checked the name on the front page and sniffed dismissively.

'Got a Pythagoras.'

'No! You lucky bastard,' said Scott. 'I've always wanted a Pythagoras.'

'In my new Proficiency class. Very studious boy, bit of a square.'

Scott grinned and nodded, acknowledging the joke. He sifted through the pile, found the one he was looking for and handed it to Oliver.

'Archimedes! Nice. Not had one of them before.'

'Clean lad, spends a lot of time in the bath.'

'Well, he would,' agreed Oliver. 'So, how's work going with you?'

'I'd rather be sitting on a beach hiring out windsurf boards, but it could be worse, I suppose.'

Oliver nodded. 'Same. Mind you, been doing some interesting old stuff with my Proficiency class. You done the conditionals?'

'Wouldn't know one if it fell on me,' said Scott, trying to get the attention of the waiter, who was hiding inside.

'Rum old stuff, your conditionals.'

'Care to enlighten me?'

'I had to teach them yesterday. Turns out there are three of them. First one, pretty straightforward: If I have enough money I will buy you a drink, so that's your possible action.'

'Possible but hugely unlikely in my experience,' said Scott.

'Second conditional: If I *had* enough money I would buy you a drink. Now there you are looking at an unreal or improbable situation.'

'You don't have the money?'

'Exactly. Now here's my favourite, the third conditional: If I *had had* enough money I would have bought you a drink.'

Scott wrinkled his brow in thought.

'So that's in the past. If say, yesterday you'd had some money, you would have bought me a nice cocktail?'

'Yep, keeping up well there Scotty. So what you've got here is a bit of grammar specifically designed to describe something that did not happen in the past!'

'That *is* pretty cool when you put it like that. Something that didn't happen in the past? Sounds like a description of your life,' said Scott. 'Oliver Pond's life is one long third conditional. That should definitely be the title of your biography.'

178

Oliver adopted a hurt expression.

'I'll have you know my past is full of interesting stuff, some of which definitely happened. Or so I've been told.'

'It's the future you've got to worry about.'

Oliver decided the immediate future involved another beer and waved to get the attention of the waiter.

Without looking up, and as casually as he could manage, Scott said, 'I got a letter from Nessie yesterday.'

Oliver stiffened. 'Oh. She have much to say?'

'Have a read,' said Scott, pulling it out of his bag.

Oliver took it from him. There were two sides of A4 paper filled with Vanessa's distinctive scrawl. He read through it. Most of the first page consisted of instructions to Scott as to which bill to pay to whom regarding her flat. On the second page she talked about England, being bored, missing Greece, and finally announced that she had been offered a new job by the tour company and would be returning in the new year. There was no mention of him. He handed it back.

'Good news that she's coming back, eh?' said Scott breezily.

'Yep, great,' said Oliver, trying and failing to keep the disappointment out of his voice.

'She'll love what's happened to Billy – can't want to see her face!' said Scott. 'On that subject, what's our next move?'

'Been thinking about that,' said Oliver, relieved to move the conversation on.

The remaking of Billy into a local celebrity was never meant to achieve anything like the success it did. What started life as a gentle piss-take had developed a bizarre momentum of its own. Each week Scott played a few more tracks of Billy doing his folk numbers, and soon the station was inundated with callers asking where they could buy it. Public opinion could never successfully accuse either Scott or Oliver of looking a gift horse anywhere near the dental department, and they were not about to start now.

'So there's the T-shirts, the CDs, the live gigs and the personal appearances. I was thinking we could also sell some posters,' said Oliver.

'As you well know, I'm prepared to do most things for money, but the thought of inflicting Billy-boy on the innocent walls of teenage bedrooms – well, seems a bit much.'

'Fuck 'em,' said Oliver.

'Very sensibly argued, Mr Pond, I find your elegant sophistry too much for my frailly constructed premise. Will anyone buy them?'

'Look, mate, ours is not to reason why, ours is just to make as much cash out of this situation as humanly possible. Besides, the only possible explanation for Billy becoming a celebrity is divine intervention. This is God's work, my friend, and I for one am not going to mess with the big fella.'

Two weeks later, they were in a studio recording the album. Christina lent the use of the radio station for a couple of nights and they recorded Billy doing ten of his usual folky repertoire and ten cover versions of funk classics. They then chose the best ten from the whole lot, burnt them onto a CD and within a week they were on exclusive sale at Taffos's cousin's record shop. Shameless plugging by Scott on his radio show saw them shift five-hundred CDs within two months, and by the time December came around they had cleared the equivalent of £1,500.

They split the profits fifty-fifty with Billy, and now had enough money to buy a sailing boat that had a reasonable chance of getting them back to England and earning the inheritance.

The run-up to Christmas left Oliver with mixed feelings. On the one hand, he rather liked the Greek Christmas as it was so devoid of the rampant commercialism of the UK. A few days before, they threw up some lights and decorations, had a few days of eating and drinking, and that was it. For the Orthodox Greek church, Easter was the big deal and Christmas had the feeling of being something of an after-thought. He did, however, miss the family element, and this would be his second Christmas away from home.

He was also thinking about Vanessa a lot more than he wanted to. Not normally the type for brooding, he just could not shake her off. As the weeks had turned into months he had gradually resigned himself to the fact that she didn't feel the same way about him as he felt about her. He'd felt sure she would get in touch after reading his message, and although his pride had been dented – or perhaps because it had been dented – he still wanted her. Ironically, he had never been more popular with the opposite sex, as the constant attention from students rubbed off on the world at large and he was conscious of a lot more glances in his direction than he'd ever had before.

Oliver's problem, when it came to girls he really liked, was that modern life didn't really suit him. He hated nightclubs, didn't like dancing and was prone to saying inappropriate things at the worst possible time. In his ideal world, he would demonstrate his love by building a trap, capturing some unsuspecting large animal, and presenting a large pile of meat and a fur coat to the object of his desires. Upon which they would retire happily to their snug little cave and live happily ever after. He had been really impressed with OddRane building his treehouse for Rikke, and had been considering a similar gesture for Vanessa, since he couldn't see her being too chuffed with a dead carcass and she seemed to be well stocked in winter coats. Even if he could build a treehouse, though, he couldn't see Vanessa wanting to live in it, and was at a bit of a loss.

Nevertheless, he ran the idea by Scott, who told him to his great surprise that she liked longbows. It seemed a strange thing for her to be into, but Scott insisted he had heard her say she liked them.

After a bit of research, he discovered an organisation called the English Longbow Society and signed up as a member for £12.50. For that he got information on re-enactments and events, and a manual on how to make and maintain his very own longbow.

The first job was to find a length, or 'stave' as the Longbow Society would have it. Yew was recommended but olive was suggested as a good alternative, which got the whole thing off on the right footing. His intention was to only use medieval tools but he had compromised on sandpaper, since the alternative was to use the dried skin of a sturgeon – which, as he didn't have his glasses on, he had read as a desiccated member of the medical profession and therefore not easy to come by.

Trying to order the right tools and get them shipped out to Greece almost scuppered the plan from the outset, but that had been solved by a rather spritely eighty-two-year-old Greek man called Takis. Takis was a wheelwright. He had been making wheels and barrels, and working on wooden sailing boats, since he was twelve years old and had never retired. He had a small yard full of cats and sat on a table rattling his worry beads from 9am to 11am every day. He hadn't had any paying customers for at least five years, but it suited his pride to say he was still working, and it suited Mrs Takis who enjoyed a couple of hours each day without having him under her feet.

On this particular December morning, he had taken to the comparative warmth of his workshop and was just firing up a portable gas stove to make his coffee when he became aware of a tall, oddly dressed stranger. Old Takis was no fashion expert but he was puzzled by his visitor's trousers. The man looked like the photo that slimming companies take whereby the successful slimmer proves the effectiveness of the programme by standing with both legs in one of his old trouser legs.

Oliver smiled and held out his hand. Takis looked at it suspiciously and said 'Albanos?' This was one of the few words Oliver knew, as it meant 'Albanian' and it was not the first time he had been taken for one. The Albanians who managed to cross the border to seek work in Greece tended not to be the best-dressed men-about-town.

Oliver raised his eyes in the Greek gesture that meant 'No' and said, 'Anglos.'

This went down well with Takis. The English were popular amongst the older generation of Greeks who had fought alongside them in the war, and Takis had been a young man during that conflict. He shook Oliver's hand and gestured towards his bubbling coffeepot.

Oliver smiled and nodded, and was ordered to sit down while Takis poured two small cups of oily black coffee.

The workshop looked to Oliver like an Aladdin's cave of tools and equipment. There was an old wooden cart in the corner, complete with wooden spoked wheels, and all the walls were covered in hooks and shelves holding tools of various shapes and sizes.

There is a book called Zorba the Greek in which two characters, a Russian and the eponymous Zorba, tell each other the stories of their lives despite not speaking a word of each other's language. They do it by dancing their stories and getting very drunk. Takis's dancing days were far in the past, but he liked a drink rather more than the next man and his eyes lit up when Oliver produced a bottle of five-star Metaxa brandy from his bag and said, 'I need some help.'

Takis understood very little English, but the Beatles had ensured pretty much everyone who had ever been near a radio knew the word 'help', and he knew a good bottle of brandy when he saw one.

He took the bottle and poured a generous measure into each of their coffee cups, then sat down calmly looking at Oliver.

'Speak any English?' asked Oliver.

'Ochi' came the reply, together with the raised-eyebrow head-tilt that indicates 'no' in Greece.

So Oliver started dancing. Well, that would be stretching the point, but he launched into a series of mimes, movements and noises that he hoped would convey his intentions.

Takis sat through the performance impassively as Oliver stood up and went through a series of movements that he hoped demonstrated a man selecting a length of wood, smoothing and oiling it, stretching it, and then firing an imaginary arrow with it. Then he eased himself out of his chair and walked round the workbench, coming back with four different lengths of wood, each about four feet long and each from a different tree.

Oliver picked up the first one and weighed it in his hand. He proceeded to examine the grain and gently flex it to check the bend. Then he did the same with the other three, after which he was absolutely none the wiser. His research had told him that the stave should have heartwood facing you for compression and sapwood facing the target, for stretching, but he was buggered if he could tell which side was which. His mime of compression would have been taken by most watchers as a charade of someone with extreme constipation trying desperately for a bowel movement. But Takis instinctively understood what he was trying to say and quickly picked up one of the pieces and nodded confidently. Takis then got out a battered tape measure and held it from the floor to Oliver's nose. Oliver shook his head and said 'Ochi', took the measure and moved it down to around his chest, which was where Vanessa's chin reached to on him.

Takis scratched his head, and looked confused.

Oliver pointed at himself and shook his head. He then lowered his hand to indicate the height of a smaller person and said, 'Filli,' which was close enough to the Greek for 'girlfriend' to be understood.

A light went on behind Takis eyes and he nodded. He put down the tape measure, pointed at Oliver and did that thing with his hands that men do when describing the curves of a woman, and then pointed to his heart. Oliver nodded and said yes. To further make the point, he looked around and picked up two small pieces of wood that he crossed to look like a kid's airplane, pointed to his heart, wiggled his fingers to indicate walking and moved his wiggling fingered hand towards the hand holding the airplane. He then waved the airplane around, successfully and succinctly getting his message across.

Takis spat on the floor. This tended to be his default response to show disappointment, annoyance or, as in this case, 'shit happens' sympathy.

Oliver grinned and passed the question back by pointing at Takis and spreading his arms while shrugging slightly. Takis did the thing describing the body of a voluptuous woman, shook his head, described a very large circle and pointed to his heart before breaking into a long wheezing laugh. An idea then hit him and he pointed to a barrel in the corner to emphasise his point, before collapsing in a laughing and coughing fit on his chair.

They continued in this vein for the rest of the morning, alternatively selecting tools and types of wood, doing short mimes and sketching things out while taking increasingly frequent nips of brandy.

After a few hours they said their farewells, embracing like old friends, Takis having conveyed the information by pointing and grunting that he was there every morning and all Oliver had to do was pop in whenever he wanted to continue.

This he did. Every couple of days they worked and happily drank together as the bow began to take shape.

While Oliver was using his free time in the construction of ancient weaponry, Scott had discovered a new and very unexpected pastime to help deal with the dull winter months. There was a morning every year, usually in late December, when the town would wake up to the mountain of Pelion sporting a rather jaunty white shower cap. This was the cue for determined activity as people rummaged in the backs of wardrobes for their ski equipment. Pelion was high enough to be snow-capped for three months each winter, and from December through to March the implausibly small ski resort, Hania, on its peak was open for business.

Taffos was a keen skier and took each Friday off during the season to get a day's piste action away from the weekend crowds. As luck would have it, Scott's timetable had conspired to give him every other Friday off, and today Taffos was taking him for his first every skiing trip. He finished his morning coffee and began searching through his limited wardrobe for something suitable to wear.

For the journey Scott employed his now tried-and-tested Abi gambit, and focused on her waiting for him at the top of the mountain in a rather fetching ski outfit. A couple of hours later, Taffos left him at the start of the beginners' slope and jumped onto the chair lift to the top.

Hania was a good place for Scott's first introduction to skiing, having just four slopes ranging from not-very-steep to something you'd need a spirit level to prove wasn't horizontal. With a drag lift and a chair lift, it was the perfect resort for learners or the terminally timid. Scott had both legs firmly in the first category but not so much in the latter, and once he realised that the rope which pulled him up went almost as fast as the skiers going down, he decided the beginners' slope was a bit dull. So he graduated to the second steepest slope, where he discovered what all learner skiers usually get taught: that the most important aspect of the sport is learning how to stop.

The technique he adopted was unique and a new entry in the skiing coaching manual. It involved using his face as a brake. At a certain speed, his skis would cross, he would be pitched headfirst into the snow and his head would slowly bring him to a halt. After six or seven performances of this, he arrived at the bottom bruised, cold and wet.

It being Scott's first time, he lacked any proper ski wear and had elected for an outfit that had drawn more than a few glances from the more fashion-conscious around him, which, in fact, was everyone. He was wearing a pair of jeans, a black leather biker jacket, woollen gloves and a fur-lined green ex-army hat which had droopy ear flaps and made him look like rather like a very sickly spaniel. The gloves were now soaked and frozen, providing the warmth one might get from wearing a bag of frozen peas strapped to each hand.

Limping into the café for a reviving brandy and hot chocolate was like walking into heaven. It had a wood-burning stove in the middle of the room, which was blazing so intensely that the other skiers had stripped off their many layers and were wearing just T-shirts, ski bottoms and boots. With his hands too numb for any useful movement, Scott managed to slide the gloves off and wriggle out of his jacket, but the hat was a bridge too far.

The rest of the room represented the elite of the local Greek populace, resplendent in the latest ski wear. Under normal circumstances, Scott's appearance as the scruffiest and least well-equipped skier in the room would have drawn a few glances. As a man wearing a t-shirt, jeans steaming so much they appeared to be on fire and a green furry hat with earflaps, he might as well have been on a podium.

Standing nonchalantly with a steaming mug gripped in both useless hands, he tried to ignore the rivulets of sweat pouring down his face from his hyper-heating head and silently willed his hands to recover. Even as they recovered some movement, it still proved impossible to undo the hat's ties, which were knotted under his chin and frozen solid. The impression held by most of the room that they were in the company of a dangerous maniac was not alleviated by Scott, in desperation, clumping up to the bar and miming slicing a knife across his throat while smiling amiably. The girl serving at the counter was just edging away when the appearance of Taffos cleared up any lingering confusion. Scott was able, with the help of Taffos, to remove his hat but had to suffer the entire room pissing themselves at his expense as Taffos explained that he wasn't mad, he was just a bit of a useless English wanker.

It may not have been the most auspicious of beginnings, but even so he was hooked. Every other Friday he and Taffos headed to Hania and once he'd worked out how to stop, he turned into quite a decent skier.

With their respective hobbies to focus on, the days passed quickly for Oliver and Scott. February soon came around and with it the return of Vanessa.

Chapter 28

It was just before the end of the month that Vanessa returned. She had stayed in England for her sister's wedding and that had run into a family Christmas, the first time in a few years they had all got together. After the disappointment of finding that Oliver had given her what she took to be a shopping list when she had been hoping for his undying devotion, she was in two minds about returning to her job in Volos. December in the UK made up her mind. The relentless grey sky and cold wind, combined with life in a small market town fifty miles from the nearest coastline, made her realise that there were better places to be, even if she had no great desire to see Oliver any time soon.

Sunny Sunshine Tours had written to ask if she wanted to return to help with the planning for the new season. This represented something of a promotion as they were asking her to travel around the area, checking out hotels and guest houses for their summer clientele. She would still have her flat in Volos as her base, but a lot of the job would entail touring. It was too good an opportunity to turn down, and so with some trepidation she packed her bags and headed back to Volos.

As the weeks passed and Oliver didn't hear from her, he reluctantly came to the conclusion that he had misjudged the situation badly and she wasn't interested. The fact that she had written to Scott and not to him was the final nail in the coffin. Maybe she had even been embarrassed by his statement of his feelings. It was therefore with a measure of unease that he heard she'd returned and Scott had arranged for them all to meet for a meal the next evening.

That morning, Oliver's waking thought was about what it would be like to see her again and how the situation might pan out. He was thinking about this and making himself some breakfast when the door buzzer to his apartment sounded. Could it be her? It had to be her. No one else would be calling him at this time. He took a quick glance in the mirror and he had to admit the face looking back was not at its best. His dull morning brain was taking in the stubble, the dark marks under his eyes and the smell coming off his unshowered body when the buzzer rang again.

After pressing the button that remotely unlocked the ground-floor entrance, he calculated he had worst case one minute, best case two to do something about his appearance before the lift arrived at his door. He grabbed some deodorant and liberally sprayed himself all over, changed into a new pair of pants, pulled on some jeans and wriggled into a reasonably clean shirt. Checking his reflection, he now looked exactly as he had before, just wearing more clothes and smelling like the cosmetics counter in the duty free section. There was a knock on the door and he took a deep breath and opened it.

'Fancy a swim?' asked OddRane, who, to ensure no one was going to miss his point, was wearing Bermuda shorts and a short-sleeved shirt.

Rikke was dressed somewhat more conventionally in a big jumper and coat and they were both grinning happily.

'Rikke, OddRane – blimey, that's a turn up. Come in, come in,' said Oliver, recovering quickly from his surprise.

They had come back to assess a few places to potentially purchase and do up, and, wisely, to check out just what a Greek winter was like before throwing themselves into buying a place.

'Rikke, girl, you're looking good,' Oliver said, giving her a hug and lifting her off her feet. 'And OddRane, looking spry I see. Give us a manly pat there,' he said, repeating the action with OddRane. 'I'll get some coffee on.'

'I am feeling a bit overdressed, it is so warm here!' said OddRane, who was not one to understate a point.

'You'll be wanting to sit outside then, mate,' said Oliver as he put on a thick coat and opened the door to the balcony.

Outside he had a hammock and a deckchair that doubled as a fairground attraction; it threatened to collapse if you so much as looked at it in a funny way. If it could speak, it would undoubtedly be asking anyone planning on sitting down, 'How lucky do you feel?' Oliver generally avoided it, but as OddRane had grabbed the hammock and Rikke the other chair, he gingerly lowered himself into it.

It was a very cold day and both Oliver and Rikke enjoyed watching OddRane's increasing discomfort as they chatted about what they'd been doing for the last few months and reminisced about Crete and the summer. It wasn't too long before OddRane, who was absolutely frozen, suggested he and Rikke should get moving as they had to hire a car and visit some villages. Oliver told them the name of the restaurant where he was meeting Scott and Vanessa that evening and gave them directions and a rough map to ensure they found it.

They were due to meet at 9pm and Oliver was there by eight. He was uncharacteristically nervous about seeing Vanessa, and decided the best policy was to get a couple of drinks on board as soon as possible. While he was waiting, he considered the best outcome and decided that ideally, when he saw Vanessa, it would be no big deal. She was just someone he had fancied but who hadn't fancied him, and so what, there were plenty of girls around who fitted that category. The best option was to play it cool and just be pleased to see her, like he would any friend he hadn't seen for a while. This thought process, together with the wine, brought him to a fairly chilled state with all nerves and anxiety banished. Then she walked in and he turned into a jabbering wreck.

Vanessa had been equally nervous about seeing Oliver and had decided the best approach was to show him what he was missing. She'd put about three hours' worth of effort into getting ready, which was two hours and forty-five minutes more than normal. Looking in the mirror she wondered why she'd bothered. She saw the pale, English winter sculpted face, the tired eyes, and the mess of a hair style. The dress was a mistake she thought, too showy. But what the hell. After a fortifying gin and the last-minute addition of a black ribbon around her neck she set off.

To Oliver she looked stunning. She had tamed her hair into coils on top of her head in the style of an aristocrat from ancient Rome, and was wearing a red dress that accentuated all the bits that benefited from being accentuated. The black ribbon added something that he couldn't put his finger on but he would very much like to. He stood up as she walked over to his table.

'Hi, long time no see,' she said.

Oliver intended to say something along the lines of, 'Wow, you look amazing. I've never seen you look so beautiful.' But to his surprise and horror, he heard himself say, 'Alright there girl, put a bit of effort in on the dressing-up front I see, smashing!'

They leaned in and did a half-hug-type clinch while kissing on each cheek.

Before the conversation went any further, Rikke and OddRane arrived, Oliver had just introduced them when Scott appeared, and further hellos, handshakes and hugs ensued until they were all seated at the corner table.

Despite his initial bravado, it didn't go unnoticed that OddRane had opted for jeans, thick jumper and winter coat, although he was still dismissive of the Greek winter as being no worse than a mildly chilly spring day in Oslo.

They chatted and caught up on what had been happening over the last few months. The stories of the radio station and Billy's success as a pop star brought gales of laughter, as did Vanessa's tales of just how dull it was in her home town. The drinks flowed and the conversation got steadily more raucous as the *tsipero* took its customary effect.

OddRane was doing a passable impersonation of Henry VIII at a royal feast. The cost of alcohol and restaurant prices in Norway were such that he and Rikke rarely got to eat out, and when they did, the most they might share was one bottle of wine. At Greek prices, he couldn't get the stuff down fast enough. He mopped one of his many greasy plates with a bread roll and sat back in his chair contentedly.

'This is life,' he said.

'You look pretty happy there, OddRane,' said Oliver, leaning over to remove a couple of unwanted chips from Rikke's plate.

'He's been working hard, haven't you, darling,' said Rikke, ruffling his hair.

OddRane had spent much of the time since they last met preparing for the renovation work he was planning in Greece by building something that sounded like a cross between a holiday cabin and a beach house.

'I am, as you say, "putting my hand in" so that I am ready for the building work here', he explained. 'I am helping my brother Bent. He is a builder so I have been learning a lot.'

Oliver couldn't resist this. 'Bent! Your brother is called Bent!'

'Ah, that must sound funny in English. It's a normal name in Norway, quite common. Much more common than OddRane Villsvin.'

'Does your name mean anything?' asked Scott. 'Like, I dunno, Son of the Viking Hammer-Thrower?'

'Villsvin does.' He wrinkled his brow in concentration. 'I don't think I know the word. It's like a pig but lives in the forest and is bigger. Asterix eats them.'

'A boar, perhaps,' said Vanessa thoughtfully.

'Maybe, I don't know. "Strange Boar" – yes, I think that is sounding right.'

'Hmm, interesting, very interesting,' said Vanessa.

Scott clapped a firm hand onto OddRane's shoulder. 'So, what do you fancy doing tomorrow?'

Vanessa stood up and to everyone's surprise announced, 'Tomorrow we are all going skiing!'

They all looked at her.

'I didn't think you liked skiing, Nessie,' said Scott.

'Have you got your list?' she asked.

'Always.' He spread it out on the table.

The labours of Hercules

1 Killed the Nemean lion
2 Killed a Hydra, a nine-headed snake
3 Captured a golden-horned reindeer
4 ~~Brought back a bull from Crete~~
5 Captured the Erymanthian Boar
6 ~~Cleaned the Augean stables in a single day~~
7 Chased away flesh-eating Stymphalian birds
8 ~~Captured the horses of King Diomedes~~
9 ~~Got the belt of Hippolyta, Queen of the Amazons~~
10 Captured the cattle of Geryon, the three-headed, six-armed giant

11 ~~Brought back the three golden apples from the Garden of Hesperides~~

12 Went into Hades and brought back the three-headed hound of hell

'Tomorrow we are doing number five,' she announced. 'I'll handle the details.'

Capturing the Erymanthian Boar was something she had already considered but dismissed on the grounds that borrowing Ma Taffos's favourite pig might not go down too well. In the myth, the boar accidentally kills Adonis by goring him through the leg. Aphrodite, who loved Adonis, comes for the boar intent on revenge but is persuaded against killing it when the boar assures her that, dazzled by Adonis's beauty, he had run towards him to kiss him and had forgotten he had tusks. Aphrodite forgives him and allows him to wander on the mountain of Erymanthia, where he grows so wild and savage that no one can go near him. Hercules captures the boar by chasing it into a snowdrift, tethering its feet and carrying it down to the sea, where it swims off to Italy. This, Vanessa thought, necessitated a trip to the ski resort at the top of the mountain.

Sitting in the back of the bus as it pulled into Hania, OddRane looked noticeably unenthusiastic about what the day held in store. Vanessa was just going over the details again:

'So, OddRane, have you got the plan?'

'I am walking along in the snow. Scott jump on me, wrestle me into a snowdrift.'

'Good, good. Then we carry you down to the sea, throw you in, and you swim to Italy,' added Oliver.

'But I can't swim!'

'You're not exactly a wild boar either, mate, so don't think we'll be following the script religiously,' said Scott.

The walk from the bus to the ski resort was about ten minutes and all uphill, leaving Scott, Vanessa and Oliver absolutely knackered when they got to the café. OddRane and Rikke, who had walked on snow for at least half of every year of their lives, were barely out of breath. Vanessa, directing proceedings, decided that it would be better to stage the scene at the top of the slopes, with a view of the sea and the bay of Volos in the background. It was a beautiful day, bright blue sky and amazing views in all directions, but no amount of loveliness was about to convince OddRane he should wear the pig mask Oliver had just plucked from his bag.

'Shame really, OddRane, I think it would add something visual to the scene.'

After being told in no uncertain terms that it would also add something visual in the form of heavy bruising to his face if he didn't put it away, Oliver decided to go ahead with the shoot *au naturel*. It was implicit in the story that Hercules had pursued the boar for some time, so therefore some kind of chase was really required.

After ten minutes which left Scott clutching his sides and panting like an overenthusiastic porn star, it had become clear that OddRane was both fitter and nippier than a wild boar had any right to be. Vanessa was delighted, though; she had shot nearly a whole film of hysterical Keystone-Cops-style chase scenes, which she knew would look fantastic when they put the story together. Calling a halt, she positioned a giggling OddRane with Scott five yards behind and suggested the capture scene should feature a full-length rugby tackle by Scott for ultimate dramatic effect. OddRane shrugged agreement and stood waiting while Scott took a bit of a run-up to get his momentum.

To that old Hollywood adage of never acting with children or dogs there needs to be added a category of large, jovial Norwegians. It's a moot point as to whether it was OddRane's idea of a good joke or his fear at the manic determination on Scott's face which caused him to skip to the left at the last minute. Either way, it left a flying Scott in mid-air with nowhere to go and nothing to stop him. He landed on his chest on a particularly icy patch of snow and just kept sliding. That it was only the intermediate run and only three-hundred metres to the bottom was of no great comfort to Scott as he shot over the edge and disappeared from view.

They found him propping up the bar of the café with a large brandy in front of him and water dripping out of the ankle hems of his jeans. This, it transpired, was from the wedges of snow that had found their way down the front of his trousers as he slid headfirst down the hill. He was not best pleased.

194

OddRane was, however, one of those people who, try as you might, it is impossible to be angry with for long. After a few beers and a few medicinal brandies, he had cheered up sufficiently to continue with an abridged version of the plan. They wandered round the corner of the café, shoved OddRane into a suitable snowdrift and slid back down the path to catch the bus.

Two hours later, they were standing on the small deserted beach that served the town of Volos, and OddRane was being reminded of some of his many comments on the subject of temperature.

'Call this cold? You don't know what real cold is,' recalled Scott from memory as a sheepish OddRane stood shivering in his pants.

'It's impossible for a Norwegian to be cold in a place this far south,' added Oliver.

'Okay guys, the point is being made. Am I really having to go in the water?'

'Well, that depends,' said Scott maliciously, 'on whether you are a man or a bit of a girly embarrassment to your Viking heritage.'

In he went – hesitantly up to his waist before plunging his head under the water, letting out a blood-curdling scream and running back out, to be met with a lot of laughter and a warm towel.

They all headed off for a celebratory drink and Scott was able to scratch out number five on his list.

<u>The labours of Hercules</u>

1 Killed the Nemean lion
2 Killed a Hydra, a nine-headed snake
3 Captured a golden-horned reindeer
~~**4** Brought back a bull from Crete~~
~~**5** Captured the Erymanthian Boar~~
~~**6** Cleaned the Augean stables in a single day~~
7 Chased away flesh-eating Stymphalian birds
~~**8** Captured the horses of King Diomedes~~
~~**9** Got the belt of Hippolyta, Queen of the Amazons~~
10 Captured the cattle of Geryon, the three-headed, six-armed giant

~~11 Brought back the three golden apples from the Garden of Hesperides~~

12 Went into Hades and brought back the three-headed hound of hell

He now only had one left to complete the deal. It was time to start thinking of buying a boat and the tricky business of learning to sail.

Chapter 29

Vanessa's reaction on seeing Oliver had been much the same as his on seeing her. Her stomach had gone into a knot and she had felt breathless and stupidly tongue-tied.

They'd seen very little of each other since that first evening and the following day on the ski slopes. Her work had kept her out of town a lot, visiting the many hotels vying for Sunny Sunshine Tours' custom. When she had run into Oliver, he'd always been surrounded by annoyingly pretty moonstruck girls gazing at him adoringly and giggling, which had done nothing for her equilibrium.

It was coming up to her birthday, and to cheer herself up she decided to have a party. The venue was near the harbour and although it had not been open long it was already gaining a reputation as the trendiest new nightspot. There were a lot of nightclub-style bars in Volos and most of the popular ones had some kind of theme or gimmick that brought in the punters. This particular venue, the Underground Bar, occupied a series of caves at the end of a strip of land that formed the southern breakwater of the harbour. The finger of land on which it sat curved slightly, so that when looking one way from the club you could see a short stretch of water and then all the lights of Volos laid out in front of you.

Not surprisingly, with such a stunning view it had rapidly become very popular. Every summer Vanessa was effectively in charge of a new captive audience each week, who were happy to spend at least ninety percent of their holiday budget getting as drunk as possible. As a result, she knew and was feted by most of the bar and club owners in town, all of whom had reason to be grateful to her for sending packs of tourists their way. Getting into any club was never a problem and the owner of the Underworld had been very happy to provide her with a private area for her party. She had a couple of tables set up in a roped-off area for her collection of assorted expats, teachers and a smattering of Greek mates. The event was actually a combined birthday and welcome-back-to-Volos party, as work demands had meant that since her return she hadn't had a chance to catch up with many of her friends.

Oliver was in two minds about whether to go or not until Scott took him to one side during their morning lessons a couple of days before the event.

'Mate, I've got a bit of a confession to make,' he said, shifting his weight from foot to foot and looking as guilty as he had when they'd been caught smoking in the third year.

'Go on,' replied Oliver.

Scott handed him the note that he had written to Vanessa the evening before she had left.

'I found this last night under a pile of papers.'

Oliver took the note and stared at it in confusion.

'You telling me you forgot to give it to her?'

'No, I gave her a note, left it outside her door – just must have been the wrong one.'

'What do you mean "the wrong one?' How many bloody notes do you carry around in that bag?'

Scott bit his lip. 'I found it mixed up with a load of our "envelope of truth" notes. It was next to your list of "women I shouldn't fancy but do.'

'Fucking great!' said Oliver.

'Well, on the bright side, at least I didn't give her that one. Look, I'm really sorry, mate,' said Scott.

'No, I mean it really is fucking great. This means she didn't get my note so she hasn't been blanking me. She just doesn't know I fancy her.'

Having digested this news, Oliver decided that what he needed was a grand gesture that would sweep Vanessa off her feet. He pondered the best approach for a day or two, but came up with nothing better than literally sweeping her off her feet by walking into the club, slinging her over his shoulder and carrying her out. The caveman approach, as he called it, had worked for him before but he couldn't help thinking that Vanessa's feminist views might make this one a less-than-successful gambit.

He stumbled across the solution in the school library.

He had been rooting around looking for something to use in his Intermediate class and had found a short book on mythological love stories. It opened at the tale of Orpheus. Two things jumped out instantly: Orpheus was a legendary musician and one of the original Argonauts who sailed from Volos with Jason. This, Oliver thought, was just what he was looking for. Vanessa had become fascinated by all things mythological, and so playing the old Greek mythology card was sure to be a winner.

He started reading and discovered that Orpheus was such a brilliant musician he could charm everyone he met, and had used this ability to great effect during the voyage of the Argonauts. They had sailed past the Sirens, the ones who lured sailors onto the rocks with their beautiful songs, and he had played and sung louder and more beautifully than the Sirens to ensure they sailed safely past.

The bit that ensured his entry into the top ten Greek mythological love stories concerned his wife, Eurydice. He had fallen madly in love with her, but on their wedding day a jealous satyr tried to grab her. While being chased, she trod on some poisonous snakes and died. Orpheus played such sad and beautiful music while mourning her that the gods took pity on him and advised him to go to the Underworld to get her back. He went into Hades and played so movingly that it had softened the heart of Persephone, the keeper of the Underworld, who agreed to allow Eurydice to return with him to the land of the living.

At that point, the bell rang to announce the start of Oliver's lesson and he put the book down with a renewed sense of optimism. The venue of Vanessa's party, the Underground, was not quite the Underworld, but it was pretty damn close and good enough for Oliver.

From various other stories he could vaguely remember about Hades, he knew that the only proper way to arrive was by boat, and hence on the evening of Vanessa's party he could be seen standing on the harbour, about to climb into a bright red pedalo. He and Takis had finally finished Vanessa's longbow the previous week, and he had it strung across one shoulder, his guitar across the other. It was all going to be down to the eye of the beholder, who would see him either as the proverbial white knight on his charger or a complete twat.

Oliver set off at 9pm and found that he had seriously underestimated the distance and the sideways drift of the current. For every ten metres he went towards the club, the current took him five to the right. After an hour, his legs had turned to jelly, he was drenched in sweat and had succeeded in reaching the harbour wall parallel but opposite the club, with the whole bay between them. There was no way he could make it across the stretch of water, so his options were to leave it there and walk back to where he had started and then on to the club, or ask for some help from a friendly fisherman. As there didn't seem to be any other boats around, the only course of action was to walk. He was next to a mooring hook and a ladder up to the top of the jetty, so he tied up the boat and climbed up, his wobbling legs just about holding his weight.

The first thing he saw, when his head appeared over the top of the concrete wall, was three men in uniform with guns at their belts, staring at him. They didn't look friendly. To their somewhat jaundiced eyes he looked for all the world like an illegal immigrant avoiding passport controls. Added to their mental charge sheet was the fact that he was also carrying a weapon – admittedly, one not used much in anger for the last four-hundred years, but a weapon nevertheless. The guitar was a bit confusing and perhaps indicated a more benign reason for his appearance, but, to be on the safe side, they promptly arrested him.

Oliver had unwittingly moored in front of the main Port Police office, where he was taken inside and seated on a chair next to three other officers playing cards. They looked up briefly as he came in. One of them said something to the others which caused them all to break into raucous laughter before going back to their card game.

It is fair to say that for a country that contributed to the word bureaucracy, Greece had not really benefited from it. The system tended to create jobs and was not always keen on people doing them very much. So it was with the Port Police. Generally speaking, a few stern words might be passed and then Oliver would be invited to join the card game and given a beer, but it was Oliver's misfortune that the officer in charge that night was Arris, Chief of the Port Police. His father had been Chief of Port Police before him and he stood out from the crowd as someone who actually enjoyed his job. It would not be going too far to say he loved it. Arris's office was filled with spy novels and detective stories, and he saw himself as the first line of defence against the forces of evil that might try to infiltrate his country. He had spent most of his working life imagining the moment when he would step up to the microphone at his very own press conference to announce to the waiting world's media how he and his crack team had uncovered an international smuggling ring that had escaped the attentions of Interpol, the CIA and a host of other intelligence services, blinking in the face of hundreds of camera flashes as he stood in front of the three-metre-high bundles of cocaine. Although he spent his days checking the catches on local fishing boats and issuing permits to people running pleasure cruises to the islands, his dreams and ambition still burned bright.

Arris came into the main room to take a look at Oliver and was disappointed to see that nothing about him suggested an international drug smuggler. He made him turn out his pockets anyway, and had his suspicions raised somewhat when he was unable to produce any form of ID papers. All he had was some cash and a Golden Virginia tin. The tin excited his interest a bit more, particularly as he noted Oliver's pained expression as he produced it. Thinking he might find some cannabis at the very least, he eagerly opened it and started pulling out the contents. Oliver let out a long, loud moan of anguish as the customs officers spread the items all over the table, peering at them with ever-increasing excitement as more and more items appeared until they had everything.

1m² tin foil
10 painkillers (strong ones from when his brother Pete broke his collarbone)
15m fishing line
10 fishing hooks
3 fishing flies
2 condoms
2 waterproof 'lifeboat' matches
12 Swan Vestas snapped in half and dipped in wax
wire saw
2 big keyring rings (for trap triggers and saw)
Guitar D string
Guitar B string
Bit of hexiblock (firelighter)
24 water purification tablets

Oxo cube
2 razor blades with tape on one edge
2 scalpel blades
3 Stanley knife blades
4 relighting birthday candles
10 split lead fishing weights
2 small lightsticks
magnetic strip glued on outside of lid
small polythene bag
sandpaper glued to inside of lid
5m dental floss
3 needles
5m black thread
5m darning yarn
sachet of petrol (Zippo refill)
sachet of WD40
a pen
swing bin liner
1 effervescent paracetamol/codeine
10 butterfly stitches
2 big plasters
miniature tube of Savlon
pocket Leatherman – pliers
small screwdriver
medium screwdriver
tin opener
bottle opener
file
6 multivitamins
3 small safety pins
1 nappy safety pin
1 diarrhoea sachet
3 2in nails
1 antiseptic wipe
credit card multitool taped on the outside of tin
5cm ruler
tin opener
awl

magnifying glass
4 spanners
butterfly screw opener
bottle opener

Arris looked at the array of stuff, looked at Oliver and decided he was almost certainly dealing with a cleverly disguised member of a terrorist cell. Granted, he looked like an idiot, but then that would be the perfect disguise, and lots of the captured terrorists he had seen on the telly had looked none too bright either.

At this stage, Oliver was more concerned with how he was going to repack his tin, but his priorities changed when Arris pulled out a pair of handcuffs. He searched his mind for something useful to say in Greek that might explain the situation or someone who could help. Taffos! Everyone knew Taffos, he thought.

'Gregoris Papadopoulos, taverna, filos moo,' he said, which roughly translated as 'Taffos with the restaurant is a friend of mine'.

Arris paused, looked at him and repeated, 'Gregoris Papadopoulos?'

Oliver nodded and pointed to the one useful thing he had about his person that would benefit the current situation, which was an old napkin from Taffos' restaurant with the phone number on it. By miming a phone and pointing to the number, he was able to convince them to allow him to make a call.

The phone rang out for what seemed like forever before the familiar voice of Taffos answered.

'Taffos, mate. It's Oliver. I'm in a bit of bother with the Port Police, can you help?'

Ten minutes later, all hell broke loose. It seemed that Ma Taffos had been dining at her son's taverna when Oliver had called, and her arrival on the back of Taffos's scooter rather changed the dynamic of the evening.

As the door opened, Arris turned from examining the contents of Oliver's tin only to be hit in the chest repeatedly by a jabbing finger attached to a small, round bundle of anger. Oliver had no idea what Ma Taffos was saying but there was a lot of it, it was very loud and it seemed to be having the desired effect. The guys at the table all put down their cards and sat quietly looking down, for all the world like schoolkids in front of the head teacher. Arris, to his credit, attempted to put up a fight and did get some words in through the tirade, but after a couple of minutes even he visibly wilted.

Taffos, bringing up the rear, grinned at Oliver and put his thumbs up. He was free to go. They scooped up the contents of his tin, put it all in a plastic bag and handed it to him on his way out.

Once they were outside, Taffos turned to Oliver and asked him what he was doing there in the first place. Oliver tried and failed to hide his embarrassment as he explained that he was on his way to Vanessa's party and thought it would be a romantic gesture to arrive by boat. Taffos looked puzzled but Ma Taffos understood everything. She grabbed Oliver and gave him two big kisses on each cheek.

'You are a good boy, you be kind to Vanessa. I take you there now.' And with that she climbed onto the scooter and gestured to Oliver to get on the back.

'What about me?' asked Taffos.

'You get taxi,' she shouted over her shoulder as Oliver perched himself tentatively behind her considerable bulk. She sped off, leaving Taffos mouthing something it was fortunate for him that she could not hear, and Oliver hanging on for dear life with one hand while holding a guitar and longbow in the other.

They made it there in five minutes. Ma Taffos skidded to a stop in front of the bemused doorman and Oliver hopped off and attempted to make himself look presentable. His legs had recovered a bit from an hour of pedalling and no longer felt like jelly, but he was conscious of an unpleasant sheen of sweat over his entire body. The owner of the club, Stavros, was the older brother of one of his students and was a keen windsurfer. He and Oliver had bonded over this during the summer and he had let him borrow a board a few times free of charge. Stavros had therefore been happy to help when Oliver outlined his plan and made the necessary arrangements. Hence the doorman did not seem remotely fazed to be letting in a guy who was carrying a bow and a guitar, and had just been dropped off by what looked like his nan.

As Oliver reached the tables where the party was in full swing, the music was turned down as planned.

About twenty heads turned in his direction.

He looked around and said, 'Alright? Right then, Vanessa, tonight I am Orpheus and I've got a song to play you. Hope you like it.'

'What do you mean, you're obvious,' asked one of the party.

'Orpheus,' repeated Oliver. 'As in Orpheus and the Underworld. Well, Underground.'

Vanessa looked blank and then her brow wrinkled.

'So who is Eurydice then?'

'That would be you,' said Oliver as he pulled his guitar down and started into his best seduction song, I Hope That I Don't Fall in Love With You, a Tom Waits number that generally had the ladies swooning over him.

In his gravelly voice, he sang the sad story of a man in a bar who sees a woman, a stranger, who he imagines is as lonely as he is. But before he finds the courage to go over to her, she's gone, and he wonders if perhaps, without speaking, they might have fallen in love, just a little bit.

When he finished, there was a round of applause and catcalls from the roped-off area. Vanessa was instantly out of her seat and over to him. She hugged him tightly and whispered into his ear, 'That was the most romantic thing anyone has ever done for me.'

Her hand slipped into his and they walked out of the club together.

It was a beautiful evening and they sat hand in hand on a small wall overlooking the dark water of the harbour and the blinking lights of the city.

'Orpheus! Wasn't expecting that,' said Vanessa.

'Seemed the best way to tell you how I feel.'

'Hmm ... I'm guessing you perhaps sort of skim-read the story?'

'Well, didn't read it all, but you know, he was a musician and rescued his love from the Underworld,' he said, jerking his thumb at the sign saying the Underground. 'Thought it was pretty close.'

Vanessa looked thoughtful. 'There's a couple of things you might have missed.'

'Oh?'

'When Orpheus got into the Underworld, he played his music and was allowed to leave with Eurydice on condition he walked ahead of her and didn't look back.'

'Ah, and I'm betting he did look back?'

'Yes, he did. Which meant that Eurydice had to go back again,'

'So still dead?'

'Yes, still dead. There's more. Orpheus from that moment on refused to play his music to any females and only took male lovers.'

'You what?'

'And eventually all the spurned ladies that didn't get to hear his music or enjoy his, ahem, attentions, cut off his head and threw it in a river.'

Oliver pondered this for a moment.

'So, you're dead, I'm gay, none too bright and soon to be decapitated.'

Vanessa squeezed his arm. 'It's the thought that counts.' She leant forward to kiss him and, as she did so, got her hand caught on a bow string.

'One other thing: why are you carrying a bow and arrow?'

'Ah, yes. This is for you. I made it,' he said, taking it off his shoulder and handing it to her.

'You … made … this … for … me,' she said. 'Do you mind if I ask why?'

'Scotty told me you liked them so I made you one.'

Vanessa's brow wrinkled.

'He told you I liked what, exactly?'

'Longbows.'

Her face twitched, her shoulders shook and her chest heaved as she sought and failed to control herself before breaking into sobs of uncontrollable laughter. Tears rolled down her cheeks. Eventually she managed to calm down enough to say, 'I like the handbags! Longbow is a bag made by the Japanese designer Aiko Tanaka.' She started laughing again. 'They have – they have – a trademark knotted bow on the – on the side,' she managed to get out before collapsing again into hysterics.

'This is going well.'

Vanessa had just about regained control of her breathing. 'Oh my, you'll be telling me you came in a pedalo next.'

Oliver looked sheepish. 'Fucking thing. Took me two hours to get here.'

Vanessa thought about asking him why, but in the end just elected to kiss him.

They stayed locked together for some minutes before coming up for air. Vanessa stepped back and looked up at him and said, 'You lovely, adorable, funny, idiot man.' She leant forward and tilted her head upwards and kissed him lightly on the lips. 'And slightly clammy.'

'Got a bit of a manly sweat on pedalling out. Oh, got you something else,' he added.

He handed her the bag that Arris had tipped his stuff into.

'Me tin.'

She took the bag and looked inside. She squealed: 'You've opened your tin for me!' And kissed him again.

'This is turning into the best night of my life!' she said, which turned out be somewhat premature as, after plunging her hand into the bag, she pulled it out with a one-inch fishing hook imbedded in the pad of her thumb.

A little later, Oliver was standing at the bar with Scott.

'Quite a night for you, mate,' said Scott.

'Yep. An hour of pedalling that bloody pedalo, arrested for spying, rescued by a Greek grandmother, and now I'm down a fish-hook, one antiseptic wipe, two butterfly stitches, one big plaster and two painkillers.'

'Worth it?'

'I'd say so.'

'Pleased for you, mate, nothing you don't deserve. You make a very nice couple.'

They clinked glasses.

Oliver grinned and downed his drink. 'Right, I'm off soon. Going back to Vanessa's ... Can you do me a favour?'

'Depends.'

'Can you drop by the Port Police office on the way home and pick up a pedalo?'

Chapter 30

Scott didn't see much of either Vanessa or Oliver for the next couple of weeks. It seemed they had some catching up to do, and he left them to it. He had a few more skiing days with Taffos until grass started showing through the snow in places, heralding the end of the season.

It felt like the first part of the adventure was coming to an end, too. He only had one more labour to complete and a boat to buy and learn to sail. He had bought a book on sailing and optimistically figured that it would be the same as windsurfing, but in something a bit bigger and with more ropes, so was feeling fairly confident.

One evening he brought the subject up with Taffos.

'I've done a fair bit of sailing look, Scotty boyo, we had a boat at our place by the sea. Tidy it is, you'll like it.'

'Is it hard to learn?'

'I wouldn't say it was hard, just takes a bit of practice. I know a man who can give you a few pointers.'

Taffos had introduced him to his friend Alexei, who ran day trips to see dolphins in a sailing boat that was big enough to accommodate up to ten day passengers and could sleep six. Alexei was preparing the boat for the new season and took Scott out a couple of times on trips around the bay. A conversation with one of the more interesting language-school lifers had informed Scott of a four-stage learning process. It was often used to describe the process of learning to drive a car.

Stage one was called *unconscious incompetence*. This was the most dangerous stage, as effectively the learner didn't know what they did not know, and tended to be overconfident.

Stage two was *conscious incompetence*. This was the point at which you recognised your limitations and understood what you had to learn.

Stage three was *conscious competence*. At this stage, you could achieve the task, but only by concentrating really hard.

Stage four, the final one, was *unconscious competence*, whereby you could carry out the task without thinking.

The conversation was something of a revelation to Scott, as it made him realise how long he tended to stay happily bobbing around the unconsciously incompetent stage when faced with a new challenge. It took half an hour with Alexei for him to jump straight into being only too conscious of how much he didn't know. There were ropes everywhere, and cleats and sails and trim, and that was before you got into the business of pointing the thing in the right direction and knowing how much water was underneath you. He had been correct, though, in his assumption that the basic principles were the same as windsurfing, and he made good progress, gradually coming to understand when to pull the sail in a bit and when to let it out and how to turn the boat around.

There was, however, still one labour left to go. He had been thinking of what he could do for it, and when Vanessa and Oliver did finally surface, they all met one evening in Taffos's place to go over the options. Scott laid his list out between the various bottles littering the table.

The labours of Hercules

1 Killed the Nemean lion
2 Killed a Hydra, a nine-headed snake
3 Captured a golden-horned reindeer
~~**4** Brought back a bull from Crete~~
~~**5** Captured the Erymanthian Boar~~
~~**6** Cleaned the Augean stables in a single day~~
7 Chased away flesh-eating Stymphalian birds
~~**8** Captured the horses of King Diomedes~~
~~**9** Got the belt of Hippolyta, Queen of the Amazons~~
10 Captured the cattle of Geryon, the three-headed, six-armed giant
~~**11** Brought back the three golden apples from the Garden of Hesperides~~
12 Went into Hades and brought back the three-headed hound of hell

'We're not going to kill anything, so that leaves us with four options,' he said. 'We could have gone to the Underground club and done number twelve if you two hadn't already played that card with the Oliver Pond Orpheus experience.' Vanessa looked at Oliver and grinned. Oliver had the good grace to look moderately sheepish.

'Chasing away birds doesn't sound so hard. I could use the bow and arrow. What are Stymphalian birds, anyway?' Oliver asked.

Vanessa pulled out her Greek Mythology for Idiots book and flicked through to chapter six.

'The Stymphalian Birds…' She licked her finger and turned the page. 'After Hercules returned from his success in the Augean stables, Eurystheus came up with an even more difficult task. For the sixth labour, Hercules was to drive away an enormous flock of birds which gathered at a lake near the town of Stymphalos. Arriving at the lake, which was deep in the woods, Hercules had no idea how to drive the huge flock away. The goddess Athena came to his aid, providing a pair of bronze *krotala* – noisemaking clappers similar to castanets. These were no ordinary noisemakers. They had been made by an immortal craftsman, Hephaistos, the god of the forge. Climbing a nearby mountain, Hercules clashed the *krotala* loudly, scaring the birds out of the trees, then shot them with arrows, or possibly with a slingshot, as they took flight.'

'Well, we're there then. We've got the bow,' said Oliver.

'You are not going to shoot any birds,' said Vanessa sternly.

'I wouldn't worry, Nessie. I've seen him practise and he's got more chance of developing some social graces than he has of hitting anything he aims at,' said Scott.

'Good point.' She continued. 'Some versions of the legend say that these Stymphalian birds were vicious man-eaters. The second century A.D. travel-writer, Pausanias, trying to discover what kind of birds they might have been, wrote that during his time a type of bird from the Arabian desert was called "Stymphalian". He described them as equal to lions or leopards in their fierceness, and speculated that the birds Hercules encountered in the legend were similar to these Arabian birds. These fly against those who come to hunt them, wounding and killing them with their beaks. All armour of bronze or iron that men wear is pierced by the birds; but if they weave a garment of thick cork, the beaks of the Stymphalian birds are caught in the cork garment.'

'I could knock something up,' said Oliver.

'Would I be correct in imagining a large hole string vest with corks shoved into each hole?' asked Scott.

'Pretty much what I was thinking.'

'Good, just wanted to be clear.'

Vanessa, still focused on the book, went on: 'These birds are of the size of a crane, and are like the ibis, but their beaks are more powerful, and not crooked like that of the ibis.'

'Size of a crane! Bloody hell, that's big,' said Oliver.

'I think that would be the bird rather than the building equipment,' Scott pointed out.

'Ah yes, right.'

'What do you think?' said Vanessa.

'If I get to take my bow and arrow, I'm up for it,' said Oliver.

'Where are they, though?' asked Scott.

Vanessa looked thoughtful. 'Well, if you're a bird you can go pretty much anywhere you want, so I say we go to Rhodes.'

This came as something of a surprise to Oliver and Scott.

'Why Rhodes?' they asked in unison.

Vanessa explained that she had been there years before with her parents and had fond memories of spending all day with her bird-spotting father, walking around with binoculars to search out migrating birds. This, she thought, would make it an ideal destination for the sixth task on the list.

'So we just need something that makes a horrible, discordant noise to scare them,' said Scott thoughtfully.

They found Billy half an hour later in his favourite café.

Vanessa recalled that most of the bird watching she had done with her father had taken place around the Kremasti river area of Rhodes, and so this was the place they should head for. She reasoned it should be easy to scare a few birds into the air. Billy, having been sold the idea of going on tour, was all over the scheme, and Oliver got busy making a few more arrows.

Their ferry pulled into Rhodes at four in the afternoon after an uneventful eight-hour trip. It had been very busy when they got on, but the combination of Billy tuning his accordion and a six-foot-two Anglo-Saxon with a bow and arrow on his back seemed to encourage people to vacate their seats. The usual scrum of room touts were waiting and they took an apartment in the centre of Rhodes town.

The first impression of Rhodes was amazing. Built by the Venetians, the town was surrounded by walls as protection against marauding pirates. Since the island was so close to the Turkish mainland, raiding parties had been common through history. Sadly, no one had possessed the foresight to protect the island from marauding North European youths and a couple of the resorts had become the go-to destination for those looking to drink themselves senseless and pick up a variety of STDs.

The first morning dawned clear and bright as they met over breakfast. Vanessa produced a guide to birdwatching in Rhodes and said, 'We've got a car for two days. I suggest we head out to a place called Plimmeri.'

'Plimmeri, eh? said Scott, picking up the book.

'Page forty-five.'

He flicked through, looked at some pictures, pretended to read a bit and said, 'Great, looks perfect.'

It took them about thirty minutes, the last ten of which was down a bumpy single-lane track which ended in a dusty parking area next to a body of water. They set off along a track that followed the water's edge.

'I hope it's not too far. This can get quite heavy after a while,' said Billy, indicating his accordion.

'It's not far now,' said Vanessa. 'According to the map, we should start seeing large flocks of birds any time soon.'

The path had taken them away from the water's edge and was now rising, giving them brief glimpses of the water through the trees. They rounded a bend and found themselves on a viewing platform with a bench and a clear sight of the water stretched out in front of them. About forty metres away was a small island which was clearly the nesting area of choice for the local bird population. This was the spot.

'Right, this is it then,' said Scott. 'Billy, can you give us one of your best tunes, mate?'

Vanessa rolled her eyes at Oliver as he enthusiastically pulled his bow and arrow from his back and started flexing his arms. 'You're not actually planning to shoot anything with that, are you?'

'Well, it does state that Hercules shot the birds, and it took me ages to make it – so yes, I thought I'd have a go.'

Vanessa slipped her camera out of her bag and fitted the zoom lens. 'I think you should leave the "shooting" of the birds to me.'

'Nice!' said Scott. 'I like what you're doing there, Nessie.'

Looking pained, Oliver shrugged his shoulders and said, 'Alright, I'll just send a couple over their heads as a warning shot.'

Scott looked at Billy. 'You ready?'

He nodded adjusted his volume knob to the highest setting and hit the opening bars of 'My Old Man's a Dustman'.

It was spectacular. The silence of the morning was shattered. As one, a huge body of birds rose from their resting places and soared into the air.

Oliver set his feet apart, threaded an arrow onto the string pulled back with his right arm, and fell on his arse as the bow split down the middle, breaking into two pieces.

Meanwhile, there was a whirring series of clicks as Vanessa zoomed in on the flock and shot the pictures they needed.

Scott tapped Billy on the shoulder and mouthed 'Enough,' but Billy, being Billy, continued until he had played out the first verse and the chorus. In the silence that followed, Scott grinned and said, 'Well, that seems to have worked out pretty well.'

'Ye-e-es,' murmured Vanessa, looking out over the lake. 'But I think it might be time to leave, and I think we should do it right now and do it quickly'.

They all followed the direction of her eyes and saw that a number of what looked like small bushes were actually camouflaged hides, each of which had people appearing from behind it, looking less than pleased. Birdwatchers are generally known as twitchers and the group of men running in their direction, waving poles, looked very twitchy indeed.

They ran, got to the car, jumped in and were on their way before the angriest of the watchers was able to catch up with them.

Back in the main town, they headed for a bar and some celebratory beers. Scott, with no little ceremony, got his list out and crossed out number seven with a theatrical flourish.

The labours of Hercules

1 Killed the Nemean lion
2 Killed a Hydra, a nine-headed snake
3 Captured a golden-horned reindeer
~~**4** Brought back a bull from Crete~~
~~**5** Captured the Erymanthian Boar~~
~~**6** Cleaned the Augean stables in a single day~~
~~**7** Chased away flesh-eating Stymphalian birds~~
~~**8** Captured the horses of King Diomedes~~
~~**9** Got the belt of Hippolyta, Queen of the Amazons~~
10 Captured the cattle of Geryon, the three-headed, six-armed giant
~~**11** Brought back the three golden apples from the Garden of Hesperides~~
12 Went into Hades and brought back the three-headed hound of hell

'That's it, then,' said Vanessa. 'You've done it, completed the tasks.'

'Just got to get a boat and sail back,' said Oliver.

'Hmm. Must admit, this is the bit I've been trying not to think about,' said Scott.

Chapter 31

Oliver and Vanessa had been thinking about it a lot. Having spent such a long time waiting to get together, neither of them was keen on parting so soon. Taffos had found someone selling a four-berth boat, which meant there was room for all of them, but Vanessa sensibly declined to spend potentially months crammed into a tiny space with two idiots who were barely on nodding terms with the techniques of sailing. At one stage, Oliver even toyed with the idea of staying, but as Vanessa pointed out – rather unkindly, he thought – as two halfwits, he and Scott only really functioned as a sentient being when together.

As a compromise, Oliver suggested that the first part of their journey should involve sailing between various Greek islands to get the hang of things before venturing further afield, and Vanessa could take the ferry and join them for a few days on each. Having decided on this course of action, they were all keen to see the boat that would be home for the coming months.

When they arrived at the marina, Taffos was already there, deep in conversation with a shifty-looking bloke whose eyes never stopped moving. Occasionally, they would flit across a listing lump of wood moored at the jetty which had 'Brigit' written on the side.

'Hello, Taffos mate, how's it going.'

'Scott boyo, this is Lefteri. Look, Lefteri, Scott and Oliver.'

They shook hands.

'Where's the little beauty, then?' said Oliver, rubbing his hands together. 'Hope it's in better shape than that raft down there.'

Taffos shuffled his feet.

'Nothing wrong with that, boyo, good solid sailor that.'

Oliver laughed. 'Yes, right. You'll be telling us that's the one next.'

'Harsh, mate. Not even Taffos would stoop to that, would you?' asked Scott.

'That's it, lads – the boat of your dreams, that is. Needs a bit of work but it's all there.'

The looks of amusement gradually faded from their faces as they realised he wasn't joking.

Oliver stroked his chin. 'I might not know a great deal about the subject, but shouldn't there be a long, thin wooden thing in the middle?'

'Something the technically minded might call a mast?' added Scott, who'd clearly been doing his homework. 'Oh, and a sail is always quite a handy addition to a sailing boat.'

'Told you already, lads, it's all there, the mast and sails and ropes and things. You'll just have to put it all together and away you go.'

In the end, Taffos and the mysterious Lefteri won on the basis that the boat had two redeeming features: it (sort of) floated, and it was all they could afford.

'Brigit' had started life as a four-berth sailing boat owned by a Swedish couple. They were schoolteachers and spent their entire summer holidays sailing between Greek islands before their two children turned into moody teenagers incapable of spending four weeks away from friends and electronic devices.

Although cosmetically it left a little to be desired, structurally it was sound and in good working order. Their first job was to raise the mast, or 'step' it as Scott's book had it. Scott had been studying books on boats and sailing for the last four months, and together with his practical experience on board with Alexei, he at least had a rough understanding of how it all worked.

Oliver's contribution during this time was to buy a captain's hat, learn to smoke a pipe and practise in the bath with a small model boat. He was keen to learn, though, and delighted in using any nautical terms he could pick up from Scott, who made up a few 'nautical expressions' of his own which Oliver had fallen for, appropriately enough, hook line and sinker. Hence Scott's days were enhanced immeasurably by the pleasure of Oliver knowledgably suggesting they 'frot the sails', 'rim the mast', or 'fromage the anchor'.

In an uncharacteristic bout of organisation, Scott had found and photocopied a book with detailed instructions on 'Stepping the mast on a Pandora 700'. He had even put the pages in a sensible lever arch file, which he was holding as he stood on the marina jetty surveying the scene. Oliver, by way of contrast, was holding his small model boat at arm's length and comparing it to the bigger version with the intention of using it as a blueprint for rigging out the Brigit. The mast had been rigged with the necessary ropes and wires and was set in position by the side of the boat. Scott's smile of satisfaction at the order and precision in front of him gradually disappeared as he opened the file and read the first line of the instructions.

'We do not recommend you attempt to step the mast without the use of a boatyard crane.'

This was a bit of a blow. The nearest they had to a crane was knowing a bloke called Derek. However, the beauty of being a mindless optimist was that situations like this merely presented something between a minor hiccup and a challenge.

As Scott continued reading down the page, however, it became evident that in addition to some hard physical labour, there was also going to be a large dose of guesswork involved.

'Ensure that the spinnaker is attached to the ...'

'On no account allow the main mast to ...'

'When anchoring the mast, ensure that the footing is ...'

The photocopier had been set to portrait and the book was landscape. Typically, each word that had been cut off was one of the crucial ones. At least the business of raising the mast seemed pretty straightforward. Taffos promised to help, and, with Oliver roped up to take the strain at the base, Scott and Taffos would, they reasoned, be able to walk the mast up and into position. Then Oliver would have to keep it vertical while they attached the wires to hold it in place. Once it was partially secured, they could then take their time sorting out the ropes by a process of trial and error.

As a plan, it wasn't great, but against the odds it worked. Scott and Taffos had the worst job as they had to walk the mast up towards vertical, which meant the closer they got to the base, the heavier it got. There were a few nasty moments when it looked like the mast was going to slip and spear itself through the floor of the boat, sinking it, but after ten minutes of swearing and grunting they had it in place and secured.

The rigging took considerably longer. Oliver's attempt to work it out by comparison to the model, or 'Little Brigit' as he called it, did not prove to be a wholehearted success.

'According to this, we've got a lot more ropes than we need, mate,' he said, peering from his model to the profusion of tackle lying on the deck of the Brigit.

'Not entirely convinced your bathtub toy is 100 percent accurate. I think we might be better going on the Sailing and Rigging a Pandora book.'

'Well, if you're sure,' said Oliver, putting Little Brigit down and scratching his head wistfully.

With the help of the book, a lot of trial and error and the assistance of a fellow yacht owner who took pity on them, they finally finished the rigging and had what looked a lot more like a fully functioning sailing boat.

'So, what now?' asked Oliver. 'Are we really planning to sail that thing to England?'

Scott stood still, looking into space.

'Urgent requires answer.'

Scott shook his head, looked back at Oliver and pulled his shoulders back in the manner of someone who has just made a decision. The thought of getting in a boat and travelling around Greek islands did not scare him in the least. Neither did the thought of taking a ferry, or a plane or anything else.

It was at that moment that he realised that he had changed: the fear had gone, and there was a world of opportunity in front of him. He thought about Abi and how he could suggest they go away together, how he could show that he was capable of adventure. He had written to her from each of the new places he had been to, not too much, just a 'here I am, it's nice here' postcard from Volos, Drama, Xanthi, Chania, Malia, and all the other places he'd visited. He wasn't entirely sure why he hadn't sent them, but something had held him back. That something had gone. Now he could let her know where he had been and, confident in the knowledge that he would be able to travel anywhere he wanted, could continue to go.

'Right now, I need to make a phone call,' he said, and with that he disappeared off towards the post office and the booths of phones that were set up for long-distance calls.

He heard the familiar English dialling tone before a voice answered.

'Salisbury 745623.'

'Hello, Dad.'

'Scott?'

'Yes, it's me'

'What a surprise, I was just thinking about you, how are you?

There was a pause as Scott looked at the receiver and wondered about what he was going to say.

'Scott, are you ok, is anything wrong?'

He took a moment to look around at everything that was different, the way people walked, the way they talked, the way things smelled and he realised that he wanted more of it.

'No, everything's great. Dad, I did it, I completed the labours, I've bought a boat and it's all ready.'

'My word, have you really? Well well, I'm very proud of you, and I know Teddy would have been too.

'Thanks.'

So, you'll be coming back a rich young man. I suppose you'll be opening that club you've always been talking about.'

'That's the thing, dad. I don't think I want to. At least, not yet.'

There was a silence on the line.

'You see, I feel I want to travel more now, I've always been scared to go anywhere and now I know I can go anywhere and do anything. This has been such an adventure and I don't want it to end.

He could almost see his father nodding on the other end of the line. 'Teddy thought – I'd say hoped this might happen. He told me to ask if you had ever heard of Odysseus.'

'Is he the bloke Homer wrote that epic about? Sailed around Greece in the Odyssey.'

'That's the one. Took him ten years. I'll break it to your mother.'

219

Scott smiled and hung up the receiver. Took a deep breath and dialled a second number. It was answered by a familiar voice at the second ring.

"Abi, hi it's Scot, I just wondered if you were free for the next year or so and fancied going sailing?"

The End.

Printed in Great Britain
by Amazon